Her Smile

By Carla Kelly

CAMEL
PRESS

Kenmore, WA

CAMEL PRESS

A Camel Press book published by Epicenter Press

Epicenter Press
6524 NE 181st St. Suite 2
Kenmore, WA 98028.

For more information go to:
www.Camelpress.com
www.Coffeetownpress.com
www.Epicenterpress.com
www.generontalbooks.com

www.carlakellyauthor.com

This is a work of fiction. Names, characters, places, brands, media, and incidents are the product of the author's imagination or are used fictitiously.

Design by Rudy Ramos

Her Smile
Copyright © 2021 by Carla Kelly

ISBN: 9781603811903 (trade paper)
ISBN: 9781603811910 (ebook)

Printed in the United States of America

To Mary Ruth Kelly Huerta

Thanks for reminding me about this little novel.
And thank you for your abiding faith in my writing.

Books by Carla Kelly

Fiction

Daughter of Fortune
Summer Campaign
Miss Chartley's Guided Tour
Marian's Christmas Wish
Mrs. McVinnie's London Season
Libby's London Merchant
Miss Grimsley's Oxford Career
Miss Billings Treads the Boards
Miss Milton Speaks Her Mind
Miss Wittier Makes a List
Mrs. Drew Plays Her Hand
Reforming Lord Ragsdale
The Lady's Companion
With This Ring
One Good Turn
The Wedding Journey
Here's to the Ladies: Stories of the Frontier Army
Beau Crusoe
Marrying the Captain
The Surgeon's Lady
Marrying the Royal Marine
The Admiral's Penniless Bride
Borrowed Light
Enduring Light
Coming Home for Christmas: The Holiday Stories
Regency Christmas Gifts
Season's Regency Greetings
Marriage of Mercy
My Loving Vigil Keeping
Double Cross
Marco and the Devil's Bargain
Paloma and the Horse Traders
Star in the Meadow
Unlikely Master Genius
Unlikely Spy Catchers
Safe Passage
Softly Falling
One Step Enough
Courting Carrie in Wonderland
A Regency Royal Navy Christmas
Unlikely Heroes
A Hopeful Christmas
The Necklace

"We will find a way to make
a way out of no way."

JOHN R. LEWIS (1940-2020)

When I was working with Oscar-winning film director Alejandro Gonzales Iñárritu on the film, *The Revenant*, Alejandro said to me he wanted to create a film that tells a story. As I read Carla Kelly's novel, *Her Smile*, I started to visualize another story where a woman's journey came to life as she experienced changes within her own understanding, along with her friendship with the Nez Perce.

My former colleague Carla Kelly opened a doorway to the life and experiences of Elizabeth Ann Everett, who finds herself pitchforked into the savage conflict of the Nez Perce Nation's flight to the Canadian border. As a scholar of nineteenth century western history, Carla allowed for this woman's perspective, which is rarely seen or recorded, to be told. It reaches the heart of westward expansion: the changing of the West between the United States and Native American relations. These changes of westward expansion and whites moving into these traditional homelands came at a high price for the indigenous people who had lived in those areas for millennia. Broken treaties, land grabs, forced removal, colonization and dependence became the norm.

Loren Yellow Bird, Sr.
Arikara and Plains Indian Historian
Trenton, ND

Prologue

September, 1904

Near La Grande, Oregon

I never planned to write an account of my summer with the Nez Perce, that summer of 1877. Even after all these years, scarcely a day passes that I don't think of the flight, but I never seriously thought to commit the whole thing to paper.

At least I didn't until last week, when my husband Duncan went to Washington state to visit his relatives. My daughter Millie was newly settled in town, and our two sons still at home were busy getting in the last cutting of hay. Nothing of importance was pressing on me, a rare occurrence. What to do?

I was looking forward to several weeks of relative calm in order to catch up on some reading, and to make those green tomato preserves Duncan likes so well. Knowing that Duncan loses track of time when he visits relatives, I really didn't expect to see him anytime soon.

You can imagine my surprise during dinner five nights later when he opened the back door and came into the kitchen. I stared at him in surprise. He limped, so I knew rain was coming soon. He kissed me on the top of my head and sat down in his usual place.

As I got up to get a plate and fork for him, he reached out and held my arm as I walked past him. "Sit down, Smiley. I have something to say."

Our sons sat there, too, waiting for him to speak, since he wasn't one to make pronouncements. He kept holding my hand, not unusual for him, but somehow different.

"He's dead."

He could only mean Joseph. Silent, we looked at Duncan, hoping he would tell us more. He said nothing, but got up and went to the foot of the stairs. We watched through the kitchen doorway as he took off his Jefferson peace medallion and hung it on the newel post.

He gazed back at me. Through the years I have become better at reading his expressions, but not this time. "It's over," he said. "I mean, it's really over."

He went upstairs slowly, hand over hand on the railing. I heard the door to our bedroom close. The medal on its leather strip swung slowly back and forth. My boys looked at each other. I knew they didn't understand why their father had done that, and I knew I couldn't explain it to them in a sentence or two.

Duncan was right. It is really over. I must now write the story as I remember it.

Chapter One

In the morning, lying so close to my good man, I asked him where I should start. He suggested the beginning, which earned him a pillow over his head but only briefly. Husbands are so helpful, aren't they?

"I may get some of the details wrong," I said, when the pillow was behind his head again. "Will that upset The People? I'm no Nez Perce scholar."

"They won't mind. You've done some tribal good, Smiley. That matters more."

Here goes. My name is Elizabeth Ann Everett Stuart, named after my maternal grandmother Elizabeth Casey, of the Albany, New York brewery Caseys. I was born in Monroe, Michigan, May 19, 1859. Monroe's chief claim to fame is as the home of George Armstrong Custer, late – very late – of the Seventh Cavalry. My daughter Millie says that books about Custer sell well, but I have only a little to say about him in this account, and none of it flattering. I trust you are not disappointed.

The Civil War broke out in 1861, when I was not quite two years old. Father volunteered, of course. He never sought active combat, but he served in a Michigan volunteer regiment as a supply officer and eventually regimental quartermaster. He attained the rank of major before Appomattox, so I assume he was reasonably proficient.

Duncan, who is – rightfully so – of a more cynical turn of mind than I am, insists that Father's rank was more likely due to his extortionist capabilities. In view of Father's subsequent career, I suspect this could be so.

My father made a number of important connections during the late conflict, his most fortuitous with General Grenville Dodge of the Union Army. After the Civil War ended, Dodge became chief engineer of the long-proposed transcontinental railroad. By the time the dust settled at Promontory Summit in 1869, Father found himself treasurer of the Union Pacific Railroad. At the age of ten, I found myself in Omaha, Nebraska, UP headquarters.

We lived in a three-story brick house on McDermott Street. It used to be in the best part of town, but as Omaha has grown, the neighborhood has begun its decline. Many of the large homes have been cut up into apartments for the less fortunate. (I could state that I was one of the less fortunate even when the Everett house was still a mansion, but why quibble?)

Our house is no longer standing. I was traveling through Omaha five years ago on one of my lobbying trips to Washington, D.C., when I was informed that several of the houses on McDermott Street were being torn down to make way for a Catholic church (Italians inhabit the neighborhood now).

I woke early the next morning, long before my train was due for departure, and walked to McDermott Street. I arrived in time to watch my childhood home under demolition.

The workmen had pulled down the back part of the house, scattering bricks everywhere. Before I even realized what I was doing, I picked up a brick and let it fly at one of the front windows. The glass shattered with a most satisfying tinkle; it was such fun that I did it again.

I would have thrown a third brick, and probably could have obliterated the stained-glass cornucopia etched in the front door, but a constable chanced along. He told me to mind my manners or he would run me in. I walked away, laughing to myself. Not everyone has a chance to fulfill a childhood dream.

When I say we lived in that house during my growing up years, I mean precisely that. We lived there. By we, I mean Mother, Father, me, my brother Philemon and my sister Eugenie. We ate and slept there, took our piano and voice lessons there, greeted company there. We never had much fun there, and I don't recall much laughter. We grew up in that house. I don't believe any of us children ever felt any emotion but relief when we left.

My mother gets most of the credit, or the blame. She did everything that a genteel mother of that era was supposed to do for her children, except that she did not love us. Granted, there were times when our own children were growing up and Duncan and I were more or less confined to our ranch that I would gladly have traded them for magic beans. But I loved my four rascals, and they knew it. We could usually end a fraught day amicably enough, sitting on the corral fence watching Duncan train one of his horses.

Mother was different. It seemed to me then that she spent a lot of her time trying to pretend we were not there. This wasn't difficult in our house, with its three stories and broad porches. After birth, she relinquished me to a wet nurse and a nanny, who gave way in time to a governess, a tutor, a dancing master and an Italian instructor. *La penna è sul tavolo.* Indeed.

Phil, Eugenie and I often went days without seeing Mother. She would get an occasional burst of motherly feeling and instruct the governess to bring us downstairs to visit with her after we finished our dinner in the nursery. These visits never lasted longer than twenty minutes, in which Mother asked us how we did. Later on, she inquired about our studies and asked if we needed anything. When conversation thinned and vanished, she put her hand to her forehead and looked at the governess, who hustled us away until her next motherly feeling.

I mustn't leave out the obligatory kiss. We lined up according to age, with the governess always cautioning us not to step on Mother's dress or muss her hair. We bent over her with our hands behind our backs and kissed her cheek, which she tilted forward slightly. I was never kissed on the mouth until much later. (That'll make Duncan raise his eyebrows and grin.)

One time when it was my turn to kiss Mother, I teetered off balance and fell into her lap. She stood up and dumped me on the floor, declaring in a high voice that I had wrinkled her taffeta.

I could continue, but you can gather from this backward glance that my childhood was not all bliss. As much as we dreaded Mother, we worshipped her, too. She was so beautiful. I have before me now a tintype taken when she in her thirties, a decade she claimed for twenty years, which must have been rewarding for her.

Tall and slender, she wore her chestnut hair swept up on her head and anchored there with a diamond pin. She had high cheekbones, and an elegant sneer. I once drew a picture of her and penciled in a bone through her nose. My governess was so horrified that I had to suffer bread and water in my room for the rest of the week. It was a good likeness, though.

Mother had the most extraordinary eyes, blue with a darker rim around the iris. Always observant, I noticed that she cultivated a wounded look in them whenever Father was around that enabled her to get whatever she wanted. Her eyes could fill with tears at the slightest provocation, real or imagined. Shortly after our marriage, I tried that look on my husband. Duncan just laughed at me. I know I must have left something out.

I am told that I look the most like Mother, with less height. I do hope to goodness I have never sneered at anyone.

My father must also receive his due for our constrained homelife, if only because he was away from McDermott Street so often that we never had much opportunity to get to know him. He spent long hours at his office, and we saw him mainly on weekends. After I learned something about life, I wondered if he kept a mistress in Omaha or its environs. Once could scarcely blame him. He helped me through a tight spot later, so I shouldn't be too censorious.

I sometimes had the feeling that he would have liked to know us children better. On occasion he came to the nursery to play checkers with my little brother. Mother considered checkers lowbrow.

Our family consisted of a modest three children: my two-years-younger brother Philemon Edward, and my little sister Eugenie, four years my junior. Phil survived a series of childhood diseases that plagued him until he started school. All through our nursery years he broke out with hives, bumps or spots. To this day, I can't look at calamine lotion without thinking of Phil and his sundry afflictions.

He was a good-natured boy who used to sit outside my door and read to me when I was confined to quarters for one or another infraction. We got through *The Man in the Iron Mask* that way. I'm smiling as I write this. Even Phil got into trouble when he pronounced the author's last name as Dumb-Ass rather than Dumas. And wouldn't you know it? I never could remember the correct pronunciation, which meant my own children still get the giggles over Dumb-Ass, even though we are all old enough to know better. Such is the trajectory of family jokes.

I last saw Phil, an Omaha attorney, a few years ago when he took a roundabout trip to San Francisco on business, via Oregon. My husband and I took him around the ranch, showed off the horses, and introduced him to all the children then currently home. He kept nodding and smiling. When we saw him off, he squeezed me tight around the middle and said, "You know, Liz, you have something awfully nice here."

Poor Phil. Strangely enough, he married a woman like Mother. His children barely tolerate him. I expect to see him more often as we all age.

By rights I should have hated my sister Eugenie. She was short and plump like Father, with an extravagant array of dimples and an honest-to-goodness beauty mark next to her right eye. Her hair was naturally curly. She was frequently called upon to entertain visitors with "Horatio at the Bridge," or "The Wreck of the Hesperus." Heavens, she clasped her hands and rolled her eyes upward and really ripped into that old Longfellow poem.

Eugenie turned into a lovely woman. I am told that her come-out was the highlight of the 1882 Omaha social season. (It had been prudently postponed from the 1881 debut calendar to give the gossip and scandal time to fade away. More about that later.) Eugenie wasn't exactly covered over with intelligence, but she was always comfortable to be around, and knew which fork to use. More important, she loved me no matter what.

That was our family, or nearly so. Let me add this about my maternal grandmother Casey: Grandpa Casey made his fortune in beer, a fact which Mother preferred to overlook. In her letters to me, Grandma Casey chuckled at Mother's snobbery. "Money's money, Lizzie, and don't you forget it. Damned stuff comes in handy."

Before she died, she turned into a true eccentric, reading French novels and the *Police Gazette* and sleeping in the altogether with the windows wide open (the drapes, too, if you can believe her neighbors). She admired my latent independence and helped me out beyond measure when I really needed it. On the anniversary of her death, Duncan and I toast her with beer. She would have liked that.

Other relatives came and went, but none of them are of sufficient interest to include here. I might add that any relative staying with us for at least six months at a stretch was entitled to a free lifetime pass on the Union Pacific. We had lots of company.

That enough about my family for now; they will show up again in this narrative. I believe you get the gist, if you have been paying attention, and I need to get on with my story.

I should state here that I never would have spent nearly eight weeks with the Nez Perce if I hadn't developed a bosom.

Chapter Two

My story is what Duncan refers to as "the ultimate tourist experience." I blame it all on my bosom. Mother never held out much hope that my bosom would exceed or even match the ordinary, and I shared her fear. I gangled though my early teen years until Something Happened. My freckles vanished, never to return, and my nose – granted, a somewhat commanding specimen – finally began to fit my face. Then, lo and behold, after years and years of staring down at my chest and waiting for some sign of maturity, I developed breasts.

I helped it along, because that bosom didn't come easily. Hiding in my closet with a candle, I wrote away for a bottle of Dr. Hardee's Female Improver. I talked one of the maids into picking it up at the post office for me. She did, after I promised to give her most of that month's pin money when she delivered that brown bottle safe into my hands.

The instruction on the label said to rub the contents in a clockwise direction over the afflicted area. I was dubious, but desperate to catch up with a fellow classmate who wore corsets already and didn't need to resort to ruffles to substitute for what wasn't there.

The mixture smelled like a combination of cod's liver oil and sour beer, but I rubbed it over my poor flat chest and waited for results. Nothing happened, except that I got my nightgown and sheets oily and the housekeeper threatened to tell Mother if I continued such quackery. My bosom finally came of its own accord one summer when I wasn't looking.

With the development of an hourglass figure and a marked improvement in my visage, Mother decided that upon my graduation in 1877 from Miss Sumner's Female Academy, I would enroll in Vassar College and catch myself an Easterner. I had been hoping to matriculate at a small Episcopal college in Lincoln with some of my chums. After Mother took a good look at me, she decreed that I could do better than St. Mary's College. At Vassar, the worlds of Yale and Harvard would be mine, and a prominent place in Eastern seaboard society.

The idea held no appeal for me. I was not averse to the notion of leaving home, but it seemed practically medieval to barter my improved looks for wealth and position. I had nightmares of some bidder checking my teeth before slipping on the ring.

Mother prevailed, using her tried and true methods of coercion. She suffered all manner of palpitations and spasms between May and June to convince me that I was an ungrateful, thoughtless daughter who could relieve her distress by saying yes to Vassar. After an endless month, I felt so guilty that I would have agreed to parade naked past Omaha Barracks if only she would leave me alone. I surrendered. Mother wasted no time in informing the seamstress to begin by sewing nametags into all my underthings. I was doomed to Vassar College.

What could I do? I mooned around the house long enough for Father to come out of his usual fog and ask what the deuce was going on. He only nodded and pottered off when I told him. Later that evening at dinner, he offered me a consolation prize.

"Elizabeth," he began, pushing away the custard pudding and leaning back in his chair, "what would you like to do this summer, before you go East to college?"

A hundred scathing replies came to mind. I almost blurted out one, when I glanced beyond him at Phil. He mouthed something. I stared at him. Phil raised his hands like something exploding, and I knew what to ask for.

"I would like to go to Yellowstone Park, Father," I replied, wiping my mouth with the corner of a napkin as I learned at the female academy. I looked him right in the eye.

You'd have thought I was seeking permission to move into an opium den. Father's eyes widened and he came down on all four chair legs with a bang that made the underfootman wince.

"You can't be serious," Mother said. She glared at me for long moments until I felt myself shrinking under her well-bred scrutiny.

I glanced at Phil, but he had that mulish look in his eyes and his lips were set in a tight line. In the past year he had become addicted to those dime novels glorifying the West. (To be scrupulous, so had I.) He was quite serious in his attempt to get Out There.

You might be wondering how my brother was able to sneak such low literature past both the butler and more particularly, the underfootman, who had come to Christ in a camp meeting and never was any fun after that. I did the sneaking. I put the dust cover of Ovid's *Metamorphosis* around the latest dime novel and brazenly carried it off past everyone. Our successful subterfuge more than justified the value of taking Latin.

In exchange for my role in the subterfuge, Phil did my trigonometry homework for me. That year, I never did exactly sparkle on examinations, but my homework shone with a light all its own. My instructor charitably decided I was one of those unfortunates struck dumb by the fear of a test; thus, I was able to pass the course and graduate.

So yes, in exchange for a year of trig help, Phil used me to get a trip to Western lands where those silly shoot-um-ups transpired. I was complacent and shallow; Phil was determined. And seriously, what was wrong with a few weeks in America's first national park?

When I didn't retract my startling request, the idea of Yellowstone Park started to soak in. All of us wandered the house for the next few days with thoughtful expressions. The more I considered the whole, harebrained scheme, the more attractive it became.

Our only previous experience with roughing it was a week spent in the Adirondacks, where we existed in canvas-walled tents and spent an extraordinary amount of time slapping mosquitoes. We took along our cook who burned everything, then resigned.

I had to admit that Yellowstone appealed to me. It had been declared a national park in 1872, the first of its kind, five years earlier by President Grant. To my knowledge, none of my friends had been there yet, a fact which heightened its attraction. I told you I was shallow.

To be frank, Yellowstone Park was as good as anywhere. For weeks I had been noisily objecting to Vassar to no good purpose. I really didn't care where I went. I knew beyond any doubt that I would be under my mother's thumb until I discovered a way to liberate myself.

Yellowstone it was. Phil and I spent the next hurried weeks outfitting ourselves in proper adventuring togs and reading guidebooks, instead of *Colonel Cody and the Indian Trap*. We learned that the park embraced over two million acres, some one hundred geysers, a few of which erupted periodically, and an interesting array of wild beasts.

By alternating threats and bribes, Mother coerced her dressmaker into running up some simple shirtwaists requiring a minimum of petticoats, new riding habits, and flannel underdrawers for cool nights. She sent for some cork helmets from Wannamaker's of New York, which we all refused to wear except Eugenie, who was pliable in the extreme.

Even Father got into the spirit of things. In his usual organized fashion, he made arrangements for us to take the UP to Ogden, Utah Territory, the spur to Salt Lake City for some sightseeing, then back to Ogden, where we would meet with a caravan hired to convey us through the park. He even arranged for an army friend to provide us with a military escort. Father took everything into account, putting together an expedition that could not possibly have met with anything unplanned.

Some of my school chums gave me a going away party the night before we departed, presenting me with several gag gifts, one of which was a popgun with string and cork plug. A note attached to it admonished me to use it on road agents and Mormons. Another friend gave me a braided, red-dyed mop to wear so I wouldn't lose my own scalp to savages. I was dubbed Omaha's Number One Tourist as we laughed and talked until midnight.

Gadfreys. Just thinking back to that night gives me a chill. We were so casual, flippant, and sure of ourselves. It really was a going-away party. In a sense, I never returned.

No early riser then, I was not at my best when we left Omaha in the morning. Phil possessed sufficient enthusiasm for all of us, allowing me to slump down in one of the chairs in our private rail car and go back to sleep.

The train ride was non-adventurous in the extreme, if luxurious. The Union Pacific Railroad spared no expense to treat the line's treasurer to the best somebody's money could buy. Even Phil began to wonder if we would have had more fun at Newport or Bar Harbor. There is possibly nothing more dull than Nebraska or Wyoming. The land rolls along in monotonous fashion from horizon to horizon and the wind blows continuously.

I had one embarrassing moment in North Platte, Nebraska. When I stepped off the train, the wind whipped my skirt nearly over my head, affording some startled and gratified cowboys with a view of my striped stockings and drawers. After that, with perception born of experience, I noted at all our subsequent stops that each platform maintained its own retinue of lounging cowboys, strategically placed to catch every glimpse that came off the westbound train, even if it was only a quick view of ankle.

The cowboys developed an unwashed sameness after a while, but we were fascinated by the Indians. They didn't so much lounge around as affix themselves. They seemed such a permanent part of the landscape that I was startled the first time one of them moved. Their ragged children crowded close on the platform, ready to plead with everyone who left the train. The regulars ignored them. The rest of us chafed and worried when the little ones held up their hands, begging for food or money.

This was naturally a severe blow to Phil, who expected something quite different, based on his reading of western potboilers. Already the cowboys he had seen were totally ordinary, and now these Indians…. His perplexed expression made me push my way through the swarm of dirty urchins, poke him in the ribs and tease, "This was all *your* idea, Phil."

"Aw, Liz, maybe we'll see some *real* Indians later."

Did we ever.

Chapter Three

We Everetts stopped in Ogden, near where the Union Pacific and Southern Pacific join, boarded another train for Salt Lake City, and arrived in the famous City of the Saints by mid-afternoon.

I know it was fashionable back then for tourists to examine Salt Lake to see if all those stories about the Mormons were really true, and I cannot deny that I was disappointed at the reality. Can I ever do enough penance for forming opinions from reading Phil's western novels? We were not abducted by lascivious Mormon men eager for wives. In fact, no one approached us, except one small boy who wanted to shine Father's shoes when we were still at the depot.

We strolled down first north, or south or maybe east or west street – Mormons lay out their streets grid-style, which seemed to suit them, but confused me, who would have failed trig without assistance. I craned my neck at every woman who passed by, wondering if she was trapped in polygamy – remember, this was 1877 – and forced to perform unspeakable acts in one of their temples.

The women all appeared quite ordinary; indeed, they were some of the best-looking and healthiest ladies we saw on our whole journey. I couldn't imagine any of them having anything to smile about in their lives of degradation and misery, but they looked quite pleasant. It was in Salt Lake City that it began to dawn on me that one shouldn't believe everything one reads.

Father arranged for an audience with Brigham Young, the Mormon "prophet." Father had met him while work was going forth on the railroad in 1868, and he thought we would be improved, or at least entertained, by an interview with one of the world's greatest rascals.

We were ushered into the Beehive House by one of the old man's numerous daughters, and invited upstairs to a spacious and well-appointed parlor, grander than anything I had ever seen in Omaha. I was amazed at such elegance in the middle of the Great American Desert. Another daughter sat down at the harp and played for us until her father appeared.

Brigham Young came into the room leaning on a cane and half-supported by a son. His eyes lit up when he saw Father. "Those were the days, weren't they, Mr. Everett?" he began, by way of introduction.

I trust you have all seen photographs of Young, but they didn't do justice to him. He was above middling height and large, with a beard I can only call patriarchal. His personality filled the room and we were captivated.

He and Father exchanged pleasantries, and then the old prophet was introduced to Mother, who did her duty. He shook hands with Phil and Eugenie, and then he came to me. He hooked his cane over his forearm and grasped my hand in both of his.

"So you're the little lady who wants to see Yellowstone Park?" he asked, still holding my hand. I suppose I should have felt uncomfortable, but I didn't.

"Yes, sir. It was my idea."

He patted my hand then let it go. "I hope you find what you're looking for there."

"Thank you, sir," I answered, awed by the force I felt. I didn't know what he meant, but I have wondered since then about the gift of prophecy.

He and Father conversed for several minutes – I heard something about an upcoming visit to Mr. Young's winter home in St. George – then another daughter served us eclairs and punch. Phil jabbed me discreetly when I took my first bite, whispering that I shouldn't eat it. He reminded me of *Abducted by the Saints*, where the heroine eats a drugged doughnut and is carried off to a harem in Utah. I made a face at him and ate his eclair, too. They were delicious.

We left soon after refreshments, when the "prophet, seer and revelator" started to nod off over his punch. We didn't know it at the time, of course, but Brigham Young had less than a few months to live. Popular opinion may brand him a thorough-going scoundrel, but I don't know.

We spent the night in Salt Lake, then journeyed back to Ogden next morning to meet our guide for the Yellowstone venture.

His name was Muskrat Watkins, a man with the distinction of possessing the yellowest teeth of any human being I have ever seen. Part of his dental challenge was due to the wad of tobacco he harbored in one cheek or the other. He chewed on that disgusting mess for hours, then suddenly expectorated a stream of yellow-brown tobacco juice. It made my stomach lurch to watch him.

The accuracy of his aim impressed me, despite my queasiness. He could nail a grasshopper at twenty paces and put such a curve in his expectoration that he practically spat around rocks.

Muskrat Watkins delighted Phil. Here, at last, was a Genuine Article of the West, easily recognizable after a steady diet of those prevaricating frontier novels. Thank the Lord Phil didn't adopt any of the man's saltier habits, the least harmless of which was chewing with his mouth open. I must add here that even loyal Phil endeavored to remain upwind of Muskrat Watkins.

Muskrat had additional unpleasant habits. He blew his nose on his fingers and wiped the results against his buckskin pants, which probably could have stood up without him in them. He also scratched in the most unseemly places. One scarcely knew where to look when Muskrat was busy digging away at himself.

He did know how to manage and hold together a caravan of greenies, though. Surely never before in the brief history of Yellowstone Park had such an outfit of tenderfeet attempted what we attempted. Perhaps I am not being fair to Muskrat Watkins.

He employed a couple of wranglers to drive the supply wagon and the touring carriages. The wranglers looked like fugitives from the law. They never offered more than their first names, and no one had the nerve or inclination to inquire more.

One of the men spent a lot of time leering at me. Miss Sumner at the female academy had never prepared me to deal with such a specimen, so I ignored him as much as I could. This was not always easy. Father sent him after me once when I strayed away during a stop for luncheon. I was sitting on a rock listening to some magpies abuse each other when he crept up behind me.

"Well, hey, missy," he whispered, and laughed when I practically jumped straight up.

I shouldn't have done that, because it was like showing fear around a moody dog. He came closer and reached for me. I drew back. I don't know what the brigand would have attempted, if Phil hadn't blundered by then. The wrangler knew I feared him, never a good thing.

Our cook was Chinese, complete with a pigtail. He spoke no English, or so we were informed, but it mystified me that he knew our business so well. He could cook the most incredible meals in a dutch oven. After several days of this, I had to strain to button my skirts.

There we were, the Everett Party: one wealthy railroad executive, his socialite wife and three children. If you are a student of history, you might find us as a footnote in a volume of the history of that summer, along with the Radenburg party or the Helena party. Or not. I never looked.

It rained the morning we left Ogden. We huddled together in the grandiosely named touring carriage, which was a modified army ambulance painted black. I'm not certain the wagon ever possessed springs, but all evidence of them as was gone by the time Muskrat hired the conveyance.

During the noon stop, and at Mother's urging, I approached Muskrat Watkins. (Cautiously, I might add.) "Pardon me, Mr. Watkins, but does it always rain like this in July?"

I don't think anyone had ever called him mister before. He stopped chewing his cud and winked at me. "Hell, no, miss, it don't ever rain like this!" he brayed, spraying me with tobacco juice and digging away at himself. I averted my gaze and vowed to ask no more questions, even if Mother insisted.

It rained all week, and not just any drizzle, mind you. It poured. I am told we drove past curious lava formations before we reached the park, but we couldn't see any of them. When Mother started giving me disgusted looks, I began to wish I had never listened to Phil.

Not wishing us to be disappointed and call off the venture, Muskrat Watkins did his best to entertain us. Every morning as he rounded up the mules to be put to the wagons, he serenaded us with the most incredible, imaginative profanity it has even fallen my lot to listen to.

Muskrat was a true artiste. He limbered up his voice by auditioning a few of the more standard four-letter curses. When he got his customary response from the mules – a blank, nearly human stare – Muskrat began what can only be described as an aria. His voice rose and fell, crooning *dulcemente* or thundering *basso profundo*. He shrieked and railed at the beasts, using the vilest words, then cajoled and caressed them into their harness with gentle bits of vocal pornography.

One could not ignore it. Mother clapped her hands over Eugenie's ears, leaving Phil and me to fend for ourselves.

Each morning when the animals were finally ready to go, Watkins hauled himself into the saddle and slouched there for the better part of the morning, the portrait of well-earned exhaustion. His profanity seemed to drain him, as if he had spent the day lying on his back painting the ceiling of the Sistine Chapel. I cannot say that we ever became accustomed to each morning's virtuoso performance, but Muskrat Watkins proved beyond any doubt that he was a Genuine Article.

Another diversion on our journey to Yellowstone Park was the addition to our party of Lieutenant Thomas McCormack. Father had pulled a few strings and obtained a more refined guide from the U.S. Army, cavalry wing.

In blinding contrast to Muskrat Watkins, Tom was the perfect escort. In 1870 he had accompanied the Hayden Expedition of discovery that initially mapped what became Yellowstone Park. Tom performed the astounding feat of starting a fire with only one match, and he kept his profanity to the bare minimum. I heard him say "shit" once when a horse stepped on his foot, but that was baby's cooing, compared to Muskrat Watkins.

I suppose that in his own way, Tom was as much a Genuine Article as Muskrat, conforming to the picture of a typical hero in Phil's detestable novels. He was well-mannered, courageous, knew sign language, was handsome and neat, even in the wilderness. He had brown hair and grey eyes that made Eugenie sigh and toss away that cork helmet. Naturally, I fell in love with him, too. Who could help it?

As soon as the rain stopped, I asked Muskrat to saddle my horse, so I could join the lieutenant and Father at the head of the outfit. Or I tried to. Father had procured a horse for me that must have been an antique when mountain men and trappers came through the region decades ago. He was an old gelding who had lost all interest in life beyond nipping our Chinese cook and gumming at the sugar barrel when no one was attending. Phil named him Methuselah.

I was able to keep up with Father and that marvelous lieutenant for five minutes or so, until that miserable nag plodded slower and slower until I could barely keep up with the baggage wagon. I eventually abandoned my attempts at flirtation with the lieutenant while on the march, and resigned myself to the bone-jolting discomfort of the touring carriage.

After several days of steady, uphill travel we arrived at Tarnation. Yes, that was the name. I doubt you'll find it on a map. While Muskrat set off to dicker for additional supplies with the local merchants, Phil and I scouted the town in search of a less daunting horse than my current mount.

No luck. A diligent canvass of Tarnation's one-block business district turned up one livery stable. The only horse for sale looked like the grandfather of the one I was trying to get rid of. I asked the owner of there were any other horses available, but he shrugged and turned back to shoveling manure. We left him to his happy task.

We chanced upon Father and Tom as they were leaving the stage office, which also housed the town's telegraph key. Father frowned and Tom shook his head.

"Is anything the matter, Father?" I asked.

They looked at us, startled. Father coughed. "Well, not really."

"What's wrong?" I asked Tom.

He attempted a smile. "Probably nothing. Seems there's a disturbance near the Bitterroot Mountains. We're not headed that way," he hastened to add.

"What kind of disturbance?" I asked.

"Indians."

The lieutenant seemed to hesitate then, as if wondering to disclose more. My father raised an eyebrow and said, "Say on, sir."

McCormack did. "It's a kerfuffle that started in eastern Oregon, as far as I know. The Nez Perce were heading onto a reservation there, when some hotheads shot up some farms and killed a few whites."

"A small tribe?" Father asked.

"Yes, sir. Some of them are even Christians." He chuckled. "Presbyterians. Apparently *they* were going peacefully enough, but the others..."

He looked at me, maybe wondering if he should stop. I wanted to know more, and thank goodness, so did Father. Tom McCormack seemed to enjoy an audience. "The others – we call them the Non-Treaty Nez Perce – took off heading east. They're being pursued right now by General Howard and his troops from the Department of the Columbia."

"I know Oliver Howard," Father said. "He'll stop'um."

"I imagine he will, sir," the lieutenant agreed. He scratched his head then plunged on. "Last we heard, though, there was another fight in western Montana."

"That's starting to sound a little close," Father cautioned.

McCormack took another look at us and smiled. "Nothing to worry about. They're not so close, and they're heading to Canada." He presented his clinching argument with some triumph. "And we're not!" (Looking back, let me add here that Lt. McCormack was none too bright.)

"Gosh and geewillikers."

I forgot for a moment that my brother was listening to all this, too. Phil's eyes widened, and I knew exactly what was going through his mind. He was hoping this summer would turn into something interesting after all.

Phil was not wrong.

Chapter Four

We Everetts looked at Tom in silence. I could nearly feel my brother quivering with excitement. I thought he was too well-mannered to dance around and ask impatient questions, but the excitement won out. "Are they on the warpath?"

Tom smiled at him "They seem to just want to get away."

"Away from what?" I asked, feeling no reassurance.

"Maybe treaties, probably reservations, Miss Everett." He shrugged.

"If they had a treaty, why this trouble?" I persisted.

I could tell the lieutenant was rapidly tiring of me. He mumbled something about settlers needing more land. At least he didn't pat me on the head and say, "There, there, little girl. The government knows what's best."

"Ought we to turn back?" Father sounded hopeful. I already knew that his idea of roughing it was sitting in an armchair in front of a fireplace.

"No, no," the lieutenant answered, his reassurance sounding anything but comforting. As for me, I was ready to throw in the towel. So far, there had been little adventure in our adventure.

"No," Tom went on, glancing at me and making my heart perform curious leaps. "We don't want to spoil Miss Everett's trip, do we? They're heading north to Canada. We are perfectly safe."

We spent the night in a wretched tarpaper shack the owner had the presumption to label a hotel. Everything we ate either swam in grease or had been drowned in boiling water. The bed clothes were a curious gray that made even Phil shudder, Phil, the least fastidious among us.

Eugenie and I shared a room. We whispered until late, then searched for a clean spot to settle into. I was dozing off and having trouble with coherent sentences when we heard strange breathing and moans on the other side of our wall. We heard booted men walking around, followed by a rustle of the straw tick mattress, then that heavy breathing.

I had my suspicions, but Eugenie was completely mystified. You might wonder at such naivete; after all, she was fourteen. Bear in mind that we were reared in a gentler era by parents who were discerning in the extreme.

Eugenie was too drowsy to be really curious, so I put her off with a few mumbled answers. Several men came and went, and one of them was familiar to me.

I heard the usual noises – boots hitting the floor, the mattress rustling like an elephant crashing through the underbrush, and funny breathing. This time was different: a crescendo of grunts and groans, strange silence, then a resounding slap, followed by the woman gasping for breath, as if someone throttled her.

That same someone must have slammed the woman against the wall. I listened in terror as her body slithered down the partition. I heard a coin drop on the floor, and this: "Hey missy, you're not even worth this dime."

I knew that voice. I could almost see the wrangler leering at what was probably an unconscious woman. I held my breath as he stomped out of the room, then started breathing again when I heard the woman stir, groan and flop down on the mattress.

Cold and shaking, I huddled next to Eugenie who, mercifully, slumbered on. When I warmed up, I tiptoed to the door and made sure it was locked. For good measure, I propped a chair under the doorknob. I didn't fall asleep until the sky started to brighten, and even then my dreams were bad.

Breakfast went down reluctantly. The coffee had a layer of grease shimmering on top, and the egg looked like a great yellow eye staring at me under a sea of bacon drippings.

I shivered as the wrangler heaved himself into the dining room for coffee and a strip of bacon he ate standing up, not encumbered by a knife and fork. He was now the proud owner of four long scratches on one side of his face, which offered me a moment of satisfaction.

The moment passed when he grinned at me, fully aware of what I must be surmising, then ran his tongue over his lips. I looked away, grateful to see him gone when I looked back.

Muskrat Watkins joined us at the long table, giving us a more than sufficient view of him as he ate. His chewing may have been audible over the loudest, most determined conversation, but at least he wasn't the wrangler.

Midway through the endless meal we were joined by the woman. She must have been made of durable fiber, because she sauntered in without even a limp, sporting a black eye. She didn't appear to be wearing anything under a wrapper held together by a purple sash. The front of it flopped open when she leaned forward to reach the cold eggs. It appeared to me that she must have used Dr. Hardee's Female Improver to good effect. She could have been anywhere between twenty and fifty, with hair about the same color as mine, but from a bottle, I think.

My discomfort increased as she picked out our lieutenant and leered at him. He blushed becomingly, which was somehow reassuring, until he gave her a sidelong look so full of meaning that I could only assume he had been one of her earlier guests last night.

Mother took none of this lying down. At every bat of that soiled dove's false eyelashes, Mother harrumphed and gave her The Look that cowered many a child and servant on McDermott Street.

The glower had no effect on that battle-tested trollop. She slapped a hunk of butter on her hashbrowns, stirred in an egg and smiled sweetly at Mother. "What's the matter, honey? Your piles bothering you?"

I nearly strangled over my coffee, then paled as Mother gave me a furious look. She stood up in awful majesty and tried to sweep out of the room, but the effect was marred when her dress caught on a nail and pulled her up sharp. She yanked it off and sailed away, as Muskrat laughed and scratched, Eugenie pounded Phil on the back as he choked over his flapjacks, and Father stared at his week-old newspaper, oblivious as always.

It was not a propitious beginning to our Yellowstone idyll, but at least the rain stopped.

We crossed Targhee Pass that day and camped on the edge of Yellowstone Park, taking Muskrat's word for it that we were nearly in the park. There were no signs, and the road was questionable. I hear the park has been much improved in recent years by roads built by U.S. Army engineers. There are even hotels now. I will never go back, however.

For the first time on our trip, I missed my bed in Omaha, where the maids always employed warming pans before I crawled between clean sheets. Eugenie yelped when I put my cold feet on her, but we gradually warmed up enough to sleep. I think it was the first week in August.

We entered the park in the morning. Muskrat Watkins told us the elk were already in the mountain valley, but we saw moose in the distance, and beaver and bears. The bears with cubs shied away when they heard our noisy entourage approaching, but some of the slightly older bandits scampered along the dirt track laughingly called a road and begged with such appeal.

We did not disappoint them. I suppose we Everetts were among the first park tourists to beguile bears with bread and scraps and turn them into lazy loafers.

We camped first at what is now called the Lower Geyser Basin, with its variety of hot springs, and gurgling, spouting phenomena. (I've never been back since 1877, but my brother Phil recently sent me the new nineteenth edition of *Haynes Official Guide*. I looked through it and identified that area where we camped.)

I recall one geyser spewing forth steam to an amazing height. If I had ever paid attention to my art instructor, I would have been sketching for all I was worth like Phil. I just stood there with my mouth open, enjoying the spectacle and the rumbling beneath my feet.

Lt. McCormack cautioned us to tread carefully around the hot springs, as the ground was often merely a crust and liable to give way with no warning. Indeed, Muskrat Watkins walked into a streamlet near a river and scorched his toes. He did not rest until he scalded the woods with a blast of his choicest profanity.

The wagon road ended at the Lower Geyser Basin, so the following week, feeling somewhat like Lewis and Clark, we loaded our belongings onto pack mules and struck out for the interior of Yellowstone Park.

We headed south and camped near the site of the famous geyser Old Faithful, purported to erupt every fifty minutes. Although not as spectacular as that northern geyser, Old Faithful's punctuality was an impressive display for people who lived by the clock, as we did.

On the Firehole River, Eugenie and I discovered the joys of hot-potting. Muskrat Watkins pointed us toward a hot water streamlet that fed into the river, where we stripped down to our chemises and underdrawers and cavorted in the sulfur-scented water warmer than a bath. Eugenie especially enjoyed the medicinal effect of the sulfur water, since she was prone to blemishes. At the advanced age of eighteen, I had left pimples behind. Still, any excuse to swim nearly naked suited a side of me I hadn't discovered before. The things one learns on vacation...

We were splashed around in our hidden hole one morning when the wrangler found us. He sat by our clothing and wouldn't leave, even though we threatened to tell Father. Eugenie and I hollered until Phil wandered by. The wrangler swore at him, but he left. As he scrambled up the bank, the wrangler turned and stared me in the eye.

"You think you're mighty fine, missy, don't you? You just wait."

I avoided the man from then on, but he gave me such looks of concentrated malice that I confess to considerable fear. I was grateful never to be alone in his company.

When I wasn't hot-potting, I fished. This caused my mother additional distress as she watched my complexion tan. Like the dutiful daughter I occasionally was, I slathered on her oils and unguents at night and literally slid into my bedroll. Still, as soon as I was out of her sight after breakfast – she never strayed from camp – my straw hat soon went down my back, held there by the ties. I didn't care what my suntan did to my chances at Vassar. The brisk air and sun-filled days in the park were so exhilarating that I couldn't sit in the shade.

I flirted with Lt. McCormack as often as I dared, but he preferred to spend his time with Father, exploring the woods and hunting. At least, he did when he wasn't sitting on his folding chair near the tent entertaining Mother, who began to take even more meticulous care of herself.

My husband likes to fish, so let me add this for any anglers who might read this account: There are several convenient hot springs near West Thumb where you can catch your cutthroat trout in the lake, skin and gut it, then boil it in a hot spring. Bring your own tartar sauce.

After a week by Yellowstone Lake, we moved camp to a spot three miles east, which became our headquarters from which we set out on daily or overnight expeditions of the park.

On one trip near Lewis Lake, we chanced upon a military party, headed by no less a personage than General William T. Sherman himself, then conducting a tour of regional garrisons. He and Father renewed a brief acquaintance from Civil War days while I was proposed to by a bachelor junior officer in the entourage. Women were scarce in the West back then, and the average enterprising man allowed no grass to grow under his feet. In the accelerated space of two days, I turned down his offer, but kindly, feeling no guilt.

Two days after the Sherman party moved on, an event occurred which should have warned us that our peaceful time as tourists was nearly at an end.

I went fishing with Father one morning, and we were angling up some nameless creek. Father waded into the middle of the creek and worked his way downstream, casting, catching, and putting trout in the creel around his waist. I sat on the bank sunning myself when I heard a noise and glanced up.

I saw a riderless horse on the opposite bank, but not just any old horse. This one was tall, with a red-colored chest, a long, handsome face, and curious liver-colored spots on its rump and legs. I had never seen a horse like that before, and I stood up for a better view. I called to Father, but he was too far away.

I had already removed my boots, so I picked up my skirt and started across the stream. The water was icy even in August, and the stones in the stream bed hurt my feet, but I was curious.

Before I was even halfway across the stream, the horse whinnied, stumbled around in the brush, then sank to its knees, toppled over and lay still. I was so surprised that I dropped my skirt and stood there. When the horse whinnied again, I hurried across and climbed up the bank, wondering what I could possibly do.

The horse died before my eyes. I'll admit I was no horsewoman then, but I could tell the animal had been ridden hard. As I looked closer, I saw marks that might have been half-healed bullet wounds.

I called again for Father and he soon joined me. He stared down at the horse much like I had, then knelt and patted it.

"Where do you suppose it came from?" I asked, a little surprised at myself because my voice trembled, and I felt tears gather. The dead horse was so beautiful.

Father shook his head. He ran his hand along the animal's neck and looked closer. He touched its mane, then felt it carefully. He lifted it and we both stared.

Someone had woven braids of tiny seashells into the horse's mane. They hung in tangled, knotted strands.

"Do you suppose..." Father began.

"Indians?" I finished.

It was most unlikely, but where would Indians around Yellowstone Park get seashells? We looked at each other and I think shared the same thought, the one better left unsaid. Maybe Lt. McCormack's Indian disturbance was closer than he thought.

Chapter Five

We hurried back to camp and told Tom McCormack about the dead horse. The lieutenant wanted to have a look, but darkness was nearly on us, and Father and I weren't sure we could locate the place again. The three of us agreed not to say anything to Mother and the others. "It's probably nothing. Why alarm them?" the soldier said, which I thought was perfectly stupid.

Before we retired to our tents, Tom took Father aside and told him that perhaps we ought to break camp in the morning – you know, nothing in a hurry to frighten the others – and head further south, just in case.

I know I wasn't supposed to overhear their conversation, but when I coughed and made my presence known, Tom tried to make a big joke of the whole thing. What sheltered lives we ladies led then! I was not so easily put off. I knew very well why we were moving.

Did I sleep? Who knows, except that I was up early in the morning. Eugenie protested and tried to roll over and return to sleep, but I jerked her bedroll around until she had no alternative. The stare she gave me was *not* friendly.

I dressed quickly. I remember I left off my corset and put on a camisole with lace trim around the neck and a light blue ribbon running through the lace. Isn't it strange what the mind recalls? I wore my brown riding habit, the one with jet buttons down the front, and pinned my watch over my heart. After a month of our Chinese cook's best efforts, I had to hold my breath to button the skirt.

I pulled my hair into its usual knot, anchored with hairpins here and there, then set my riding hat on top just so, as I always did. As it turned out, it hardly could have mattered.

Our plans for an early start sprang a leak. That disgusting wrangler had lit out on his own during the night, taking with him several pack mules, some supplies, and two good rifles. When Muskrat Watkins interrogated the other wrangler, the man mumbled something about his colleague saying he'd had enough of prissy travelers and wanted to cast his lot with the army detachment we had come across earlier. He thought they paid better than Muskrat Watkins, which sent Muskrat into a profane tirade until Father told him to shut up. I had never heard Father speak that way before.

For myself, I couldn't help but feel relief at seeing the last of the wrangler. I silently wished the army well.

We made a cold breakfast of leftover biscuits and canned peaches, then Phil went to help Muskrat and the other wrangler ready the remaining horses and pack mules. Our hardy frontiersman summoned the animals with less vulgarity than usual, which added to my unease. I wanted to be out of that clearing.

Tom helped me saddle Methuselah, who groaned like an old man and broke wind with every tug of the cinch. The lieutenant bent down and cupped his hands. Wasting not a moment, I let him toss me into the saddle. I hooked my leg over the lower pommel, straightened my skirts, nodded to the lieutenant and waited for the others.

As I had earlier, Eugenie was having trouble with the hooks and eyes on her riding skirt. She started toward me, needing help.

Every moment is still clear in my brain. I had just swung my leg out of that lower pommel to help her, when I heard more horses and looked up.

All carrying rifles, four Indians walked their horses into our clearing. One of the men propped the butt of his gun on his thigh while the others rested their weapons across their laps as they rode toward us.

Unnerved, I had the presence of mind to swing my leg back across the lower pommel as before. I froze as four pairs of eyes followed my movement. I heard a click as one horseman cocked his rifle. When Eugenie started to whimper, I nudged her with my boot and hissed at her to be quiet. She shuddered and clung to my stirrup in silence.

Phil stood on the other side of the clearing, as motionless as when we used to play Statues on the side lawn at home. He carried his saddle and stood there, his face chalk white. I had read that phrase before in an overheated novel and scoffed. No, it is possible to go chalk white.

He would have gone even paler if he had looked over his shoulder. Behind him in the trees I saw other riders.

The original four riders walked their mounts into the center of our camp. Two of them rode brown horses and the other two rode spotted horses similar to the one Father and I had come across yesterday.

I thought at first that the Indians were entirely naked, but as they came closer, I saw they wore loincloths. Three of them wore their hair hanging down in thin braids on the sides, with hair on top swept back in a pompadour and the rest hanging free. The fourth man wore his hair straight. It came only a little past his ears, and looked as though it had been lopped off in a dark room with pinking shears.

Their faces were painted for war, but not recently, as it had rubbed off in spots. They looked somehow rumpled, as if they slept in their clothes, but since they weren't wearing many clothes, I know my description is hardly apt. Perhaps the better word was tired, as if they were part of a camping trip that had gone on too long.

As the four braves filed their horses into our clearing, the others rode in, too. I counted seventeen in total. These were dressed, or undressed, like the original four, with the addition of a blue flannel shirt on one man, and another with leggings. Several of them had cropped hair. One horse carried two riders, which made me wonder if the horse we saw yesterday belonged to one of them. Some men had saddles; others rode bareback.

Father has always looked like a natural leader. One of the four kneed his horse closer and stared at Father, who started back. He had been shaving, and he was all lathered up, presenting a ludicrous appearance, if anyone could have seen any humor in the moment. I know I couldn't.

Someone did. I heard a chuckle and looked around to see an Indian not far from me and Eugenie. He smiled at Father.

Since I didn't know where to look, I looked at him, noting his interesting war paint. One half of his face was painted a dull white, and the other side a deep red. Little dart-like arrows on his forehead crossed over from the white side to the red side. I didn't see a rifle, but his bow was slung over his shoulder.

Muskrat Watkins broke the silence. He walked toward the Indian who had moved closest and held up his hand. "What Indians are you?" he asked in English, which I thought positively foolish. It seemed unlikely to me that any of this barely clothed bunch had ever been near a mission school.

I was wrong. The Indians looked at each other and at their leader.

"We are Nimiipuu," he said. "Sometimes you whites call us Nez Perce."

Weren't those the Indians Lt. McCormack had told me not to worry my pretty head about? I shifted in the saddle to look for our lieutenant, well aware that the Indian – the Nez Perce – with the curious paint watched me.

Tom sat on a camp stool near Mother, who had been buttoning up her shoes. She still bent half over with the button hook in her hand, afraid to move. Her face was red from the exertion and she didn't show to advantage. I turned away and noticed that the Indian was smiling again.

I couldn't resist. "You must have a sense of humor," I muttered under my breath.

I know he heard me. He took his hand off his bow and leaned forward as if to reply. We were both distracted then by a sudden move from the remaining wrangler.

The man stood to one side by the pack mules, partly hidden by the supply wagon. He raised his rifle and aimed it at the head warrior. Phil gasped and dropped his saddle, which made the leader jerk his horse around as someone shot the wrangler.

It roared like a double-barreled shotgun, nearly cutting the cowboy in half. I watched in horror as he worked his suddenly blood-filled mouth a couple of times, tried to grasp what remained of his middle, then seemed to collapse inside himself.

Mother shrieked like a banshee, which was echoed and outdone by most of the Nez Perce. Eugenie sobbed and clutched my stirrup, and Phil vomited. Trust Phil.

Methuselah shivered and I patted him. He seemed undecided what course of action to take, and I fully expected him to fall down in a heap. It would certainly have been in character.

I think he would have, if the smiling Indian near me hadn't let out a scream that fully described and amplified the term *blood-curdling*. Call it a cliché if you must, but you weren't there and I was.

Old Methuselah turned into another horse. With a scream of his own, old Ancient of Days reared back. Eugenie was thrown to the ground as I reached for her. As the horse reared farther and farther back, I clung to the saddle with both hands. Above the shooting and the din, I heard Father hollering at me to let go. If I had possessed a grain of sense at the moment, I would have. Instead, I threw my leg over the side saddle and gripped Methuselah tight with both knees as he went up and up.

When it seemed Methuselah would topple over backward if he reared any farther, he came down with a great thump that jarred my teeth and gave me a three-day headache.

We were off. The Nez Perce were already leaving the clearing at a gallop and that fool horse Methuselah joined them. I yanked back on the reins as I swore at that nag with some of Muskrat Watsons's choicest tidbits. It did me no good. I was at a definite disadvantage. Methuselah obviously had a highly honed sense of herd attraction and he was constrained to follow the Nez Perce.

When I dared raise my eyes from the bald spot between Methuselah's ears, I saw that I was surrounded by Nez Perce. One of them came close as we pounded along leg to leg. He leaned closer as I drew back and snatched the gold watch pinned to my riding habit, taking a circle of material with it. (Incidentally, he later returned the watch and apologized, but it had run down by then and I had no idea what time it was. I let him keep it.)

I was joined on the other side by a fellow who appeared considerably exercised. He shrieked and screamed in my ear, shaking a hunting knife in my face as we tore along. I cried and pleaded with him, but he kept that knife right under my ear.

All this time I thought I was still pulling back on the reins, but Methuselah ignored me completely, charging on like one possessed. Detestable horse. The Nez Perce with my watch fell back, to be promptly replaced by the man with the strange war paint. He leaned across me and shouted something at the Indian on my other side, the one with the knife against my jaw. With a wolf's howl, he sheathed his knife and shot ahead.

The red and white painted Indian rode by my side as we galloped on. I suppose we passed some of Yellowstone's most magnificent scenery, but I don't remember any of it. As a tourist, I was a positive failure that morning. I cried and still sawed at the reins. Nothing. Finally, the Nez Perce took the reins from my hands. He had to pry my fingers loose.

Methuselah came to himself then. With the Nez Perce warrior in the lead, he trotted along like a colt and left me to my thoughts.

Chapter Six

My thoughts were not profitable. In this part of my narrative, it will be hard for me to express on paper how I felt. I assure you, I still remember those feelings. I am sitting here at the rolltop desk and I am sweating, even though the room is cool with that early morning breeze so welcome in Oregon.

As we rode, I said, "No, no, no," over and over again like a two-year-old ordered to eat her beets. The word eventually had no meaning. I felt almost claustrophobic, as if I had been crammed into one of those new-fangled phonebooths I noticed a few weeks ago on our trip to Portland. I was smothering in terror almost as if someone were wrapping me tighter and tighter in a blanket.

I am certain you can gather what topic fully occupied my mind. The Indians hadn't killed me outright; as we loped along, I wished they had. There could be only one reason they were keeping me alive and I did not want to think about it.

Even in my sheltered life in Omaha, we had heard about the last bullet that the husband ordered his wife to save for herself, in the event of Indian attack. Women never talked about it, but we all knew it was better to die by one's own hand than suffer that fate worse than death.

That highly charged phrase cropped up occasionally in whispered conversations with other girls my age, and more frequently in those insipid dime novels Phil and I read. In our early teens, we girls weren't entirely sure what the fate worse than death was, but by the time I graduated from Miss Sumner's Female Academy, I had a pretty good notion.

My speculations were gleaned from snatched of giggled conversation behind the stacks in the library when we were supposed to be studying or reading improving works. These ideas were further substantiated by contributions from home.

We Everett children had a series of governesses in our later years from whom we learned a great deal, Miss Parmlee in particular, who took it upon herself to educate me and Eugenie in the ways of the world. In hushed tones, she told us of young girls led astray in dark alleys who ended up in Persian harems, or maidens who took that first drop of liquor and gave themselves over to all manner of licentiousness. She was rarely more specific than that. I tried to look up licentiousness in the dictionary and remained mystified because I didn't know how to spell it so I could look it up. (I told this story to my husband. He laughed so hard I thought he would do himself an injury.)

We gathered from Miss Parmlee's dire tales and dark looks that men were depraved beasts who Took What They Wanted from innocent virgins and left them ruined forever. She frightened me so much that I was over sixteen before I left Charlie Rigmore kiss me under the mistletoe. Even then, I worried for days if I was going to find myself "that way," all because I let him plant a hurried kiss on my cheek while the others were singing Christmas carols in the church.

We didn't regret Miss Parmlee's sudden departure. Mother claimed she fired our governess because she was caught dipping in the cooking sherry. Phil told us the real reason, how she let herself into his room one night and, as Phil put it, "bothered me." As that incident is not the direct subject of this narrative, we will allow it to rest.

Later, Mother sat Eugenie and me down and tried to explain the facts of life to us, but she spoke in tongues and we found it perplexing. She carried on about bees taking honey from blossom to blossom, asked us if we understood her meaning, then beat it from the room before we recovered enough to ask her any questions.

I received the remainder of my knowledge about love and life from the other girls at the female academy. Someone had a distant relative – it's always a distant relative – who let a man take advantage of her and ended up in the family way. We giggle and tittered and shivered with delicious excitement in anticipation of our own initiation into lust and desire, and if we were lucky, love. Sex was a popular schoolgirl subject even in those protective days, and don't let anyone tell you different.

But I wasn't giggling now in some dark corner of the library. The full horror of what awaited me settled down and stayed for the afternoon. I had heard the word rape before, when we were studying early Roman history and ever so lightly touched on the Sabine women. When the obviously uncomfortable teacher corrected himself with a harrumph or two, and settled on ravish instead, I naturally looked up both words after class.

While *rape* was grim and matter-of-fact, *ravish* was milder, as in "seize and carry off someone by force," and almost pleasant: "fill someone with intense delight." I spent some time wondering about point of view, and those noble Roman republicans. The thought never crossed my mind that I would be no better off than those poor Sabine women. I didn't think the Nez Perce had intense delight in mind.

As we pounded along, I spent a disquieting amount of time wondering what it would be like. Would all of them rape me? Would they kill me when they were done? Would they leave me to die?

We rode all afternoon, stopping for nothing. The horsemen were tireless. They gnawed on what looked like beef jerky, hung in pouches over their saddles, if they had them, or around their necks if they didn't. We kept a steady pace, not fast but not slow, and Methuselah astounded me by keeping up.

I watched the riders as we traveled farther away from my family, who, for all I knew, were dead. I watched in fear at first, terrified one of them would make a sudden move my way, and then out of curiosity, because that seems to be how I am constructed.

The Nez Perce who had held his knife under my throat rode by me occasionally, muttering something under his breath until I was nearly reduced to tears. He wore the most vivid war paint, but he kept wiping his nose with the back of his hand. I wondered if he was allergic to the goldenrod that carpeted the meadows and passes.

The two Indians on the same pony were only boys. They sometimes rode ahead or behind the main body of warriors until the man I thought was the leader hollered at them. I didn't know what he said, of course, but they didn't stray from the group again.

The warrior who ripped away my watch pinned the timepiece to the front of his loincloth. He held up the loincloth to put the watch to his ear, giving anyone with any sensibilities cause to blush.

The red-and-white-painted man eventually gave me back Methuselah's reins and rode by my side off and on throughout the afternoon. He whistled to himself part of the time; I thought I recognized the tune, but that couldn't be. He held the reins loosely and carelessly, as if riding were second nature. When I felt brave enough to look around, I saw that same stance among the others.

The red and white warrior seemed to have appointed himself my chief jailer. I noticed with puzzled gratitude that he always kept himself between me and knife-wielding Nez Perce. As the shadows signaled late afternoon, Red and White rode more often with the leader. I watched their earnest conversation, complete with gestures and sharp words. I wondered only a little about the subject of their discussion, especially when Red and White kept looking back at me.

As darkness began to settle, we passed through a stand of pines that opened onto a meadow. Several warriors rode to the front and talked with the head man, and we went on a little farther. After a mile or so, the leader raised his hand, the signal for the warriors to get off their horses, stretch and walk about.

My stomach knotted into a ball and my throat went dry. I wanted to leap off old Methuselah and see how far I could run, but I couldn't even move. My legs were both numb from the unaccustomed ride. I couldn't have escaped even if the Indians told me to leave.

The man with my watch walked toward me and took the reins from my hands. He let them drop on either side of Methuselah, then spoke to me and gestured. I know he wanted me to dismount, but a tornado couldn't have dislodged me from that nag. I shook my head, even as tears came to my eyes.

He stood there a moment, repeated his command, then turned and walked to Red and White, who squatted on the ground with some of the other braves. They conversed, then Red and White stood up and glared at me. When he spoke, I was so surprised I nearly fell out of the saddle anyway.

"Haven't you been enough trouble already?" he asked, his English impeccable.

I stared at him as he came closer. "You speak English?" I asked in a voice not my own. What a stupid comment. Miss Sumner would have tsk-tsked at me, but I wasn't at my best, conversationally or otherwise.

"Get off the horse," he commanded. As terrified as I was, I couldn't help noticing a lilt to his voice.

I shook my head, utterly at my worst.

"Kindly get off the horse," he repeated slowly, as if to a child or a halfwit.

I shook my head again, dreading the way he pursed his lips in a tight line.

"Get. Off. The. Horse."

I heard no kindness this time. I winced and leaned over, speaking in a whisper. "I would love to oblige you, truly I would, but my legs fell asleep somewhere back down that trail and I can't even move them."

He laughed, which made me so angry that if I could, I would have landed him a good jab with my boot.

The others seemed to want to know what was so funny, so he told them what I said. Some of them chuckled, and the rest turned away, talking among themselves, on to a new topic apparently. As I look back at that moment, I think it may have been the best thing that could have happened. The tension vanished.

Red and White held up his arms. "Come on," he coaxed, the kindness back in his voice.

"When in Rome," I muttered, leaned out of my saddle and dropped on top of him. He steadied me and held me up, then let go. I crumpled in a pile at his feet. This time he grinned.

"I guess you weren't kidding," he said, and helped me to my feet.

I started brushing the grass and dirt off my skirt. "If you think I would joke at a time like this…" I began, then stopped when he turned me around and swatted at the dust on my back. I know I should have been grateful, but I kept waiting for a knife between my ribs.

He finished to his satisfaction apparently, and turned me around. I looked at him, all fight and energy gone, totally defeated. I held my hands out. "Please don't hurt me," I said.

He shook his head. "No one is going to hurt you. It's my fault you're here. If I hadn't screamed, I doubt this old specimen would have bolted."

He ran his hand along Methuselah's flank. My useless nag quivered, too tired to move. "That's some horse you have," Red and White said. His back was to me, but his shoulders shook, and I knew he was laughing. I couldn't blame him. Compared to the horses around him, Methuselah was a poor relation.

He gave Methuselah another pat and looked toward the men adding twigs to a small fire. "Walk around. Loosen up your legs. There are some bushes, so you can take care of any private business." He paused, then looked me in the eye. "Don't do anything sudden. You don't know how hard I had to talk to keep Tall One over there from shooting you and dumping you off back there."

He left me alone and joined the others. I limped over to a large rock and sat on it, my rump on fire. I must have made an awful face, because when I came away quick from the rock, one of the Nez Perce grinned at me.

Aching from muscles I didn't know I possessed, I hobbled around until walking changed from torture to mere agony. I desperately needed to relieve myself, but the thought of squatting somewhere set my teeth on edge. Nature continued to call, however, so I found some handy underbrush and took care of the matter, all the time swearing to myself that they would have to tie me up to get me on that horse in the morning.

I thought about that. They could also just leave me here, wherever here was. Yellowstone Park is a big place and I didn't even know north from south then. The chances of being found by something on four legs rather than two was a distinct possibility, one I relished even less than keeping present company. Maybe.

With no choice, I wandered back to the Indians. They ignored me, which was a relief. I glanced about for the Indian who spoke English, then saw him at a stream with steam rising from it, washing the paint off his face. When he noticed me, he dried off his face with his loincloth – I looked away discreetly – and came closer, but not too close.

"You certain you do not wish to sit down?" he asked. I couldn't tell if he was joking.

"Positive," I answered crisply.

He stood there with his hands on his hips, as if waiting for me to say more. He looked better with the paint off his face. Not any less Indian, but better.

"What's your name?" I asked at last, knowing in my civilized heart what Miss Sumner would think if she ever heard me initiating a conversation with a man.

"Kaya. What's yours?"

"Elizabeth Ann Everett."

"People call you all that?"

"Well no," I said, amused at his plain speaking. "Only my mother and teachers call me Elizabeth Ann. To my friends, I'm Liz."

"What should I call you?" he asked, perfectly serious.

What, indeed? I couldn't lump him in with relatives or teachers, and certainly not with friends. And yet, he had argued to keep me alive, and admitted he never should have startled my old horse. I knew right then that it was possible I would never have a better friend than this man. I couldn't tell him that, of course, but there it was. I took a deep breath, not knowing then that it would be one of many during the next six weeks, as my mind and heart changed in unexpected ways, all because someone screamed and my horse was stupid.

"Call me Liz," I said simply.

He motioned me toward the campfire, where he handed me a piece of brown, dried bark. I sniffed, and felt the saliva start to flow over... bark?

Kaya obviously knew skepticism when he saw it. "Camas root. Ground up, dried and baked. Try it."

I took a cautious bite into something that tasted vaguely like turnips. I downed that morsel in three bites and looked around for more. There wasn't any. That was another lesson in a day of hard education: Eat slowly and make it last.

A peculiar thing happened. I watched the others eat, making it last, and burst into tears. You know. The loud kind. I was hungry, getting cold, standing heaven-knew-where, surrounded by savages in war paint. It had not been a good day. I stood by the campfire and wailed.

Men being men, they were unsure what to do. Then another thing happened that made me feel that matters might work out. One of the older warriors, a man with gray hair, came close and put his arm around my shoulders. I cried harder. He said something and Kaya translated. "Liz, hush a minute. He wants to tell you that he has a daughter your age in camp."

I looked at the older gentleman. I saw a father with a daughter instead of an Indian with face paint. The moment didn't last long, but long enough for me to dry my tears. The man patted me on the back, and everyone looked relieved that I had dried up.

I did feel better. Trying to regain a little dignity, I walked back to the warm water stream and washed my face. I scrubbed at the layer of grit I had accumulated in the day's travel. Maybe I scrubbed away a little immaturity, too. Time would tell.

I dug a comb out of my pocket and dragged it through my tangled hair. My hairpins were all long gone, but I pulled the hair back from my face and started to unlace one of my boots. Maybe I could cut off part of the shoestring to work.

Kaya saw what I was doing. He consulted with one of his brethren and in a moment brought me a suitable length of rawhide, which worked wonders. "Thank you," I told him, which he passed on to the owner.

I wanted to take off my boots and stockings and stick my feet in the warm water, but someone brushed dirt over the campfire. I felt a moment of fear again, the earlier fear, but it passed. The Nez Perce who had comforted me handed over a blanket. It must have been his own, but I was not about to insult him by refusing it. I nodded and smiled, well aware now that until I got myself out of this fix, I was going to do a lot of nodding and smiling.

I wrapped myself in the blanket and lay down as far away from everyone as I could, and not appear impolite. Kaya sat cross-legged by me, saying nothing, but I had questions.

"Tell me something, Kaya. That man…"

"His Heart Is Brave," he supplied. "He has a strong name."

I knew that would never be my name. Granted, I felt better, but there was nothing about this situation that reassured me. "His Heart Is Brave mentioned a daughter back in camp. This isn't the whole group?"

"Oh, no, no. Maybe there are six hundred of us, maybe more." He rubbed his chin. "After Big Hole, maybe less." He stopped talking, but this time I waited for him to continue. Maybe I was going to learn something about manners. "We are only the decoy."

"Decoy?" I began to get that sick feeling all over again.

"Yes. Haven't you noticed how much dust we have been raising?"

"Well, no." I hardly thought it worth mentioning to him that my mind had been otherwise occupied all day.

"We are counting on the soldiers and scouts to follow us instead of The People."

"What people?" Kaya must have thought I was an idiot.

"*Our* people. Liz, for some weird reason known only to them, French trappers named us Nez Perce." He chuckled. "No one pierces their nose in this nation. Oh, well. We are Nimiipuu, The People." He patted the ground. "Go to sleep. We'll start early in the morning."

I lay down and wiggled a bit until I found a good spot. Kaya lay down not close but not far, but between me and The People. Poor man. He felt responsible that he had got me in this fix, I know he did.

Before I drifted off, I had another question. I tried to open my eyes, but that didn't happen. What a long day this had been. "Kaya, where did you learn English?"

"From my father. He was a Scot who came to the Blue Mountains to trap and met my mother."

"Oh." That explained his curious accent and the way he rolled his r's. I had more questions now. Maybe one more. "What does Kaya mean?"

"Hawk. Go to sleep."

Chapter Seven

I was prodded awake the following morning by someone, a soft moccasin prod. I rolled over and tried to go on sleeping, but the prod continued until I sat up. His Heart Is Brave walked away, his duty done. I wondered if his daughter liked to be prodded awake.

I closed my eyes again and opened them slowly, hoping that when I looked around, I would be back in my own bedroom in Omaha, and the whole episode a silly nightmare brought on by too much ginger fizz. No luck. I was still somewhere in Yellowstone Park, surrounded by men in war paint. My only consolation was that some of them didn't look like early risers, either.

I tried to stand up, rethought the matter for a moment, then gritted my teeth and stood, my body one enormous ache. If I thought my muscles were sore last night, they were screaming now. I felt faint and wanted to sit down, but that would only mean I would have to stand up again. Nope.

My faithful nag was saddled and waiting for me, looking truly repentant in the half-light of dawn, his head hanging down. I am certain if he could have talked, he would have begged my forgiveness for yesterday's folly. He whinnied and tried to nuzzle me as I hobbled to him, but I was in no mood to be jollied by such a deceiving hunk of dogmeat.

As I contemplated climbing up, a rider came tearing down the trail we had covered the day before, silent and swinging a red blanket in circles. The others leaped on their horses with an agility I could only envy.

Kaya – I will call him Hawk – was already in the saddle. "Come on, Liz. We must ride."

I shook my head. "Leave me here, won't you?" I hoped he would. If the soldiers and their Indian scouts were coming at us, I figured I could remain behind and this whole adventure would be done. I could be back catching trout with Father.

Hawk shook his head. "We can't do that."

"And pray why not?" I didn't mean to whine, but there you are.

He leaned over until he was nearly in my face. "The scouts will reach you first and you will die. If you are lucky."

That hardly seemed logical and so I told him. Hawk narrowed his eyes, dismounted and started toward me. I backed away. If he thought I was going to let him toss me onto that saddle and jostle about for another day, he was sadly mistaken. I would take my chances with the Indian scouts.

The Nimiipuu were already heading north at a gallop. Several of them looked back at Hawk and laughed, which didn't do much for his disposition. "Look!" he shouted. "I'm responsible for you!"

I kept backing up. From the way he kept glancing behind him, I knew Hawk was none too eager to be found there arguing with a girl when the whole US Army thundered up. I wasn't willing to get back on Methuselah for more punishment. I turned to run, but I could barely shuffle my feet.

Hawk grabbed me around the waist and lifted me onto my horse. "You have no idea what the scouts will do to you. Please believe me," he said.

I had barely got my leg crooked around the lower horn when he slapped the horse and I was off again. Only a complete greenie who has ridden for nine hours straight, and forced to ride again can fully appreciate my situation. I felt myself falling, even as I jerked myself upright. As I did, I looked over my shoulder and saw something that put my heart in my throat and kept it there for the whole day.

A cluster of yelling warriors came at us riding fast. They looked pretty much like Nimiipuu to me, but then all Indians looked alike to me then, so perhaps I can be forgiven my error. They yelled, yipped like dogs and shot at us. Hawk was right. In the early light of dawn, I was just another body on a horse. My life would be worth less than nothing if I hung back and tried to tell them I was Elizabeth Ann Everett from Omaha, Nebraska.

One scout raced into the clearing ahead of the others. Hawk fitted arrow to bow and let fly. The arrow slammed into the man's chest and he fell off his horse. I figured Hawk had taken complete leave of his senses when he jumped off his mount, ran to the fallen scout and tugged on the arrow.

"What on earth are you doing?" I shrieked at him.

"Getting the arrow out," he grunted as he yanked. "Cannot waste'um."

If ever I needed convincing that Hawk had the blood of a Scot in his veins, that did it. I covered my ears as he tugged out the arrow, bringing with it innards I had no desire to see.

Hawk leaped on his horse again, bloody arrow in his hand. From the noise coming through the pines behind us, the clearing was about to become as crowded as our parlor on Thanksgiving. Hawk let out with his patented shriek and Methuselah was energized all over again.

My horse was as frightened as I was. His long legs ate up the ground in a fierce desire to put as much real estate between him and those scouts. "Death, where is thy sting," I muttered as we galloped and bounced after The People. My body was in such desperate shape that I wished I could have cached it somewhere and picked it up later.

I must give Hawk credit here. I know his horse could have outdistanced Methuselah without even pausing to take a deep breath, but he stayed behind me all the way. I know I should have been more grateful, but all I wanted to do was crawl away and suffer in peace.

Gradually the distance between us and the scouts lengthened. After more hard riding, they could no longer be seen or heard. We caught up with the decoy party as the sun cleared the eastern mountains.

The rest of the day was one of unrelieved torture. We rode forward, we doubled back, we milled the horses around, we dragged brush, we did everything but ride our horses up into the pines and swing from the branches. I should have been more impressed by the superb horsemanship I witnessed, but I was wrapped up in my own misery and barely polite. Hawk tried to make conversation, but I only answered with nasty looks. He ignored me after that. I couldn't blame him. I didn't like me, either.

We stayed a jump ahead of the soldiers until the sun was low in the sky, when we doubled back in absolute silence and hid in the tall pines as they passed us. The Bluecoats were so close I think I could have touched them. The column was long and noisy. We heard their jingle, clink and creak long before they were in sight. Any element of surprise was wholly on the side of The People.

The soldiers were a hard-bitten crew, their uniforms torn and dirty, their faces hairy. They looked as though they had been following their quarry all summer. Even through my inexperienced eyes, I knew the troopers had been drinking from a bitter cup.

The men looked mostly the same to me, except for the man with stars on his shoulder straps who had only one arm. I knew I had seen him before. "Who is that?" I whispered to Hawk.

"General Howard, Old Day After Tomorrow," he whispered back, his lips practically on my dirty ear, his eyes on the column.

"Goodness. Oliver Howard. He had dinner at our house last winter," I whispered.

Father liked to entertain, and many of our guests were government dignitaries and soldiers. I remembered General Howard in particular because he was missing his right arm – a result of the Civil War – and because he gave the blessing on the food one night. The potatoes were cold before he finished.

Quiet, I watched the column pass. I thought about calling out. I guess Hawk knew what I had in mind because he stayed close to me, knife in hand and pointed in my general direction. I thought it prudent not to abuse his hospitality.

After the troopers were well beyond us, heading in the wrong direction, we backtracked and rode steadily until after dark. One of the horses gave out and was left by the way. Methuselah profited by the example; he was a model horse.

When I was about the relinquish hope of ever getting out of the saddle in this life, we slowed to a walk and topped a small rise. Dogs barked.

Below me was a bowl-shaped meadow surrounded by low hills. I squinted to see a camp in the failing light. Fired dotted the ground here and there by tipis and brush shelters.

I was now in the camp of The People.

Chapter Eight

We rode to the edge of a huge pony herd, took off those saddles – those who weren't bareback riders – and turned the animals loose. I never saw so many horses in one place at once, many of them those lovely spotted creatures that intrigued me. Although it was too dark to pick out individual horses, the bulk of the entire herd took away my exhaustion for a moment.

"How many?" I asked Hawk as he handed me my saddle.

He shrugged, so I guess no one had bothered with a census. I would have thought far more than a thousand horses, probably the wealth of an entire nation.

We carried our saddles to the ring of shelters, me lagging back not out of fear now – I had been beyond that since our mad dash away from the scouts – but shyness. I looked around at tipis and brush shelters bunched together in separate encampments. I stumbled along behind Hawk, trying to hold up the train of my skirt and manage the saddle growing heavier with every step.

Hawk led me to a shelter made of partially burned canvas and set down his saddle at the entrance. I did the same. He ducked inside the shelter and motioned me to follow.

A woman knelt over a small fire in the center of the shelter, dropping stones into a tripod affair holding up a brass bucket. The woman rocked back on her heels and stood up when Hawk entered. Her smile lit the shelter. I waited for her to hug him, but she only touched his shoulder. Her gaze was so deep into his eyes that it went beyond touch.

Hawk turned to me. "My mother, Blue Mountain Woman." He said it simply, but I heard all the love.

If Blue Mountain Woman was surprised to see me, she didn't show it, which made me think that Hawk was the kind of kid who probably brought home strays when he was younger. She looked me up and down, but I saw no hostility.

Hawk spoke to her, telling her where I had come from, I suppose. When he finished, she touched my shoulder, such a light touch. (As a side note, let me mention a comment from a white friend only a year ago, who complained about how light Indian handshakes were. I said something placating, but I was thinking, "Dummy, did you ever suppose maybe they're not used to touching in that way?")

When Hawk left the shelter, I couldn't help my tears, the quiet type this time. I already knew that the men didn't raise their voices, so I doubted Blue Mountain Woman would have cared much for histrionics.

Instead, she gestured for me to sit by the fire. She pulled off my boots and stockings and rubbed my feet between her hands, chatting all the while. I nodded and smiled back and wished I understood. I did hear a few English words. The way she gestured toward the shelter opening with her lips made me think she was irritated that her son hadn't treated me better. It's only a guess, but since I have sons of my own, I can own to motherly irritation now and then.

She turned back to the brass bucket, which simmered now. As I watched with interest, she used two sticks to remove stones that upon closer inspection looked volcanic. She set them in the fire, then added other hot stones. I gasped in surprise as the water bubbled immediately. She repeated this addition and removal several times until I found myself salivating at the wonderful aroma the cooking had released. My stomach rumbled in uninhibited fashion, which made her laugh and pat my knee.

While dinner simmered, Blue Mountain Woman sliced off several pieces of what I already knew was camas root bread, and set them on a polished piece of wood close to the fire. It was all I could do to keep my hands off. I hadn't eaten since last night's mere appetizer. As I watched her deft motions, I vowed that if I ever returned to civilization, I would never turn up my nose at beets or pears, foods I detest. Brussel sprouts, too.

When I didn't think I could stand it any longer, Hawk returned. He sat cross-legged by the fire and waited. Using those sticks, Blue Mountain Woman took out a slab of whatever-it-was from the pot and laid it on another piece of wood, along with a portion of camas bread.

I did my best not to wolf down my portion. Was it salmon? A discreet glance at the pot told me there were no seconds, so I made firsts count. Another lesson learned.

When Hawk finished, he leaned back on his buffalo robe and propped himself up on one elbow. "I told the chiefs about you, Liz."

My stomach slid around and landed somewhere south of my knees. I must have looked pretty stark, because Blue Mountain Woman touched my arm.

"They weren't too pleased, but they were mostly angry with me," Hawk said. "They want to see you."

What could I say? Of course they wanted to see me.

Hawk stood up, brushing flecks of food off his chest. "I will come back for you when they are ready. Maybe you can straighten yourself around a little?"

"That bad?" I asked, trying to keep my tone light.

"Pretty much," he said. When I frowned, he had the wisdom to leave.

He was right. I nearly shrieked when Blue Mountain Woman found a scrap of mirror so I could survey the damage. I knew I was sunburned because my face felt hot and tight. Some cosmic being must have taken an eggbeater to my hair, which was scrambled all over my head. Yes, I was sunburned, but my face had more layers of dirt on it than unexcavated Pompeii. Tears had streaked the dirt down my cheeks, one of which sported a bruise from where a branch had snapped at me.

I didn't know where to begin. Blue Mountain Woman took the brass pot off the dying fire and motioned me to take off my clothes. I smiled inside at the thought that I was going to smell like salmon pretty soon. Hopefully there were no mountain lions skulking about. I stripped down to my drawers and camisole while Blue Mountain Woman held out my riding habit by the front of the shelter to give me some privacy and beat it with a stick.

I started to scrub at the top, merciless to my face and thinking about impressing some Indians who I was certain didn't want me in their camp. A warm cloth down my breasts was bliss in a salmon sort of way. I rinsed off my arms and legs with the now-brown water and promised to do a better job when I could.

Comb in hand, I attacked my hair. I lost. A handful of my hair eventually ended up tangled in the teeth, but at least I didn't look like a freak in a sideshow. I finished it off with the rawhide strip in a bow.

Hawk barged into the shelter then. I still suffered from the effects of the camp cook's meals, but at least the buttons on my camisole weren't straining now and my bosom was more under control. *C'est la vie.* To his credit, Hawk backed right out of the shelter as his mother gave him The Look and handed me my riding habit.

Word traveled fast in the encampment, but I already suspected I was going to be a nine-day wonder for as long as the Nimiipuu suffered my presence. A little knot of people watched me as I left the shelter. Hawk led the way, and I followed him, my eyes on the ground, too shy to look at anyone. I felt dreadfully out of place and so unequal to the situation. Miss Sumner had hammered into our skulls that good manners allowed anyone to fit in anyplace. I'd like to have seen *her* in the Nimiipuu camp.

We walked to a campfire at the edge of a v-line of tepees, followed by Blue Mountain Woman and what looked to me like all the Indians in the western Hemisphere. Journalists have said since then that there were some 250 warriors and 500 women and children in the five clans of Nimiipuu who fled from their homeland in eastern Oregon. I don't know. I would have thought more, but I was scared and they weren't there.

They were an orderly crowd, as opposed to, say, the French rabble lining the streets on Marie Antoinette's tumbril ride to Place de la Revolution. No one talked or jostled for position. I felt the excitement in the air.

There were at least fifteen men seated around the fire. If I name their names, you will know them…. White Bird, Looking Glass, Joseph, Ollokot, Toohoolhoolzote. There were others you wouldn't know…. Many Wounds, Poker Joe, Tom Hill, Husishusis Kute. I didn't know them at the time, naturally, but they were obviously men of authority. Anyone could have discerned that by the way they sat and the gravity of their expressions.

As Hawk and I entered the circle, one of the men motioned us to sit. I did so as gracefully as possible, trying not to wince or grimace on the way down. Methuselah had a bony back.

I sat directly opposite a truly splendid-looking man. He was tall, even sitting down, with a broad face and high cheekbones. His eyes quite captured me. I saw serenity, which was a comfort. I learned later that this was Joseph, a distant cousin of Hawk's and a chief of the Wallamwatkin family of the Nimiipuu.

To his right sat a younger man who resembled him. I think he was the handsomest Indian I ever saw, and the Nimiipuu were, on the whole, quite handsome. He was Ollokot, Joseph's brother.

By contrast, seated next to Ollokot was perhaps the homeliest person I ever laid eyes on. Toohoolhoolzote was the leader of a clan of Nimiipuu that roamed between the Snake and Salmon rivers. He was tall like the others, but hunched over to one side and cursed with thick lips and a nose that looked like it had been broken in several places. Chief Looking Glass had a long face and mournful eyes. And White Bird? He looked at me and I saw compassion.

I could tell you something about each man in the circle, but it's too hard for me. I sit at my desk, aching inside, because all these men are dead now, with the exception of Hawk. I regret their passing. They took something good with them when they left.

The interpreter was Kinikinik Hototo, also called Poker Joe, a mixed blood like Hawk, but French. I learned later that he had lived with the

Flathead Indians for several years, and was famed, for good or ill, by his love of playing cards. He had a thick accent, as did Hawk, but I understood his English.

After a gesture from one of the men, Hawk spoke first, retelling the story of how they had acquired a white female captive. Poker Joe knelt by me and interpreted while Hawk spoke to the chiefs and war leaders.

One of the chiefs, if I remember right it was White Bird, asked him why they had not killed me or left me behind. Hawk seemed to think about that for a moment, and then he lied. "He says, 'We traveled for some distance before we realized she was with us,'" Poker Joe whispered.

I nodded, struck by the fact that Hawk had known I was there from the start. I knew it was not my place to correct him, however, especially not in that tight circle where I think my fate was being decided.

Hawk's lie seemed to satisfy White Bird, one of the war leaders, who clearly had plenty of acquaintance with reactions in the heat of excitement, such as generated by the death of that wrangler back in the camp.

Joseph asked the next logical question, an extension of White Bird's. When they realized, why hadn't they just left me behind? With no hesitation this time, Hawk replied that they thought about leaving me, but were afraid General Howard's Bannock scouts would kill me.

"What of it?" Toohoolhoolzote grumbled. Poker Joe almost didn't translate that for me, but I asked him to.

Silence, then Ollokot gave an impatient sigh and said something pithy. "He says, 'You are too much a white man, Hawk,'" Poker Joe translated.

Hawk snapped something at him that Poker Joe refused to translate, then he spoke again, his voice calm. I looked at Poker Joe, who nodded. "'No, Ollokot, I am too much one of The People. No good would come of killing a white woman, or leaving her behind for Bluecoat scouts to do what they wanted.'"

When Hawk mentioned the scouts again – I was beginning to know that word – Toohoolhoolzote spit into the fire. I surmised that his opinion of General Howard's Indian allies was on par with mine.

Nothing more was said. Hawk knelt on one knee beside me and waited while the chiefs conferred. I was too tired to feel any more afraid than I already did. I was between a rock and a hard place and I knew it. This dilemma had no easy answer, no poof of a wand to make it go away. If they decided to leave me alone in this wilderness, there was no telling what would become of me. If they took me along, who knew what would happen? Would I drag down their entire flight and make it more precarious? Would one of them turn on me, fearing what I would say when the Bluecoats found me?

Finally, Ollokot stood up and spoke for them all. "You will come with us," he said, as Poker Joe interpreted. "At the first chance, we will leave you with white settlers or travelers. We would rather not keep you at all. Only remember that we do not make war on women and children. Only white men do that."

He waited until Poker Joe finished, then shifted his gaze to Hawk. "And you will remember who you are, if you even know." Poker Joe shook his head at that one, but interpreted.

Ollokot sat down and Hawk helped me to my feet. As I was leaving the circle, the chief called Joseph touched me on the arm. He murmured something. Hawk smiled for the first time and told me, "He says, 'You will be all right with us. Not to fear.'"

I followed Hawk from the campfire, unsure of everything except that I wasn't going to die that night.

Chapter Nine

The meadowlarks were beginning to tune up when I stuck my head out from under a buffalo robe and looked around. Hawk still slept on the other side of the shelter, his mouth open slightly. I heard Blue Mountain Woman moving around outside and talking in low tones to her friends.

Her face was half hidden in shadows and I saw Hawk's profile in hers, with her long, straight nose and close-set ears. Her hair was pulled from her face like mine, but held back by the basket-like head covering the women wore.

My riding habit lay near her buffalo robe. She had patched a bright piece of cloth over the tear in the bodice where that warrior had ripped off my watch, then trimmed it with a circle of white beads. The beaded flower inside the circle looked like a daisy. She must have stayed up late doing it.

How kind of her. I propped my chin on my hands and regarded her now in a new light. She smiled at me and started to hum.

Hawk stirred and woke. He coughed and rolled over on his side. I pointed to the lovely beadwork. "How do I tell her thank you?" I asked him.

"Just tell her. She understands some."

"Did your father teach her?" I asked, remembering his absent parent.

"Yes. Some."

"Who was he?" I knew it wasn't polite to ask prying questions. I reasoned that since I was forced to cast my lot with this family, like it or not, I wanted to know something about them.

57

"He was a Scots fur trader from Vancouver, Washington Territory. He lived with us in the Wallowa Valley until I was eight years old, then he returned to Vancouver. It was called Columbia City then."

That was not enough information. Hawk was going to get tired of me really soon, but I wanted to know more. "How did you learn such good English if he left when you were so young?"

He raised his chin and gave me a down-at-the-nose look that suggested I might be teetering on the edge of his personal commentary. "He married a white woman and talked Mother into letting me go there."

"Married a white woman? But…but…"

He reached across the space between us and tapped my wrist with one finger. It was an odd gesture, as if he were trying to tell me that he was about through. "Mother was called a Country Wife," he said, still tapping. "It happens." He stopped tapping and assumed a position much like my own, his chin on his hands. "The mystery to me is how he convinced her to let me go."

I thought I'd try my luck with another question. "Did you like it there?"

"For a while, until I began to miss the valley of the Wallowa and the Blue Mountains. Then I hated Vancouver."

"What did you do?"

"You're determined, aren't you?" he asked, not in exasperation, but as if he were my nonexistent big brother tolerating his upstart little sister. (I had no idea how old he was, and still don't know.) "Really determined?"

"Why, yes, I am," I said in a perky way that made him laugh.

"He died. I left the night after the funeral."

"How far was it?" I know I was beginning to sound like the prosecuting attorney in Spanish Inquisition versus Poor Sinner, but Hawk fascinated me.

"You're a little bulldog, aren't you?" he asked, but I heard the humor. "You dig in and don't let go." He turned over and stared at the burned canvas overhead. "Four hundred miles, give or take. Took me a long time to get home. I followed the big river you call Columbia."

"How old were you?"

"Twelve summers."

Twelve years old? When I was twelve, Mother had just begun, under protest, to let me pick out my own clothes. I started to wonder what I had been missing out in life, not that I would have carried to walk four hundred miles. But the idea of it!

"Look away."

I turned away from him as I heard him get up. There was a rustle of buckskin and a tuneless whistle, followed by a metallic clink and another rustle. I smiled when he swatted my hip with his moccasins. "All right."

I turned around as he pulled on the blue shirt his mother had left for him. I wanted to ask him about the medallion and the shells he wore on a rawhide thong, but I figured I had interrogated him enough for one setting. He ate something outside by the fire, then headed for the horses.

I dressed next, pleased with Blue Mountain Woman's neat stitches and the beads. I was still stiff and sore, but decided that youth was on my side and my backside would get used to days in the saddle. Surely we would find some settlers willing to take me in until the army showed up.

I was buttoning my bodice when I heard a rustling sound in a shady side of the shelter. Someone giggled. I looked closer to see an old woman. She favored me with a smile, then smoothed back her hair much as I has just done. She cleared her throat.

"'Fear not, for I bring you good tidings of great joy.'"

I blinked. "Excuse me?" I couldn't have heard her right.

She repeated the verse again. Blue Mountain Woman must have heard the old one. She came into the shelter and knelt in front of the woman, then patted her head. "My mother. Her name is Catherine."

I smiled at Catherine. She grinned back, showing gums with teeth either missing or worn down. Even a nearly toothless mouth couldn't hide the fact that Catherine had to have been a beauty a number of years ago.

"'Fear not, for I bring you good tidings of great joy.'"

Blue Mountain Woman listened gravely, then looked over her shoulder at me. "She speaks good English, yes?"

"Yes," I agreed. I didn't know when I had been more enchanted. "Where did Catherine learn such fine English?"

Blue Mountain Woman asked me to repeat the question, and I did, using fewer words this time. She nodded. "Reverend Spaulding. He sprinkled her head."

So Catherine had been baptized by Marcus Whitman's old missionary companion? My United States history instructor would never believe I was staring at history.

Catherine sat up, and Blue Mountain Woman pulled her deerskin dress down to cover her pipestem legs. She picked her up easily and carried her into the sunlight. I followed.

By morning light, I saw that there weren't as many tipis in the camp as I had thought. In fact, from the evidence in the clearing, most of The People slept outside, or under rude brush shelters. Consciously or not, I was still under the spell of those western dime novels, so I confess I was not impressed with my first look at a real Indian encampment.

Children and dogs were everywhere, the former underfoot near the cooking fires or rounding up horses, and the latter yapping around the former. The prairie grass was pretty well eaten down and trampled near the cluster of tipis. The grass in the distance looked waist deep and almost blue-green.

A fair-sized stream rippled through the meadow. Indian youths had planted themselves along the bank, spears held high, as they stared into the water. I watched in amazement when one of them thrust in his spear and bore it up seconds later with a struggling fish. The lad looked about Phil's age, Phil who can't even thread a needle. Other impromptu fishermen were equally successful. They were no doubt dexterous, and had the added encouragement of hunger, I am certain. My own stomach was telling me to do a little foraging, too. I watched the boys and girls and had to admit I was ill-prepared to survive anywhere outside of Omaha, Nebraska.

Ever-hopeful, I walked back to Blue Mountain Woman, who sat her little mother on a folded buffalo robe and motioned me to join her. She handed me a sliver of camas root bread and I made myself eat it slowly this time. When I finished, she gave me a bit of boiled salmon from the brass pot. This time I knew better than to look inside and see if there was more; I knew there wasn't.

Blue Mountain Woman ate her own tiny portion then popped another piece of the bread in her mouth. As I watched in amazement and then humility, she chewed, took the food from her mouth and put it in Catherine's mouth, which was open wide like a bird's. I know it was rude to stare, but I had never seen anything so kind and practical. With hardly any teeth, I suppose it was the only way Catherine could eat.

Blue Mountain Woman looked at me with a smile. She chewed more food for her mother, then touched my hand, always such a gentle touch and much like her son's, I had discovered. What was I learning in so few days? I knew that once I was home safe in Omaha, it would take a winter to absorb it all.

"Would your mother not do this for her mother?" Blue Mountain Woman asked, moving me out of my odd reverie. I didn't know what to say. She would never understand if I told her that my mother complained when she got a letter from Grandma Casey, saying she wanted to visit. That Casey side of the family owned a successful brewery, which fact Mother had never admitted to her Omaha friends. No. My mother would gamble at cards before she would feed her mother from her own mouth.

I had to ask myself – would I?

When I said nothing, Blue Mountain Woman gave me a charitable smile and went into the shelter to fold robes and blankets. All around me women were pulling down tipis and shelters and packing. The lodge poles formed the frames for their pony drags. I don't know what had happened to Blue Mountain woman's tipi, but she still had lodgepoles. While she expertly readied the horse and travois, I folded and packed. My efforts were decidedly puny, but I knew I would be better the next time, if there was a next time before the chiefs found a place to hand me off to others.

There was so much to see. I held onto the folded canvas as Blue Mountain Woman lashed it to the travois. Children ran and called to each other, mothers nursed babies, and old men rounded up horses. As they talked and laughed with each other, I could barely hide my growing unease. I had seen Howard's troops yesterday. Didn't The People understand the need to hurry?

When the travois was packed and met her specifications, Blue Mountain Woman picked up Catherine and set her on top of the bundle in a space she had hollowed out. She smoothed her mother's skirt and spread a blanket over her lap, as Catherine sat there with her hands folded. Mother and daughter touched foreheads. With a pang, I wanted her to touch mine, too.

How to find Methuselah? As I stood there, one of Nimiipuu came toward me through the confusion of the breaking camp. I thought he was one of the men from the council last night, but I wasn't certain. I'm embarrassed to admit that I still thought they all looked alike. When he held out his hand, I shook it.

"Good morning, Liz," he said, as though we were meeting in an office to begin the day's work. "I am Poker Joe. Do you remember me?"

Yes, I did. Poker Joe interpreted last night. He was dressed in the usual loincloth and moccasins, with the addition of a blue wool shirt with beaded designs on the sleeves. His hair was cut short like a white man's. Without the war paint, he looked quite congenial by morning light. With a suit on, I think he could have worked in a newspaper office.

"Thank you for your words last night," I said.

He made a dismissive motion with one hand. "I am sorry it has come to all this, but right now you are safer with us."

I nodded and looked across the smaller horse herd. "Where are the young men?"

"They have left already to play with General Howard." He grinned when he said it, but we both knew it wasn't funny. We knew what playing with Howard meant.

He turned from me as if the subject were too large, and shouted in his language to The People. I didn't need to understand the words to know that he was trying to hurry them in their preparations to leave this pleasant valley.

I had questions for him, and he seemed to understand. "Liz, it is this way," he began. "Joseph and I have been chosen to lead the people. We are not the warriors. We are here to move them along, even when we know they are tired of moving along."

I understood him completely. I had seen both sides of this already and I felt the urgency. I also knew this was my one chance to show off a little, since he was part white like Hawk. "Mr. Poker," I started, which made him laugh, as I hoped it would. "Mr. Joe then?" Another laugh. "Have you heard of Ralph Waldo Emerson?"

Admittedly, it was a strange conversation in an odd setting. He nodded, his eyes merry.

"He once wrote that traveling is a fool's paradise."

Another laugh, followed by a sigh. "Would he understand this?" was all he said, before he gave me a small salute and hurried off to irritate some more unwilling travelers.

I looked for Blue Mountain Woman and joined her as she started to the horse herd. To my surprise, an old fellow with flowing white hair walked toward us leading Methuselah. He touched Blue Mountain Woman on the shoulder and she touched back.

"My father, Meopwits," she said.

My adopted family was larger than I had first thought. I hesitated, then touched his shoulder. He said something quite lengthy in his language, which I didn't understand, except that now I was listening. I heard the name "Kaya" several times, and wondered again if Hawk was decoy. I nodded and smiled back, adept now at this sort of non-communication.

Methuselah greeted me like a long-lost lodge brother. He would have been cut to the quick if he could have understood in his dim little brain how I felt about his duplicity. I also understood by now how The People felt about horses, so I stroked the rascal and murmured, "You are the worst nag I ever knew."

Meopwits beamed at my evident love for horses and insisted on saddling that hell beast for me. He also insisted on helping me into the saddle, even though I hesitated because I knew I outweighed him. He wouldn't back away, so I let him, hoping his old bones could stand the strain.

We left our valley before the sun was much over the trees. Once in motion, The People kept up a steady pace. When horses tired, other fresh mounts were cut loose from the herd without any loss of time. Since I didn't have another horse, I spent a lot of time walking Methuselah. My shoulder ached from tugging him along like a big, reluctant dog.

Some children teased and taunted Methuselah, which irritated me until I saw the humor in it. Those little snobs were accustomed to good breeding in horses and obviously didn't know what to make of such a nag, and anyone – even a white woman – who would ride it. I laughed along with them, and eventually they tired of the game.

I have no idea where we were, or if we were even still in Yellowstone Park. I know now that we must have been traveling the secret paths of the Absaroka wilderness, according to Hawk. I knew I could never retrace the route.

Poker Joe led the march, avoiding the easy trails and taking us into dense forests, along narrow ridges, and through unknown canyons. If there was an impossible route, he found it. As the day passed, I understood why The People pulled such long faces when Poker Joe tried to hurry them.

Methuselah and I were both grateful when the sun was high overhead and we stopped. Blue Mountain Woman handed me some camas root and I crammed it in before I remembered there would be nothing more until sunset. She looked at her own piece of bread and with a smile, held it out to me. I shook my head. No sense in letting my folly infect everyone.

She ate her bit of bread slowly. "You will learn, Liz." She fed her mother, who ate with her eyes half-closed, then curled up on the travois for another nap.

It felt like the cruelest kind of punishment to have to start again, when

I wanted to hole up somewhere for a nap of my own. I knew Poker Joe would have none of that, so I followed.

We rode into the still of afternoon. To keep myself awake, I tried counting Indians. I arrived at around three hundred women, children and old men. There were no warriors in sight. The young boys and girls were in charge of the horse herd, which they kept together with real skill, the girls riding as easily as the boys.

I tried not to be rude as I watched The People. It was a bewildering thing to be coasting through the age of Victoria for eighteen years, then find oneself thrust back among Stone Age people that one has been conditioned from the crib to fear, or at least be wary around. My curiosity generally overruled my hesitation, but not at first, not before I invested myself in them.

That moment came twice that afternoon. I have never forgotten either event.

Poker Joe generally rode with Joseph toward the front of the untidy, straggling body. They took turns riding back through the moving clans, greeting friends, hurrying stragglers, counting children, observing the horses, encouraging the old ones. Joseph waved to me once. I felt shy about his dignified acknowledgment, but I waved back and felt better for it.

The pace never let up. Poker Joe was leading us in a northeasterly direction, the sun at our backs now. I didn't mean to complain, especially when only the thinnest of margins kept me in the good graces of people would could have cut me loose any time they wanted, but I was tired. When Poker Joe passed me, I called out, "Do we get to stop for the night?"

He looked back at me, a sharp expression on his face, and waited for me to reach him. "Come with me, Liz. I want to show you something."

There now. I had finally done it. He must have noticed the fear in my eyes. He held up his hand. "I won't hurt you."

Did I have a choice? I followed him back down the trail, with older youths accompanying us. My uneasiness only increased. I told myself that if I got out of this mess I had blundered into by my complaints, I would not repeat it.

He led out little party to a nearby bluff. He dismounted and I followed him to the top of the ridge, where he bellied down. I dropped down, too, and looked where he pointed.

Directly parallel to us and not far I saw a great cloud of dust. Behind the cloud about a half mile was another cloud. Poker Joe pointed to the first fast-moving cloud. "Our men have tied branches behind their horses," he explained. "Old Day After Tomorrow thinks he is following many Indians."

I nodded, too frightened to speak, lesson learned. I had no more argument in me. In silence we returned to the travelers and I did not complain again.

The other lesson, a worse one that still haunts me, happened as we were winding down an anonymous ridge toward a river below, probably the Yellowstone. The trail was a figment of someone's imagination so I closed my eyes, hoping Methuselah would dig deep into his tiny mind and keep us where we belonged. I shouldn't have worried; he was as scared as I was, if his quivering was any indication.

Not wishing to appear totally bereft of brains, I opened my eyes and began to relax a mite. Blue Mountain Woman rode ahead on the trail in front of the family travois, looking over her shoulder often to watch Catherine, who was singing, but softly.

I rode directly behind a young mother with a little one, maybe a year and a half old. The child had been patient in the cradleboard all afternoon, but I saw unrest brewing. During a brief pause, the mother took her little one from the cradleboard and held him in front of her to nurse. Later, she shifted him to her shoulder for a burp, and kept him there as she adroitly handled the reins and he played with her hair.

My auburn hair, wild about my head again, must have caught his eye. I waggled my hand at him and he smiled, showing off big dimples and two teeth. We spent a few minutes shaking heads at each other and laughing softly. Well, softly on my part, after I intercepted several glares from other travelers. I became aware then how quiet everyone was. This was not a regiment of noisy Bluecoats with banging canteens and creaking leatherwork, but people fleeing in silence.

Chastened, I knew I could easily have beguiled away the remainder of the afternoon entertaining that little fellow, or entertaining myself, if the truth be told. I never got the chance.

One moment he and I were making big eyes at each other, and the next, his mother's horse stumbled and went down hard on one knee. I watched in horror as she was thrown in one direction toward the trail's edge, and her boy somehow clung to the horse's saddle.

I was nearest to her so she pointed to her horse, who struggled to regain its footing. My heart in my throat, I leaped off Methuselah, who was stepping around now in agitation, and ran to the struggling horse, who struck out wildly, slowing me down.

"Please, please, please," went through my mind as I edged toward the flailing horse. I reached for the child just as the horse gave a mighty heave and flung itself into the canyon. I came away with a saddle blanket only.

We all watched in horror as the horse sailed out and down, the child still hanging on to God knows what, until it was too much. He let go and with arms outstretched and screaming, plummeted beside the horse, as if in a weird race to the bottom. I watched the baby fall, tumbling against rocks, bouncing off trees until what was left of him splashed into the river. I could not look away, as badly as I wanted to. None of us could.

I screamed, but only once. Poker Joe was beside me then, his hand over my mouth. "No, Liz, no," he whispered in my ear. "No." He took his hand away after giving me a good shake.

All around me was silence. The mother was still too out of breath to get to her feet, but she crawled to the edge and peered down, all in total silence. The only sound was her ragged breathing.

An older woman dismounted and dragged her away from the precipice. When the mother pulled out her knife, I shook off Poker Joe and ran toward her, determined that she wouldn't kill herself, even if I had failed to reach her son. Poker Joe yanked me back with a hand in the waist of my riding skirt. I watched as the mother, her face stony, her eyes fixed, sawed away at her long hair, then gashed her face and arms. She held her arms out as the blood dripped onto the stones. Silence filled the trail until it seemed to hang over the whole canyon. I know that sounds silly, but I swear to God, that was a terrible and lonely silence.

Utterly defeated, I bowed my head. By now, Methuselah had calmed himself and edged away from the rim. Someone helped me back into the saddle. I watched the older woman give the bereft and bloody mother a hand up behind her, and we continued a journey suddenly and everlastingly more terrible than anything I could have imagined.

When we reached the bottom of the canyon and the trail widened, Joseph rode back slowly. He spoke a few words to the mother riding double. Then he rode back to me.

He said nothing. He looked at all the bewilderment, anger and shock on my face, shook his head and touched my hand. That was all he did, but it was enough. I looked into his face, and saw my expression mirrored in his own eyes.

As I think of it now, the death of the little fellow changed something else in me. I no longer saw the people as Indians who all looked alike. I saw them as mothers, fathers, children and babies. I saw a mother who had lost her baby in a terrible accident. And over there was a young wife, quite pregnant, who kept looking back down the trail. Was her husband one of the decoy party? She worried for him; I could tell. And there was Blue Mountain Woman with her kind eyes on me. They were individuals; they were The People.

In silence we backtracked at least twice over the trail we followed. At one place, the youngsters and old ones milled the horse herd around until God Almighty himself couldn't have picked our tracks among all the hoofprints.

I couldn't tell you where we camped that night; it didn't matter. No one put up shelters. No one started cooking fires. We ate our morsels cold, then rolled up in blankets and buffalo robes. The decoy was somewhere, if they were even still alive.

There was no gentle talk, no friendly exchanges, only silence. I was a long time getting to sleep, even though I could smell exhaustion in my very pores. That awful night, I knew beyond any doubt that I had turned the last page in my childhood. What lay ahead was a blank space. I grew up that afternoon.

Chapter Ten

Wʜat can I tell you of the next few days? After the misery of a silent night, we gathered ourselves together as one, even me, and rode on. I saw The People in a new light, noting how many of them had short hair.

I know I broke with tradition that next morning when I left the line of march and rode to the front beside Poker Joe. He didn't seem surprised at my impulsive action, which put the heart back in me. I needed to know more, and he knew it.

"I know I am out of place, Joe, but tell me something about the last month," I ordered. It was no half-hearted suggestion.

"Ride with me," he said, after a few words with Joseph, who obligingly fell back a little, after a good look at Methuselah, who was amounting to even less than usual.

"What do you wish to know?" Joe asked.

"Hawk told me that you were all to go onto a reservation, but a few tribal hotheads killed some whites and everyone took off," I said. "This was a plan?"

He smiled at that. "Perhaps we can say that no one was much in favor of the reservation."

"Was it a bad place?" I asked. I was so innocent still.

"Not really."

"Then why?"

He was silent for a long time and I feared I had either offended him or asked a question so stupid that he was hard put, polite man that he was, to answer without making me feel like an idiot. "Do you ever get weary of being told what to do?" he asked me finally.

"All the time," I said. "I'm a woman and I am always told what to do."

"What happens?"

I saw where this was going. "I grumble but I knuckle under."

"Then what?"

I had never answered a question like this, because no one had ever asked it. "I...I suppose I hope that I will meet a kind man someday who will marry me and treat me as though my opinion matters."

"And if he doesn't?"

"I will hope better things for my daughters," I said firmly, even as I realized that was no answer at all. I gave Poker Joe a sidelong glance, hoping he wasn't laughing at me. He wasn't, and I knew I had a friend.

"What about you, Liz, the you of your universe?"

I didn't know. I had nothing to say except, "The People want to have their own say in the matter, and guide their own destiny, don't they?"

"We are looked upon as charges of the federal government and treated as children," Joe said. "This order and those killings were the final burden." His voice hardened. "And there was a treaty in 1855 that we signed, giving us so much land. Enough land for our horses. All gone now."

"But why?" I know I was starting to sound like a three-year-old, and I am being generous here.

"The white men took it back."

"That was definitely unsporting of them," I said, indignant.

He smiled at that, patient with me. "We will meet the soldiers again. We are probably leaving the Department of the Columbia, General Howard commanding. We are heading into another department where another regiment of troopers, fresh troopers, will pick up our trail." He looked back at Joseph, who watched us. "Knowing General Howard, he will keep following. Now we will travel north to Canada, the land of the Grandmother, which last year took in Sitting Bull and others from the Little Big Horn fight." He raised his hands, frustrated. "There are only so many buffalo in Canada! I don't know what will happen."

"You have no allies here?" I asked.

"We will see when the young men return. For years we have traded with the Crow to the east. They know our hearts, but they also know the Bluecoats. Some are scouts."

I understood what Poker Joe was telling me. When we took the Union Pacific west from Omaha, I saw miles of tidy farms and ranches. Someone had lived on that land before the settlers. All were gone now, herded onto reservations, out of sight and out of mind to most Americans. Sitting in a private railcar, I had been an observer. Sitting on my creaky horse, I was a participant.

"So many have lost so much," I said. "Only yesterday…" I couldn't continue. I knew I would see that falling baby in my dreams for a long time.

"That was a terrible thing, but a small event," Joe said. "Now, now! Hear me out! Three weeks ago we were surprised by another Bluecoat and his troops at the valley of the Big Hole."

I looked at his face, then looked away, because I could almost see that battle on his face. His hair was already short in the white man's way, but I asked anyway. "Who did you lose, Joe?"

"My wife and daughter," he said.

"Oh, God," I whispered.

"They cried out to God, they did, Liz. They were Presbyterians. Maybe like some of the soldiers." He visibly gathered himself together. I wanted him to stop; I had heard enough, but I wasn't rude enough to stop him. "Sixty women and children gone and thirty warriors, but we stopped that Bluecoat." He sighed. "And here we are, the victors and still retreating." He gave me a searching look. I knew better than to turn away this time. He deserved more from me. "You are a bright woman. We will meet more soldiers and more soldiers, won't we?"

I nodded. "No matter how many you defeat, there will always be more."

"More and more until we are gone, because we cannot replace our-selves. All this because we wanted to be left alone. Some thought leaving Idaho for Montana Territory would accomplish that. You and I know bet-ter, don't we, Liz?"

I had all the education I needed from Poker Joe. I fell back and he rode beside Joseph again. As we parted company, I knew I had an ally, even if he had none.

Another thing of merit happened that day, a much smaller thing, but one which further my education in the ways of the Nimiipuu.

After the sun was directly overhead and sliding down, I felt that familiar trickle of moisture on the inside of my thighs that heralded the arrival of my monthly. I had lost track of the days, so it came as an unwelcome surprise.

I didn't know what to do. At home I would have gone to that special box in the linen closet, but here I was in the middle of nowhere. Blue Mountain Woman's English was somewhat south of adequate, and I dreaded having to corral Poker Joe into interpretation. I did the time-honored thing and tried to ignore the situation.

It wasn't going away. I was looking around for Blue Mountain Woman when she rode up beside me. Poker Joe was nowhere to be seen, so I edged Methuselah closer to her horse. I lifted up my skirt and showed her my problem. She nodded and motioned me to follow her.

We left the trail, Blue Mountain scanning the ground as her horse picked its way through the undergrowth, as if looking, too. She dismount-ed and gathered handfuls of moss, so I did the same. When we had gath-ered a goodly amount, she motioned me to dismount. We walked farther into the trees, where she smoothed together a smallish handful, gestured between her legs, then handed it to me. I lowered my drawers and applied the moss to the critical area, then cinched my drawers tighter, hoping they might hold the moss in place. I must admit that the moss did fine, and certainly felt less scratchy than cotton or linen.

We gathered more moss and tucked it in my saddlebag. On the way back to The People she asked, "What you do before now?"

Through elaborate gestures that made her smile, I explained how we tore up old sheets, used them, washed them – me scrubbing an imaginary washboard – dried them – I pinned them on my imaginary clothesline – and used them again – me sticking a wad where the moss was. It was a virtuoso performance in feminine hygiene. I told my husband about it a few years later, and he just shook his head.

Blue Mountain Woman wasn't amused. She looked shocked. "Same rags over and again?"

"Well, yes."

She shuddered. "Not clean," she stated, with such a look on her face. I'm certain she thought my method was a relic of barbarism. She probably wondered how I had arrived at the advanced age of eighteen with such unhygienic monthly practices. She rode a little ahead of me, shaking her head over the mad methods of white women. I laughed to myself. So much for civilization.

I rode into our new camp by my myself, not because I was embarrassed, but because Methuselah could barely clop one hoof in front of the other and he worried me. The sight of a new camp going up relieved my mind. I was admiring the view – camp activity, horses cropping grass, the jagged peaks of the Absaroka range, wildflowers here and there – when Methuselah started to stagger. When he began to sway, I got off quickly and dropped the reins. He looked deep into my eyes, gave a belch, broke wind, then toppled over, dead.

I own to being startled but I felt no remorse. He had caused me nothing but trouble from the beginning, by thinking he was Pegasus and charging after the Nimiipuu. I pulled the saddlebag and saddle away and walked into camp. For a nitwit of a horse who was the author of my current troubles, I don't know why I cried, but I did. Poor Methuselah. Poor me.

When I dried my tears and told Blue Mountain Woman what had happened, she sent several of the older children on horseback to tow old Ancient of Days into camp. She handed me a knife and told me to get to work. I shook my head and backed away, so she commissioned some young women my age to introduce me into the mysteries of butchering. Methuselah was going on the Nimiipuu menu.

Talking to each other and laughing, they gutted the horse, tossing entrails to the omnipresent pack of dogs, who snarled and fought over Methuselah's tidbits. When the women started to dismantle him, I came closer, took back the knife and knelt next to Blue Mountain Woman. She showed me how to separate the hide from the flesh and I did my best, skewering myself a few times until I got the hang of it.

Blue Mountain Woman was an excellent instructor. She guided my hand when it looked like I needed help, and encouraged me with throaty sounds like, "Ah ah," and "Oh oh." At one point she sat back on her heels and asked, "You are good. Who was your teacher?"

I wanted to assure her that Miss Sumner at the Female Academy only believed in meritorious, Christian works for the deserving poor. Blue Mountain Woman didn't understand me, of course, but she wouldn't have understood someone like Miss Sumner. Instead, I smiled and said, "You only," which was true.

When I was elbow deep in blood and muscle, I had a fleeting mental picture of dressing for dinner in Omaha. I wanted to laugh, but as I looked around, I knew that none of my fellow diners would get the joke.

Dine, we did. Methuselah in small strips was better than Methuselah on the hoof. As I chewed, I practically growled over him like the near-wolf pack picking at his insides. He made a satisfying meal. He would have been improved somewhat by salt, but we had none, so that was that.

Hawk and the others rode into camp as we were wiping off the knives. He didn't look like the same man who had ridden out two days ago, covered with dust now, his eyes red-rimmed and bloodshot from dirt and lack of sleep. He saw to his horse, waved aside a hot handful of Methuselah, crawled into the shelter and fell asleep before his mother had time to greet him. We continued arranging more strips of Methuselah over low-burning coals. By morning he would be fit to travel again, although in a different form.

After we finished, there was time before darkness ruled to sit by myself and look over the encampment. As I looked upon people I was beginning to recognize, I felt a mellow sort of peace descend on me. I somehow managed to overlook the growing unease that a terrible evil waited in a not-so-distant room, ready to pounce on the quiet calm I now observed. Like the mother I saw singing to her baby, or children playing what I would have called dodge ball, or older men smoking, I consciously put myself into the here and now. From force of habit, I glanced down to where my watch used to be. I smiled inside. Time no longer mattered. I stopped smiling. Yes, it did, and I feared time was short for The People.

Considering the state in which Hawk retired the night before, I was surprised to find him up and gone in the morning before Blue Mountain Woman and I stirred. This vexed me, because I needed to discuss the matter of a horse for me.

After a better breakfast than usual, thanks to Methuselah, Blue Mountain Woman went with her father to the horse herd. I sat with Catherine and gently tugged at her tangled hair with my trusty comb. I knew enough of sign language now to understand her when she put her fingers to her mouth. Without giving the matter much thought, I chewed some horsemeat for her. She leaned against me as I fed her, and my heart was full.

We had finished when Hawk came back to our campsite with a frown, his lips in a tight line. He looked like he wanted to kick something.

"What's the matter?"

"Looking Glass is back."

This meant nothing to me. I didn't know he was gone. "Explain?" I asked.

"After that council for you, he rode to parlay with the Mountain Crows toward the rising sun." He pointed with his lips. "He thought they would help us. We have traded with them for years. Buffalo robes for horses..." His voice trailed off.

"I take it that the Crows had nothing for you."

He shook his head. "Nothing. We have no friends. The world is changing." He seemed to notice who I was. "Come with me."

He walked toward the herd and I walked beside him. I had noticed in my brief time with The People that men and women walked side by side, and not women behind the men. It was another thing to like about The People.

"I never thought any good would come of it," he said out of the clear blue, after we had walked shoulder to shoulder in silence. He had even nicely shortened his stride to match mine.

"Why not?" Everything I had observed since my family arrived in Yellowstone Park – already it seemed like another world – pointed toward the indisputable fact that there was a lot of empty space out west. What could it possibly hurt if The People moved onto some of it?

"Remember when I told you about Vancouver?" I nodded and he continued. "It is a small town, according to my father. What I saw was many people, ships on the river, activity, movement. I wasn't more than ten years old then, but it seemed to me that white people were filling up all the empty spaces. I wondered then if there would be anything left for The People, except that reservation in Idaho." He shrugged. "But who listens to a ten-year-old boy of mixed blood?"

I could have asked him who listens to a woman of *any* age, but I was smart enough to remain silent. "Has Looking Glass ever been to Vancouver?"

"I doubt it." He stopped and faced me. "Something else that makes my heart bad: However this ends, I do not think that the reservation in Idaho will still be given to all The People."

"But...but you've been promised," I reminded him.

He only smiled at me, then turned to look for his horse. Perhaps I could have told him that the government would never cheat The People, except that I wasn't so sure. I was smart enough not to say it was a free country.

He whistled and his horse came trotting toward him. He put the bridle on that he had slung over his shoulder at the shelter, then whispered a few pleasantries in his language to the lovely spotted horse.

Speaking of horses... I almost hated to bother him about a horse when he had so much on his mind, but I had to say something. This would be a good time to leave me behind, but I didn't relish the thought. I had heard wolves howling, and knew to a painful degree my tenderfoot status. I might have had a few useful skills in Omaha, but none here in the wilds of wherever we were, maybe Montana, maybe Wyoming. I was also beginning to wonder how the Crow would regard a footsore white woman who could sing and crochet and paint on china, but not much else.

"You know, you were eating my horse this morning," I started out.

He chuckled, and his expression brightened. "And..."

I wasn't about to defend the defunct Methuselah, but I needed an answer and not a tease. "And what am I to do now?"

"We could leave you here," he offered.

I took heart because of his lurking smile. "Thank you, but no."

He pointed with his lips toward the rest of the herd, and crooked his finger. We kept walking. I saw Joseph and his children rounding up their horses. Poker Joe was already on horseback and starting to nag The People to move. They were heading north and not east now.

"Canada?" I asked Hawk.

"Ah, yes, where the people of Canada will be so pleased to see us."

In the interest of keeping the peace and solving my own problem, I thought it best not to comment.

Another whistle, and a different horse came forward, a little mare with a spotted rump. I hadn't noticed until then that he had been carrying another bridle. It was a moment's work to put it in place and hand the reins to me. "Her name is Fair One. Treat her nice. She won't take a saddle."

"Thanks, Hawk."

He did something then that touched my heart. It still does. He gently pressed his forehead to mine.

I abandoned my sidesaddle in the encampment. Like the proverbial bad penny, it turned up weeks later at the Bear Paws. General Howard himself returned it to me. I felt far from grateful then and said some hateful things, none of which I ever retracted. Come to think of it, I said some dreadful things to quite a few Bluecoats, none of which I regret, either.

I'm jumping ahead, but I don't suppose it matters. This account is for my family alone; besides, everyone knows what happened.

We were on the march before the sun rose much higher. I shivered through the morning, wondering whether it was still August or September now. The morning sun burned away the chill, but a coolness lingered, almost like a warning. I wished Joseph and Poker Joe would come across some white people to take me in. At the same time, I wished Canada were closer.

The terrain changed from the heart-stopping canyons and rims of the Clark's Fork region, as that later geophysical map showed me, into the broad valley of the Yellowstone River. Wind played freely over the buffalo grass, whispering secrets. This was buffalo country and we had left most of the trees behind.

We hadn't left any soldiers behind. Thanks to the miracle of the talking wire, we were about to meet up with a new enemy, the Seventh Cavalry, Department of the Dakotas, bent on revenge for something The People never did.

Chapter Eleven

Wrong place. Wrong time.

I have never been able to understand how generals and historians tie up battles in neat bundles. To study Chancellorsville or Gettysburg, one would think that battle is well-defined and rational. I cannot agree. My first taste of action against the Nimiipuu was of such complete confusion that I can't tell who did what.

I know this exasperates my husband, who has a real eye for detail (ahem, except when he went a whole winter without noticing that I grew out my bangs). All I remember is that men I hadn't even met were firing at me, and that I was trying my dead level best to get into a canyon before I went the way of Methuselah.

Such singleness of purpose was rarely a feature of my life until Canyon Creek. I mean, I had a drawerful of unfinished samplers back in Omaha. I was never considered by any Everett as a sterling example of perseverance. I wish my family could have seen me in Canyon Creek.

The People made a rapid march that morning in the valley of the Yellowstone. My adopted family – well, they were – had trouble getting started. Catherine refused to get on the pony drag. Blue Mountain Woman argued with her, but Catherine folded her arms and sat on the ground.

Meopwits entered into the discussion, but Catherine wouldn't listen to her husband, either. At last he said something that sounded final, at least to my ears, picked her up and set her on the travois. He must have meant whatever he said, because she stayed there. I did notice that Blue Mountain Woman kept a closer watch on her mother that morning.

Once underway, I idled away the hours watching the youths keep the horse herd in line and enjoyed my new and unaccustomed smooth ride on Fair One. To be sure, riding bareback required more of an effort at first, until I started to imitate the rhythmic, hip-gliding motion of the riders around me.

If you are wishing for something exciting here, there was nothing. Travel is travel, in this case, dull and slow. I started fixing my sight on a distant landmark, but ended that pretty quickly after years passed until I reached it.

Call it impolite if you wish, but I spent a lot of time watching Hawk. He fascinated me. After he told me that his father was a Scot, I frittered away boring stretches of the march sneaking surreptitious glances, trying to see in Hawk's appearance any resemblance to Scots I knew or had read about. I saw none. He was a pleasant shade of tan like his friends around him, and his eyes were the color of good chocolate. His hair did look a little lighter than some and showed a tendency to curl over his shoulders. He mostly wore it hanging free, or sometimes tied back like mine.

The only real difference I discerned was his build. For the most part, Nimiipuu are tall people, men and women. The men tend toward stockiness, which provides a majestic appearance. Hawk was tall but lean, and longer through the legs than the chest.

Nope. No Celt in Hawk that I could tell. He'd never be mistaken for Robert the Bruce. He was sociable, which could have been any group of people. He rode with Poker Joe, and riding close together, they laughed and talked in an easy way that I envied. Husbands and wives rode leg to leg, chatting as amiably as old married couples on a dining terrace at Newport.

That morning, we were strung out all over the valley, General Howard somehow a distant memory. We didn't know that he had forwarded a series of messages to the Department of Missouri, which meant we had been handed off to another unit. Ignorance truly is bliss. Scouts loped far to the front until they were specks in the distance. Most of the women and children kept together in the center, with old men and boys circling on the fringes. No one's guard was down, but I saw no particular concern.

People generally banded together in family groups, which meant that I rode among Joseph's people. A little to the rear of us were families of White Bird's clan. Poker Joe usually stayed with the scouts, but he sometimes traveled by Joseph.

After I had looked over the Nimiipuu I was familiar with, I concluded that slow morning by a mental review of the multiplication tables. I finished them and was starting on conjugations of Latin verbs when I noticed great clouds of smoke northeast of us. I wondered if the Nimiipuu scouts had started the blaze as a warning or if the fire was an example of simple Indian cussedness.

It was a little of both. The braves fired a stage station and also a nearby saloon, which were the two principal businesses of Coulson, called Laurel, or maybe Billings today. They found a light wagon, hitched it to the horses from the stage station's corral and raced back and forth in front of the rest of us. It looked like great sport, with the driver taking some hair-raising turns. Several of The People clambered for rides when the wagon slowed down.

We all slowed as The People ran to watch or participate, and I dismounted to give my backside a rest. I lagged behind, kicking up dust clouds with the toe of my boot and wondering if this was a good opportunity to take French leave of my hosts. Everyone watched the wagon antics; I figured no one would miss me.

I probably would have left then, but I wasn't at all sure about the condition of whoever belonged to the burning buildings. I didn't fancy an afternoon or a day or two spent in the company of smoldering corpses.

I ambled along, staring at the grass in front of me. I looked up when a meadowlark cut loose with its surprising song. The clear notes hung in the air. I listened in appreciation, then consternation, as the sound turned into the tinny blast from a bugle not far away. I looked back and saw something that got me back on Fair One in record time and with no assistance.

Some of The People noticed, too. Outriders started to wave their signal blankets in wide circles. Mothers darted about for their children. Babies cried until hushed, and big-eyed older ones wandered and looked for a familiar face. People ran to their horses.

Bluecoats bore down on us from several directions. I didn't stop to pass the time of day, but followed the rapidly moving herd. We headed for a gap in rimrocks that looked miles away. It was a wide opening and we aimed for it. A creek flowed into the canyon.

Fair One and I fled past the abandoned wagon. Already, The People's proven sharpshooters were firing steadily from the outcropping of rocks inside the canyon mouth. I ducked every time the guns went off, feeling foolish, but ducking anyway.

This could have been another opportunity to turn around and ride toward the Bluecoats, but by now I understood that I was just a body on horseback with Indians fleeing a reservation, and not Elizabeth Ann Everett.

I was close to the rocks and almost in the comparative safety of the canyon when I nearly ran down an old woman kneeling by a clump of brush, wailing away in the oddest fashion. Her back was to me – she didn't want to look at the soldiers, either – but when my horse dislodged some rocks near her, she turned around. It was Catherine.

Heaven knows what possessed me, but even as frightened as I was, I reined in Fair One and leaped off. Catherine took scant notice of me. She started to sing louder, and I listened.

"Come thou fount of every blessing, tune my heart to sing thy grace, streams of mercy never ceasing, call for songs of loudest praise.'" Catherine understood loud praise, this Nimiipuu who had been baptized by Reverend Spaulding and who probably attended the Presbyterian Church in her Blue Mountain homeland. I could almost hear small coins clinking in the offering plate.

I looked around for Meopwits or Blue Mountain Woman to help me.

Where were they? People on horseback streamed into the canyon, now that most of the pony herd was through. I saw no one familiar.

I grabbed Catherine by the arm and tried to pull her to her feet. She wouldn't budge. I plucked at her sleeve like a child. "Now look here," I argued, screaming to be heard above the rifles and horses. All she did was shake her finger at me and said, "'Fear not, for I bring you good tidings of great joy,'" over and over. I might as well have addressed the sagebrush, for all the attention she paid me.

I dug in my heels and tried to yank the old lady to her feet. The memory of the falling baby was fresh in my mind and I was determined that this would end differently and I would be of use.

People rushed past me and still I hung onto that stubborn woman, intent on my good works. I can't imagine why I wasn't trampled or gunned down.

My Christian efforts came to an end as an Indian rode toward me. He didn't look like the Nimiipuu I was used to, with his hair in tight braids and not painted for war. I noticed his army forage cap too late. He dismounted and walked toward me in the calmest way, pointing his rifle at Catherine.

I must have been out of my mind. "You put that thing down before someone gets hurt," I snapped at him as he advanced with some confidence, I might add. "I am Elizabeth Ann Everett and my father will hear about this!"

He stared at me when I addressed him in English, stopping momentarily. I'm not certain what he would have done, because he never had the chance to take another step. The expression in his eyes fixed and hardened. He grabbed his throat and fell face down in the dust, an arrow in the back of his neck. He flopped a moment like a trout on a bank then lay still.

I gawked at him in horror, but Catherine never missed a beat, returning with another verse of "Come, Thou Fount of Every Blessing," with a martial beat this time, if anything. I turned around to thank whoever had polished off the Bluecoat scout and there was Hawk, fitting another arrow against his bowstring.

"Liz, will you get the hell out of here?" he yelled.

I refused to let go of Catherine. "I can't leave her here! Help me!"

He leaped down, pried me from his grandmother and almost threw me on my horse. "She's singing her death chant. Leave her alone!"

"It's a church hymn!" I shouted back.

He grabbed my leg and gave me a shake. "Maybe that's her death chant, Elizabeth Ann," he said. "Go now."

He slapped my horse and Fair One leapt to his bidding, but not before I hollered, "Don't forget to take out the arrow, you old miser!"

Thank God the horse had sense superior to mine. I leaned forward, sobbed into her mane, hung on and let her carry me away from the dead scout, an angry Nimiipuu, and an old woman who liked hymns and was ready to die.

I was mortified, aghast, saddened, angry at myself, sorry for a kind old lady, and worried for the man who only wanted me to find safety, and who knew better than most the high cost of dealing with the white man. The whole matter was sad beyond belief and embarrassing. If the earth could have swallowed me, I'd have been glad to go.

That was my experience with the Canyon Creek fight. Colonel Sam Sturgis commanded the Seventh Cavalry, having succeeded to regimental leadership after last year's death of Colonel George Custer, and Sturgis's own son, among many others. The ranks were now filled with troopers called "Custer Avengers," soldiers only too happy to vent their rage on any Indians, even those who had nothing to do with the deaths of five companies of cavalry on the Greasy Grass about a year ago.

Later newspaper reports indicated that Colonel Sturgis played up Canyon Creek as more of a fight than it really was. I believe he claimed sixteen dead Indians, but the only one I am sure of was Catherine, Presbyterian Church member, who decided her time had come. I saw several wounded, mostly women and children. Need I add that the injured children caused us all the most anguish. Now that I am a mother many times over, I know there is nothing more horrible than watching little ones in pain and knowing there is nothing that can be done.

Canyon Creek turned me into a war veteran, although I didn't know it at the time.

Chapter Twelve

Exhausted and numb, we hurried along until several hours after dark, picking our way among the brush and rocks and continually climbing. The gradual incline took us from the floor of the Yellowstone Valley onto the plateau of high plains broken by isolated mountains, that stretched all the way to Canada.

All credit for our escape goes to Joseph and Poker Joe that night. The war chiefs remained in the rear waiting for Sturgis; Joseph kept us moving. The wounded were placed on pony drags and had to bear the rough journey as best they could.

The moon wasn't up yet; I barely saw anything of the trail we followed. I expected any minute for the Custer Avengers to pounce on us out of the dark, shouting and shooting. I didn't know it at the time, but they couldn't possibly have driven us to extinction that night. Fresh companies of infantry and cavalry would be waiting for that privilege several weeks to the north.

Blue Mountain Woman was nowhere in sight, and I feared for her. I began to dread that she was a casualty along with her mother, until I heard someone calling to me. Relieved beyond measure, I turned aside and waited. Soon Blue Mountain Woman and Meopwits rode up beside me, she leading his horse, Meopwits with head bowed. Her tears mingled with blood from her gashed face and arms as she held my arm. "I was afraid for you," was all she said. It was enough.

I let them ride slowly past me, Meopwits in tears.

We rode slowly on and on that night until the moon final rose. I could barely hang onto Fair One, but I had to keep looking down the trail for Hawk. He didn't come. Other warriors were returning to their families. We learned from them that one brave named Teeto Hoonnad picked himself a good sniper's nest and held off Sturgis's entire regiment while the rest of the fighting men slipped away up the trail. They dragged brush and timber and rolled down rocks to block the path of the troopers, who turned back eventually.

Joseph called a halt when he figured we had put enough distance between us and the soldiers. Horses were tended to first, as always. Mothers shook out buffalo robes and their little ones slept as soon as they burrowed down into the dark skins. Campfires were forbidden that night. The moon kept disappearing behind clouds, making the air chilly.

I ate my usual tiny portion of camas bread on the half shell with gently braised Methuselah. Not caring what anyone saw, I unbuttoned my bodice and wriggled out of my riding skirt. I waited until it was dark enough before I patted in the last of the moss from several days ago. Last week, I would have been paralyzed by mortification over exposing myself. I didn't care now, and no one seemed to mind. I sat on Catherine's buffalo robe – that gave me pause – and tried to untangle my hair.

Hawk came out of the darkness. With a sigh, he took off his moccasins and unbuttoned his shirt. He sat, leaning forward, elbows on his knees, and watched me. He looked weather-beaten in the moonlight, not at all the subject of an elegiac poem about the Noble Red Man on the shores of Gitche Gumee, or something equally stupid composed in Massachusetts by someone who knew nothing about riding with The People and suffering. Hawk had daubed on red and white paint –half white man, half Indian – at some point during the canyon fight.

He must have been dragging brushing on the trail to cover the retreat, because his hair had knotted into tangles of twigs and bits of bark. He began to pull twigs out, flicking the little sticks in my direction. It was an absent-minded, brotherly sort of gesture that for a moment he reminded me of Phil. I felt a huge wage of homesickness over me that left me speechless to offer comfort or commiseration.

"I'm sorry," he said finally. Long pause. "For getting so angry at you in the canyon." Another pause. I knew better than to interrupt and fill the space with words. "My heart was bad."

In this narrative, written some twenty-seven years after the event, I have naturally paraphrased conversations. I'm not vain or smart enough to pretend I could possibly remember all that was said to me. I'm not even sure I want to, but I do remember when Hawk said that his heart was bad. His words touched me because he looked so defeated, and also because I remember my own unkind words. His hands trembled as he pitched those silly twigs at me. I knew he was ready to drop from exhaustion, but there he was, telling me he was sorry.

I tried to be rational about the whole situation, but he had caught me in my own backlash of a surge of loneliness and I melted into tears. He quit fooling with the twigs and put his arms around me. Mindful of people nearby, I cried as quietly as I could. I told him how frightened I was and how lonely, as he let me cry all over him.

I finally blew my nose on the hem of my skirt – Miss Sumner, what would *you* do if your only handkerchief was still in Yellowstone Park? – and sat up straight.

He released me. "Liz, you have strong *wyakim*."

"*Wyakim*?" I asked. I rose to my knees and started picking the leaves and brush out of Hawk's hair. I couldn't have explained what just happened, but something had changed. He made no objection.

"Guardian spirit. One who watches."

I thought about the Crow army scout in the canyon. I suppose he could have killed me and Catherine, scalped us both and called it a well-rounded day. But that didn't happen. *Wyakim*. I doubt my Episcopalian priest would have been impressed, but I was.

"I don't believe in things like that," I told him, belying my own thoughts.

"Do you believe in God and Jesus and the…the *wyakim* that no one sees?" he asked.

I hesitated, my fingers in his hair. I believed in the Holy Trinity, One and Inseparable, on McDermott Street, but out here I wasn't so certain. If there was a God, no matter in how many pieces he found himself, he certainly wasn't smiling on the Nimiipuu. And weren't they his creations, too? This was too much theology for me on an empty stomach.

"I thought I did," I answered slowly, "but now I am not so certain."

He took my hands from his hair, squeezed them and released them. "You need more faith."

How strange to hear that coming from a warpainted man. He must have gone to church in Vancouver with his father. Maybe he went with Catherine. I realized how little I knew about this person who had saved my life only this afternoon. I wanted to ask so many questions, but nothing came out except, "I am so tired."

"You and all of us," he said. "Look away."

I did as he said, knowing he was removing his loincloth and crawling under the buffalo robe. For a moment that luckily passed – should I even write this, if my children are going to read it? Oh, why not. – I didn't want to look away. I did, though, then looked back before I moved to my side of the shelter, the safe side. "Hawk, is your *wyakim* Kaya?"

"Yes. Hawk. I had an earlier name, a Christian one from my father. I haven't used it since my vigil when *kaya* swooped down and carried me to another peak."

I didn't laugh, although I might have a few weeks ago, when I was only Miss Elizabeth Ann Everett of Omaha, Nebraska. I suppose a hawk swooping down was no stranger than a virgin birth or three people being one person.

He touched his chest. "My medal has strong medicine, too," he said. His voice sounded drowsy, and I knew he would soon sleep.

I knew he meant the copper-colored medallion he wore on the rawhide strip about his neck. He always wore it.

"Tell me."

"It was given to my great grandfather, father of Meopwits, by Meriwether Lewis."

Lewis and Clark. My goodness. I recalled the stories of the Nez Perce aiding the starving Corps of Discovery as they struggled toward the Western Sea. Why should they not be held in honor in their own valleys, and not hunted through Montana Territory now?

Hawk slept, but I lay there with my hands behind my head. Blue Mountain Woman came out of the night. She knelt by her sleeping son and touched his head as gently as if he were a newborn. She pulled the robe higher around his bare shoulders and touched his cheek.

She did the same thing to me. I reached up and patted her arm. Mother might have flinched if I ever did that to her, but not Blue Mountain Woman. She smiled, then put her finger to my lips.

I knew I was safe with this family, no matter what the U.S. government threw at us. I can only blame that foolish thought on the longing of an almost-woman, Miss Elizabeth Ann Everett of Omaha, Nebraska. Somewhere, though, in that part of my heart that yearned, I knew I had another name. I didn't know how to find it.

Chapter Thirteen

In the morning, I stuck my head out from under the buffalo robe to steady rain. I pulled it back under again, not because I hate rain, but because the partially burned canvas of the shelter had no waterproof qualities.

This was no day to hit the road, in my opinion. I was stiff as a poker from sleeping on rocks and a clump of rabbit brush. I hadn't even noticed them last night when I flopped down, exhausted, but there they were in the morning, grown to the size of boulders and a Christmas tree.

I protested when Blue Mountain Woman shook me awake, but since she refused to stop prodding, I got up. The ground all around me had turned to mud. When I took a stop, I promptly fell down.

A word about Montana mud is in order here. It's the closest thing in nature to concrete. Walking in the gumbo is nearly impossible, as you soon perceive that you are getting both taller and heavier with every step.

It was cold, thick rain, the kind that turns to snow. I was soaked through in no time. The prospect of getting either warm or dry that day looked extremely bleak. I complained about the weather to Blue Mountain Woman, who favored me with an indulgent smile, the kind you use to humor toddlers.

"You talk talk about what you cannot change," she reminded me. (Dear reader, she said "talk talk" to emphasize whiners, of which I appeared to be the chief offender. If it was "cry cry," I knew it was time to dry up.)

I guess I did talk talk. She was correct. What good did it do to jaw about it? I might have looked skeptical – who knows – because she continued.

"This is time of rain. It rains. Mother earth is still our mother. This is our circle."

"Don't you get tired of riding in rain?" I persisted.

"If no rain, I mourn," she said firmly, in that motherly tone I recognized in coming years when I urged my children to eat that spinach because it was good for them. I decided not to complain complain about the weather anymore.

One of the men wounded in the Canyon Creek skirmish died last night. He was an old one, strictly a noncombatant, who had fallen off his pony during the retreat and suffered a blow to the head. Colonel Sturgis probably claimed him as a victim of the canyon fight, and I suppose he was right.

The young men wrapped the body in a blanket and carried him away for burial. I watched them go through the grey scrim of rain until they vanished. Why go so far to dig a grave? I asked Hawk about it when he returned from wrapping the body.

He was scraping mold off a piece of camas root bread. "They must do that, Liz. They must find a secret place."

"Why?"

"If they do not, the Crows or Bannocks or other scouts will dig him up, scalp him, and his spirit will wander."

I was shocked. "Surely they wouldn't desecrate a dead man. Would they?"

Hawk gave me a sour smile and returned to doctoring breakfast.

Blue Mountain Woman found me a piece of moldy bread, too, and I scraped at it with my fingernail. We had reached the bottom of the barrel, so to speak. The blue slime felt like the side of a fish pond and smell like an old closet, but I was too hungry to care.

"Hawk?"

"H'mm?"

"Are you a good hunter?"

"When I have time."

"Oh."

The prospect of anything else to eat today was discouraging in the extreme. I closed my eyes and held my breath and popped in that disgusting morsel. It went down like a raw oyster, so it could have been worse. My stomach protested, but I reminded it that this was all part of the great circle.

I nearly told Hawk about the many-course dinners that formed our usual gluttonous habit in Omaha, but figured he wouldn't believe me. When I think about all the food we wasted in one sitting, I don't believe it even now – steak, fowl, venison, pork, and that was just one course.

I used to dabble with this and poke at that, then slide it all away and settle for a nibble of vegetable cloaked in a white sauce, with maybe a macaron to finish it off. I had set myself a determined goal to achieve the appropriate sylph-like thinness for fashion's sake. And now here I was, getting thinner by the minute, surrounded by slim people and babies crying because they wanted more. I don't know what The People looked like when they began their flight in western Idaho, but here in Montana Territory, there were no plump Nimiipuu.

We made slow travel in the rain. I will always remember the suck and pull of the horses as they stumbled through the glop. Every moment we expected for the troopers to ride out of the mist. Hawk rummaged around and found me an antique musket that was probably made especially for the War of the Roses. He loaded it and handed it to me carefully, telling me not to shoot anyone who looked like one of The People.

I got a little sharp then as asked what in the Sam Hill I was supposed to do with the thing. With that superior look he was so capable of flashing my way, he told me again to save the ball for unfamiliar Indians. When I laughed, he frowned and rode into the rain, making a point to avoid me for the rest of the morning.

I used to think that misery was having to help the second parlor maid polish the silver. That only goes to show you the scope of my life before

September of 1877. Misery was an empty stomach and riding all day in cold rain. And of course, constant fear.

My hair hung in lank, ugly strings, rain dripped off my nose, and I felt a cold coming on. I debated all morning whether to beg Joseph or Poker Joe to just leave me behind here. I had stood all the adventures with The People that I wanted. I said nothing, though, because I was more afraid of what lay beyond that gray curtain of rain.

I rode close to Blue Mountain Woman, who had whacked off her long hair in mourning. Out of long habit, she kept looking back at the pony drag where Catherine had perched until yesterday afternoon. I didn't know how to comfort her and felt too shy to try. I knew it would help if I did not complain, so I didn't.

We made only a brief noon halt because most of us had nothing to noon with. The rain eventually slackened from a torrent to a drizzle, with watery sunlight seen here and there among the clouds. The old ones started to laugh and talk among themselves, as if this was a big improvement. I felt more and more out of sorts, with Hawk still ignoring me. I was rehearsing all manner of biting remarks and trenchant abuse on him when I saw him next. It was silly of me, I know, but it helped pass the time.

Then Sturgis's Crow scouts rode down on us.

They appeared suddenly out of the gloom, loping along not very fast, looking not too concerned, maybe trying to blend in between moments of sun and shadow. I didn't realize they were the enemy until a shot sang out and a young girl herding ponies slumped forward and fell off her horse into the mud. She struggled, then sank face down in the ooze, silenced forever.

The scouts were more interested in the ponies than The People. Prolific horse thieves (according to Hawk), they waved blankets and slapped at the horses with their hands, cutting off a sizeable chunk of the herd before the Nimiipuu went into action.

I reined in my horse and stopped, uncertain what to do, as the Crow tried to run off as many horses as possible before they were driven away by the Nimiipuu, who were far superior riflemen. There was no way the fewer number of them could have overcome The People, but I was amazed at Crow audacity.

Not far from me, I saw a scout dressed in a private's uniform blouse and little else, pounding an old man with the butt of his rifle. When he drew out a knife, I came out of my fog.

"You there! Stop that!" I spurred my horse forward toward them. "What do you think you're doing to that old man?"

It sounded ridiculous to me at the time and even more so now, as I had not a single notion how to help. I just couldn't sit there and watching that scout beat the old man senseless. Something must have snapped in me. To this day, I don't understand why that sparked me to action I was unequal to handle.

The Crows raised his knife, balanced to throw, and held it there. Indecisive? Unsure of his target? I have no idea. He looked back at me and said something that didn't sound polite in any language. He wheeled his horse and started toward me, his knife back and ready to throw. I raised that old gun Hawk had loaded for me, took serious aim because it mattered, and fired.

The force of the explosion threw me off my horse and I fell backward into the mud. The knife whizzed past my horse and landed behind me with a squish. I groped around in the mud for it, desperate because the Crow was nearly upon me. When it began to rain blood, I wiped the mud from my eyes and looked up.

The Crow scout still sat on his horse, his posture impeccable, but his head had disappeared, blown completely off his shoulders. Blood spouted skyward with a force to rival any geyser, then splattered down around me. I was warm for the first time since crawling from my buffalo robe.

He sat there – it sat there – never wavering for what seemed an excruciatingly long time, then toppled in the mud next to me. I probably would have screamed like a banshee – maybe I tried – but my mouth was full of mud and my teeth felt jarred loose from my fall. Instead, I lay there in what must have been shock, marveling at the whiteness of his neck bones.

After I could breathe again, I climbed back on Fair One. I was beginning to think I was made of sterner stuff than I knew, or my parents even imagined.

The raid continued only a few more minutes. Another Crow died and the others fled into the sheltering rain. It was a hasty retreat, but nothing to rejoice over, because their object had been realized. They escaped with more than one hundred horses The People could ill afford to lose.

Hawk dismounted in a hurry and stood over the Crow I had decapitated with my one lucky shot in a million. He toed the body for no discernible reason. God Almighty, his head was gone. I knew he was dead. Hawk did a peculiar thing, something that confirmed the other half of his origin that a mere glance would never have seen: He shook my hand. I was surprised and relieved. At least I had killed the right Indian.

Joseph joined us, demanding to know what happened, from the tone of his voice. Hawk told him, sparing no detail, but that was only my surmise from the intensity of his voice and his numerous, emphatic gestures. I thought Joseph would be pleased, but he wasn't, not at all. He said something biting under his breath and stared at the dead man. I wondered where I had gone wrong.

When he spoke to me this time, Hawk interpreted. "He says, 'I am sorry it came to this.'"

"I couldn't let him beat that old man to death," I explained. "Tell him that."

Talk talk as Blue Mountain Woman would say, and then, "'You are good, but our fight is not your fight.'"

Joseph regarded me for a moment, a long moment, with a solemn face. He mounted his horse and rode to the dead body of the young girl, whose parents were kneeling and wailing.

Hawk came closer. "He said he will try to find some white people to leave you with as soon as he can. He sees this now and he is afraid for you."

"I thought he would be happy that I killed the scout," I burst out.

"He is glad for the old man. He fears now that if something happens to *you*, the white men will make the most of it. He says you must leave."

"Do you feel that way?" I hadn't meant to ask such a personal question – at least I didn't think I did – but the words came out.

He thought a moment. I had learned by my weeks with The People not to interrupt thought, so I waited with patience, well, patience for me. He surprised me.

"You have seen my paint for war. Half of me is red and half is white. One side tells me no, the other side says yes."

"Which side do you listen to?"

He smiled. That was no answer, but I was too shy to ask for more.

We walked by the old man, who was being attended and scolded over by his relatives, I assumed. "Do you know who that old man is?" Hawk asked me after we passed.

I shook my head.

"He is Halatookit – Daytime Smoke – the son of your William Clark, the partner of Lewis. They were lonely men several months in the camp of The People."

"You can't be serious," I exclaimed, then knew I had earned the fishy stare that Hawk turned on me.

"I don't lie," he said pointedly. "I leave that for treaty makers."

I figured I had offended him again, and that he would call it a well-rounded day and ignore me for the afternoon. He chose to be more magnanimous.

"He has over seventy years and many daughters who mother him, as you can see."

I could see. A couple of them were coaxing him toward a pony drag, with the obvious intention of making him perch on the pile of household goods like...well, like an old man. The old man would have none of it. He broke loose and moved toward his horse, mounting unsteadily, then settling down, in control again. He, too, was made of sterner stuff, the same as I. I watched him ride into the drizzle that was turning into a downpour again.

"It seems strange..."

"...that he is hunted by the white man," Hawk finished, reading my mind to perfection.

"Nothing about this makes sense," I said. "You'll have to explain it to me sometime."

"I would if I could. My people have helped the white men at every turn, taken on their religion in some cases, and still we are hounded." He shrugged. "And now hunted."

He rode with me a little way, but I noticed he didn't reload that ancient rifle and hand it back to me. I couldn't fault him for that. I didn't want to touch it again, either.

The rain stopped before sunset. Blue Mountain Woman rode with us, exchanging sharp words with her son. My head started to ache. Would this awful day never end? Hawk snapped back at her, then dig his heels into his horse's flank and left us behind. I assumed she had berated him for giving me that musket in the first place.

She rode knee to knee with me, as if to protect me. I sensed that she wasn't about to let me out of her sight again, at least as long as there were Crows around, circling the pony herd like wolves. There was no need for her to fear that I would attempt anything so foolhardy again; I had no dead wish. "I am all right, Blue Mountain Woman," I assured her. "You can look after Meopwits."

"I watch you," she insisted, taking my hands in hers. "Like my own."

Poor lady, but she had Meopwits and me to worry about. Her father rode with his head down, crying off and on. Cry cry. He had cut off his hair, too. Because his hair was already thin with old age, he looked plucked.

The Crow scouts made another attempt to capture the herd before dark, seeming to rise out of the ground. They rode in a wide circle to the west of the herd, flapping blankets again and yipping. They killed a young warrior and raced away with a few more horses before they were beaten back.

The People were tiring. Even I could see it. We were all glad when the sun went down. My teeth chattered and my stomach hurt so much that I wanted to cry. I think I could have eaten anything. I had a sharp longing

...chicken smothered in mushroom gravy, topped off with a big serving of mashed potatoes with a glob of butter melting in the middle of it. Why quibble? I would have settled for a bowl of cold oatmeal.

I was about ready to yank off my remaining bootlace and suck on it when Hawk rode by and handed his mother two rabbits. Their fur was blood-soaked and cold with death and rain, but we weren't picky. Blue Mountain skinned one of the rabbits. I watched her, then worked over the other one under her direction. It wasn't even a good first attempt, to my view, but I could identify all the parts and my fingers were still attached to my hand. Looked like progress to me.

We put up our pathetic shelter, then Blue Mountain Woman unwrapped a small bundle of blessedly dry twigs and cow chips from an oilskin packet. More interested now, Meopwits started the fire. The kindling gave out too soon, but while it lasted, we managed to get the chill off the meat at least.

I had never eaten anything so close to raw before, but I wasn't about to stand on ceremony. We waited until Hawk returned from the diminished horse herd, then dug in. I know I presented quite a sight, with my hair wet and tangled and my clothes muddy. Blood dripped down my chin from the rabbit. Miss Sumner would have retreated into the solitude of the Sinai Desert if she had witnessed the way I attacked that main and only course.

Since it was barely cooked, we had to gnaw pretty hard at the meat near the bones. I even scraped at it with my fingernails to detach every bit of flesh.

I say we. After only a few bites, Meopwits refused to eat any more. He sat hugging his knees up to his chin, staring into the dead fire. Hawk sat by him, saying nothing. After a short time, the old man leaned his head against his grandson's shoulder. They sat like that together until the stars began to peek through the clouds.

Chapter Fourteen

Perhaps I should speak of calendars and watches and time. I've looked back through these pages and sense a sameness, as in, we traveled, we ate when we found something to eat, we tried to mask our fears (I was never good at this), and we slept. I had no idea what day it was.

At first it bothered me when I couldn't tell the time. Our house in Omaha seemed to have a clock in every room, as if exhorting that we be busy and doing and mindful of each moment. There was none of that on the march toward Canada. Our lives were governed by the rising and setting of the sun, and a watchfulness borne of the real fear that any moment, an army could appear and ride us into the ground.

The extent of that possibility came home later, when we learned that our enemy had wired ahead to other departments and stationed troops all along out supposed line of march. Colonel Sturgis at Canyon Creek should have been Sturgis farther north at Judith Gap, except that he probably consulted a watch, felt impatient and moved south.

Montana is a large state – territory then – and we traveled through space mostly empty. I began to pay more attention to sun and rain and clouds and darkness. Time held no particular fascination, because I was busy watching The People and observing nature around me. And I was thinking about myself and how I felt. Me! I didn't try to see myself through the disapproving eyes of my mother, or even the camaraderie of my younger brother and sister, who probably thought I knew everything and possessed all wisdom. I stopped worrying if my father saw me and my pleasant face as an asset to his position with the UP Railroad. The question of what do they want from me, had somehow turned into what do I want for myself? I had no answers yet, but I didn't expect any. Riding knee to knee with Blue Mountain Woman, listening to Hawk's deep breathing in the shelter, it was enough to be alive and aware of myself and where I fit in the larger scheme of things. No, the smaller scheme of things. Most lives are modest, with modest ambitions.

I suppose this is murky thinking to you who were not part of this tragic slice of American history. I knew I was involved in something not of my choice – blame Methuselah – but something told me there would be consequences to influence my life ever after. What they were, I did not know yet.

The rain had stopped, thank goodness. This morning was the first morning I noticed frost on the buffalo grass. It shimmered in the weak light and became more than a subtle reminder that winter was coming, and we had miles to ride.

Even after the passage of time I am hard pressed to describe this part of Montana as anything more than a bleak parcel of the United States of America. In fact – excuse my cynicism, but it is well-earned – I have since wondered why the government in its infinite wisdom didn't put an Indian reservation there. The land we traveled was indented and scarred by coulees and cutbanks in various stages of erosion. Buffalo grass covered everything, and there were few trees.

I haven't been over the terrain since 1877, but I doubt it has altered much. Ranchers probably own the land, but it takes a lot of acres to feed one cow. Have fun, gentlemen. Perhaps I am too harsh. I suppose every portion of the country has its admirers. Still, I dare anyone to leave that land, then look back with longing. No one wanted it then; I know I didn't.

The morning was distinguished from the sameness of others by another incident with the Crow scouts of Colonel Sturgis. We had just finished off a hearty breakfast of water and questionable rabbit scraps when we heard horses running through the encampment. The scouts trampled an old woman and scattered possessions before they were driven away. The Crows seemed to enjoy what they were doing, rather like pesky hoodlums tipping over outhouses on Halloween.

We packed in a hurry – it took less and less time because each day we seemed to have less and less – and left the area heading north, always north. I looked back and noticed with dismay that we had left several of the old ones behind. I tugged on Hawk's shirt. "Shouldn't someone go back for them?" I asked.

"No. Their time has come. They want to die."

I was such an annoyance, such a white woman. "But the Crows will get them. Doesn't anyone care?"

He looked at me without speaking and I was shamed to see tears in his eyes. Everyone cared, but there wasn't a lot they could do about the old people who cared more deeply about their children than themselves.

There were no more raids that day. Hawk and other young warriors followed Ollokot and White Bird to the rear and prevented the Crow scouts from inflicting any more damage. One brave came back with a fresh scalp. That was the only time on the journey that I knew any hair had been lifted by one of The People. There may have been other scalps taken, but this is my narrative of what I saw. You want another story? Find another account.

Poker Joe rode with me off and on that day. He had a blow-up earlier that day with Looking Glass, who wanted to slow the pace, despite the threat of the Crow. No one had seen hide nor hair of Sturgis since Canyon Creek, and General Howard probably lurked somewhere, but even I, a novice at anything connected with this flight, knew this was no time to linger.

Poker Joe nodded at my commentary. I realize now how kind he was to let me talk, even when he knew I knew nothing. Perhaps he was merely humoring me. I never asked.

I could not deny that Looking Glass had his reasons. Anyone with eyes could see that the families were worn down to the bone. Little children tossed and turned at night, and old people thought more and more of death as a relief. Most were out of food, as our family was, and some resented Poker Joe's constant hurry that gave no one time to stalk game.

I had begun to adjust to the prospect of no food, but the little ones cried so quietly and fretted. I dreaded the look of despair in their mothers' eyes as they had nothing to offer. Nursing mothers drying up gave their babies sticks to stuck on. I watched one toddler chewing on grass. The sight made me close my eyes and look away.

Still, I had to agree with Poker Joe. I know I owed some of my sense of urgency to those calendars that had ruled my life and still did. I could see days flipping by, as on that daily desk calendar in my father's office, all heading to winter.

"You are right," I told him. "As sad as it makes me to see grass-eating children, we cannot linger."

"How can I convince them, Liz?" he asked me. "I cannot blame them for wanting to slow down, but they do not understand."

"It's because they don't see calendars," I said, knowing even as the words left my lips that they sounded monumentally stupid. "Oh, I mean..." I looked at him. "You know calendars, don't you? You said you are part French."

"I know calendars." He chuckled. "My father kept a calendar, the same calendar, for years. Every month he turned a page. I had no idea why then. I understand now. Time is passing on white man's paper in ways that The People do not understand."

When he spoke again, I knew he was not talking to me, but thinking aloud. "When we fled, our leaders assured The People that there was room for us here in the buffalo country with our friends and brothers the Crow."

I let that sink in, and felt a chill deeper than a breeze or frost on grass. "Poker Joe, when we took the train from Nebraska to Utah Territory, I saw piles of buffalo bones and mounds of buffalo skins at every depot. They're going."

"They're gone," he said.

I heard all the sadness. Cry cry, I thought, remembering Blue Mountain

Woman's quaint English. I felt like apologizing for the whole United States of America. It was plain to me that the Nez Perce (oh, why not call them by an erroneous name?), were being crushed, and there wasn't a thing anyone could do. We – I had included myself because I was there – would have to play out this whole drama for formality's sake. These people were doomed. I saw it. I knew it. Canada wasn't close enough.

We rode through Judith Gap a few days later. It was a wide spot between two mountains. I wondered who Judith was. We continued in a northeasterly direction, heading for a crossing of the Missouri River. Chief Joseph made a point to have Poker Joe tell me that we would surely find some whites who would take me in.

Poker Joe dined with us that evening on a memorable stew that Blue Mountain Woman whipped up, possessing all the consistency and flavor of a cow's cud. I would be hard put to describe it, but I think the main ingredient was that moss left over from my monthly needs several weeks ago. No one complained, but I wanted to. Instead, I tried to think about my puny place in Blue Mountain Woman's great circle and act a little Nimiipuu for a change.

After dinner, Poker Joe pulled out a deck of cards. He spoke to Hawk, who nodded and walked with him to another campfire. Blue Mountain Woman watched them go, a frown on her face.

"I hope he remembers that is his only shirt," she muttered to me.

We sat by our own small fire, listening to camp sounds. I was ready to sleep, but too tired for the exertion of going inside the shelter. This lethargy had been growing on me with each day there was less to eat. Oh poor poor me! I had only been traveling like this since Yellowstone Park, and not on the move for months. I stayed where I was, piling little bits of pebbles into groups of ten, thinking about decimals, of all things.

When I was just about to force myself to go inside, Hawk returned barefoot, but still wearing his shirt. Blue Mountain Woman looked him up and down, sniffed, and went inside the shelter. I couldn't help myself.

I laughed as quietly as I could. Hawk mumbled something about white women and stalked back into the dark.

I would prefer to forget what happened the next morning. I cannot. As it is part of the journey, I must be honest and include it in this account.

Meopwits had been lagging behind, ever since Catherine's death. This morning, he shook his head when Blue Mountain Woman offered him the dregs of our cream of moss soup, and started singing to himself.

We broke camp that morning in a cold drizzle, Meopwits watching us and not helping. He motioned to Hawk, who squatted on his heels by his grandfather. They sat together, not looking at each other, but with their shoulders touching. Blue Mountain Woman called to Meopwits, but the old man shook his head and stayed where he was. His daughter paused in the motion of mounting her horse, then went ahead and threw her leg over. She looked back once, then sat straighter and rode away from her father. Meopwits pulled his blanket over his head.

I had been watching this scene play out for more than a week now, but this was Meopwits. When he didn't get up, I ran to Hawk, who had left his grandfather and was walking to the horse herd.

"You can't just leave him there," I said, grabbing his shoulders.

He shook me off. "I do not have a choice, Elizabeth Ann."

I jumped in front of him when he kept walking. He wouldn't slow down, so I found myself backing up toward the horses. I heard them milling behind me.

"What kind of man are you?" I asked too loud. "That is your grandfather!"

He stopped and yelled right back. "Do you imagine for one moment that I like leaving Meopwits? Do you think I enjoy watching young ones starve, dogs limp away to die, old people wander off? Do you think any of us like being hungry and cold?"

He jabbed me with his finger as he spoke and walked me backward. My cup finally ran over and I raised my hand to slap him. He grabbed both of my hands and held on tight. We stood glaring at each other and practically snarling.

"I can't understand why you didn't just kill me back in Yellowstone Park?" I raged at him. I was nasty and hateful and so hungry and tired.

He let go of me. "Don't think I haven't wondered about that every step of this journey!" he raged right back.

Naturally, this little contretemps did not go unnoticed by the entire functioning Nez Perce nation. There we were, sniping at each other like ill-mannered children and almost coming to blow over something neither of us had any control over. I felt miserable beyond words. I had compounded my wretchedness by verbally bludgeoning the only person I could turn to.

Through misty eyes I watched Hawk find his horse, jerk the poor beast around, mount and ride north without a backward glance. There I was, afraid to follow, frightened to remain behind with the nearly dead.

The People passed me. The Nez Perce are a polite nation. No one gawked, even though none of them could have avoided hearing that stupid battle. They left me to my own thoughts.

All except one old lady. I recognized her as Mary, one of Catherine's Presbyterian friends. Like others, she had rudimentary English skills. As I watched her in total misery, she dismounted, rubbed her back and knelt beside me. "'Make a joyful noise unto the Lord,'" she said cheerfully, which makes me smile now, even though it didn't then. She astounded me by leaning closer until our foreheads touched. "He loves you," she said. "You love him."

That was all, and so utterly, completely wrong. Couldn't she see that I had just driven away my best friend in the world? I couldn't speak so I turned away. She patted my shoulder and mounted her horse. "You'll see," she said as she rode away.

I stayed by Meopwits until everyone was out of sight. It started to rain again, I felt bowed down by the weight of the water on my back, and if I am honest, by my sadness at losing a friend in Hawk. The old lady didn't know what she was talking about. The silence overwhelmed me. No birds sang; no wind ruffled the buffalo grass. The only sound was Meopwits's muffled breathing as he sat with that blanket over his head.

I decided at last that I was more afraid to stay than to move on. I stood up and brushed at the mud on my dress. As I did that, I wondered with a certain bitterness if my mother and sister were warm in the parlor back in Omaha. Omaha? Was it still in Nebraska? Did it matter? Was it Tuesday? Who cared?

"Wait."

Consumed by my own pettiness, I had forgotten Meopwits. Had he decided maybe today wasn't the day? I turned back, hopeful.

But no. He rustled a little under his blanket, then put his moccasins out of his little haven, his last earthly lodge. I knew they were for Hawk. I wanted to cry cry.

I did what I knew he wanted. I picked up the moccasins. "Thank you, Meopwits. I love you."

I squared my shoulders and held the moccasins close to my magnificent shrinking bosom, the author of all my troubles, along with Methuselah. Fair One had remained faithful through the whole ghastly scene and the retreat of The People. Head down, forlorn, she waited for me. I looked down, too, and leaned against her.

I looked up to see Hawk riding back over the coulee. He reined in his horse and watched me from a safe distance. I wondered if he had come back to kill me, and the idea was almost welcome. I was less afraid at that moment than I had been on the whole miserable journey. I stood calmly and waited for him to select an arrow.

As he sat there, I saw his shoulders move in a great sigh. He started walking his horse toward me. He stopped when we were close. I reached up and handed him the moccasins. "He wanted you to have them."

He took them, and looked past me to Meopwits still sitting there, then turned his head away.

"Come on, Liz. We'll never get to Canada if we dawdle."

"I'm sorry," I whispered.

"I am, too. Forgive me." He gave me a nudge with his shoulder. "Let's not do that again."

We rode back to the line of moving people. I didn't want to look at anyone, but I couldn't overlook the broad grin on Old Mary's face.

They found someone the next day to leave me with. I can't blame The People for what happened, but I wish they had been wiser in the ways of the white man.

Chapter Fifteen

I have debated whether to include what happened next. As I have written, this account is for my children. My husband knows what happened, but I have never revealed this incident to anyone else. When I finish this portion, I'll show it to him for his opinion.

I am still ashamed to admit it, but after my fight with the man I had come to respect and even admire (except when he lost his moccasins gambling), I decided The People were finally as tired of me as I was of myself. Like a child, I wanted to whole ugly business to end.

One bright spot was that a beautiful day followed the drizzle and we all perked up. You know what I mean, September days so warm and sunny that you forget for a while that Thanksgiving is less than eight weeks away. As we started out, I remember watching great flocks of birds flying south in wedges. The sun was warm on my face, and I felt like I was finally drying out after days of rain.

Even better, Hawk traded some ammunition for jerky, so we had a side dish to the usual breakfast water. As we finished, Poker Joe took Hawk aside for a conversation that seemed to involve glances at me. They rode away together shortly after the day's march began.

They returned when the sun was high with the welcome information that they had located a white man who assured them he would take me in. He told Hawk and Poker Joe that he had a wife and child nearby at Bowles Trading Post, and it wouldn't be any trouble to help out.

"We will take you to him," Poker Joe said. "His heart is good."

"Why didn't he come here with you?" I asked, even as Blue Mountain Woman looked away at the news of my leaving, hopefully because she was going to miss me and didn't want to show it, and not relieved that I was on my way.

"We asked him to come with us," Hawk explained, "but he thought it would be more prudent of he stayed out of sight." He looked around him at the others and lowered his voice. "Some of The People would not be happy in their hearts to see a white man right now."

I understood that, but the scheme bothered me more than a little. I strongly suspect The People wanted to see me gone, but I knew I was going to miss Blue Mountain Woman, and maybe Poker Joe. As for Hawk, I knew I had embarrassed him yesterday, with my whining and shouting. If it was any consolation, I didn't like myself, either.

My head told me there wasn't anything else to miss. Except for a few words, I did not speak the language of the Nimiipuu. I had been subsisting on less than starvation rations. I had been shot at and chased, and fear had become my constant companion. Why I should suddenly draw back when my rescue was so close puzzled me.

I can see it now, even though I couldn't then. I had become accustomed to Blue Mountain Woman's welcoming smile each morning, even as she prodded me awake. I remember even now her relieved expression that night of the Canyon Creek fight when she found me. And there was Hawk, riding behind me when we fled from the Bannock Scouts, even though he easily could have passed Methuselah. Leaving them was going to be harder than I reckoned.

As it turned out, I couldn't say goodbye to Blue Mountain Woman because she had joined her friends and I was too shy to intrude. I decided to tell myself that she didn't like farewells, either. I mounted Fair One and followed Hawk and Poker Joe as they turned east and headed for a small stand of trees I could see if I squinted.

No one spoke, although I did wonder why Bowles Trading Post was so far from what I knew was a river. I got off my pony when they stopped and handed the reins up to Hawk.

"He said he would be near that tallest cottonwood," Poker Joe said, and pointed with his lips. "I think I see him. He said he has a horse for you."

I shaded my eyes with my hand. Yes, there was someone. I saw only one horse and wondered. "Can't I stay with you?" I wanted to ask, but I saw nothing in either man's face that indicated they were receptive to such an idea. Hadn't this been the plan all along?

They were no better at saying goodbye than I was, apparently, so I made the first move. "Well, if you're ever in Omaha, I live at 303 McDermott Street." I've seldom felt more foolish, but at least I could be polite. "Thanks for taking care of me."

Poker Joe turned to leave first, and Hawk followed, but not without several backward glances. I almost called him back, but I did not feel like rejection, not after my silliness yesterday. I watched them ride away, then walked into the trees toward the tallest cottonwood.

Where had he gone? I walked through the few trees and into the prairie on the other side. Where was this white man who was going to take me to his wife and child? A stream cut through the empty land. I knelt down Indian-fashion and lapped up some water. Something made me look to the side and there he stood.

The other wrangler, the one who had left Muskrat Watkins in the lurch, was leading a horse with an army saddle. How he had acquired that outfit was a mystery to me. I felt my insides turn to jelly as I sat there on my haunches and looked at someone I had no wish to ever see again. Wife and child, my ass. A slow smile spread across his face as I stood up slowly, prepared to run.

I took a step and another one but that was all. He rode his horse directly in front of me and planted it sideways, eyeing me like a bird of prey watching a mouse blundering about. "Well hey there, Missy," he said. "When ol' Poker Joe described you, I figured we'd met before." He ran his tongue over his lips and smiled until his gums showed. "This is some howdy do."

I ran, knowing it was utter folly, but determined not to give up easily. I snatched up the long train of my riding habit and ran. Screaming was pointless. I had been left behind by Poker Joe and Hawk. We both knew it.

He let me run a little way, maybe to tire me out, or maybe to toy with me like a cat with a mouse. I aimed for the little gap in the coulee I had ridden through so recently, hoping for someone to ride to my rescue. I wouldn't have minded the Seventh Cavalry about then.

The wrangler played with me until my side started to burn. I had reached the point when I wanted to surrender when a rope dropped around me and I was thrown to the ground like a calf ready for branding.

I hit the ground so hard that my teeth bit through my lower lip. My mouth filled with blood and I struggled to rise. It was a pointless attempt; I knew it and he knew it. The wrangler flipped me on my back and yanked the rope off my legs. "Please no," I managed to gargle through the blood, polite to the end.

When he put his hand on my throat and clamped down, I remembered similar sounds coming through the thin wall when he attacked the prostitute, so many weeks ago. I clawed at his hand and tried to bite him until he cuffed me on the side of my head. He jerked out a knife, transferring it to the hand pinning me down, and slammed his knee between my legs. When I tried to push him away, the knife bit into my neck. I lay still then and closed my eyes, not ready to give up, but out of ideas.

With his free hand, the wrangler grabbed the front of my dirty, now-loose riding habit and ripped it down to my waist as the buttons flew off. I cried and he laughed. I still remember that laugh, which was accompanied by his dirty fingers fondling my breasts. I heard someone laugh like that at an auction once. My husband had to take me home because I was physically sick.

When he couldn't rip through the waistband of my skirt, he bunched it up around my chest. As the knife bit deeper in my neck, he tore my raggedy drawers away. He stared down at my nudity and salivated. That may have been the worst moment of all. As blood dripped down my neck from that knife point, I knew I had to stop struggling to stay alive. As for why I wanted to stay alive… well, the urge remained strong. I have never been one to fold, although I was close to it, there on my back with that disgusting man forcing my legs wider apart.

He fumbled with his trouser buttons and let go of my throat for an instant. I stared right at him and let go with the loudest scream I ever thought I could produce. Everetts didn't scream, but I screamed so loud that even the meadowlarks stopped their bubbling notes.

He punched me hard in the eye and slapped that great big hand back on my throat again, even though it was slippery with my blood. He pushed down harder, forcing me to turn my attention to breathing and not what was going on between my legs. Maybe that was a blessing.

Rape is difficult to describe, so I will spare you. He was going to what he wanted and there wasn't anything I could do to stop him. Rape is rage, and don't let anyone tell you otherwise.

As the wretched man readied himself, I bore it as best I could, trying to think of something else, anything else. Lying on my back, I even started imaging I heard a horse galloping. I closed my eyes, fearing another eager wrangler, and another. I cannot describe my panic at that thought.

He had barely begun his assault on me, when I heard someone running and then yanking the wrangler away. The awful hand left my throat and I gulped air, even as I grabbed my skirt with shaking hands and fumbled to cover my nakedness. I couldn't do anything about my bodice but that was a minor concern barely worth consideration.

I struggled to sit up as Hawk snatched the wrangler to his feet, took the man's own knife and dragged it down, gutting him from throat to pelvis, as the wrangler stared down at his spurting insides. This was the work of mere seconds. Hawk slammed him facedown to the ground and let him writhe.

I stared at Hawk. I opened my mouth to scream again, but he took my bloody face in his hands and pressed his forehead against mine. "Shh, shh,

shh," he crooned, doing a fine imitation of the Nimiipuu mothers who rode so patiently day after day with hungry little ones.

When I was silent and breathing regularly again, he turned his back to me. He looked toward the wrangler, who was making horrible gargling noises. "I could kill him, but he's doing such a fine job right now that I will let him continue," he told me in a most conversational tone.

Hawk gave me time to pull my skirt down the rest of the way and try to cover my bare front before he turned around again. I might have been more successful at covering my breasts, but my hands shook too much. Silently, he took off his blue shirt and helped me into it. He did up the buttons as I shivered, then rolled up the shirtsleeves. He brushed the hair out of my eyes, and tied it back again with the rawhide strip that had fallen out in my struggle.

I flinched and drew back when he gently touched my swollen eye that throbbed and pounded. The blood started to dry up where I had bitten through my lip, but the pain, oh the pain. The wrangler lay still now. Hawk tore off a hunk of the dead man's shirt, and soaked it in the stream.

"Wipe your face, little one." He could have been Blue Mountain Woman, speaking to a child.

After I did as he said, he returned to the stream, washed out the blood, then put the cool cloth over my eye, swollen shut. He gently tugged my hand to my eye so I could hold the cloth in place.

Poker Joe galloped into the clearing then. He leaped off his horse while it still moved, and ran to us. For you readers (if anyone reads this except my Stuart relatives) who might have been nourished in the myth that Indians never show emotion, I wish you could have seen Poker Joe. I feared he would burst into tears. He went to his knees and whispered, "Liz, I thought he was a good man. I thought…"

I made a clumsy attempt to pat his shoulder. "Oh, Poker Joe," was all I said. My throat hurt as much as my eye and my knees, where he had dragged me down with his rope.

I knew it was no consolation, so he stood up and kicked the wrangler's body. Poker Joe turned him over. I gasped and looked away at the gory sight of a man disemboweled. Hawk put his arm around me and turned my face into his chest.

From the amazing safety of Hawk's arms, I watched Poker Joe, his back to us, as he whipped aside his loincloth and urinated on the dead man's face. The sound of his water splashing on the corpse was more than I could stand. I vomited up mostly nothing, then clutched my throat.

Thinking back on something I try never to remember, I have to admit that I felt a tiny bit better as Poker Joe watered the wrangler with liquid contempt.

The two men helped me to my feet. Poker Joe held me while Hawk picked up the rifle lying nearby. He stared at the dead man's horse, then went through the saddlebags, finding ammunition and a bag of jerky. He stood a moment over the wrangler, then spit on him. He spoke to Poker Joe in their other language, and Joe shook his head. They left the dead man's horse there, quietly cropping grass. As much as anything, that act illustrated the measure of Nimiipuu contempt. No man of that tribe would ordinarily have left a sound horse behind.

After Hawk mounted his horse, Poker Joe handed me up. I saw Fair One at the top of the ridge, but I was in no condition to straddle her. I leaned back against Hawk, filled with more relief than I knew was my fair share. I wanted to live, and I had another chance.

We rode slowly back to The People, no one speaking. Poker Joe peeled off to talk to Chief Joseph and the other leaders. The discussion sounded a little heated. Shock and anger on her face, Blue Mountain Woman rode beside us. She leaned over and touched me several times. Like a wounded animal, all I wanted to do was hide.

When we made camp after sundown, Blue Mountain Woman and her friends hurriedly put up our canvas shelter and spread out a buffalo robe. Hawk carried me inside and laid me down. He knelt and touched his cleaner cheek to my bloody one, then left me to the women.

With gentle murmurs and warm water, they cleaned me of blood and somehow also of shame. Blue Mountain Woman and her friend Mary shook their heads over the deep finger marks on my shoulders and inner thighs. I told her what Hawk had done in retaliation, and they nodded their approval. "Sleep now," Blue Mountain Woman said. "You are safe."

I could open my one good eye in the morning. I decided against asking Blue Mountain Woman for her little scrap of mirror, and felt my face instead. My closed eye had swelled like some strange appendage, matching my puffy lips. I still couldn't swallow well, but Blue Mountain Woman pounded dried camas root really fine and mixed it with someone's liquor. Hawk held my head steady while she poured the mixture down my throat.

Hawk left the shelter with my skirt and petticoat, soaked with the wrangler's blood. I knew I never wanted to see them again. When he was busy outside, Blue Mountain Woman handed me a deerskin dress as soft as butter, and nearly that color. She helped me pull it down over my head. With her assistance, I stood up carefully and let the dress fall and cover me just past my knees. She handed me a pair of beaded moccasins. They fit.

She helped me down again then knelt behind me and carefully combed my hair, singing to me now. She used a cleaner leather thong, this one decorated with beads and shells, to tie back my hair.

Arm in arm we walked slowly to the pony herd. Other women joined us so kindly. I saw no judgment, which surprised me not in the least, not from the Nimiipuu. I was surrounded by love.

With their help, I was able to mount Fair One. Blue Mountain Woman took the reins from me and led my horse behind hers. Hawk rode close beside me on one side, and Poker Joe on the other.

And so we traveled.

* * *

I finished the above passage just before my husband returned late from horse trading. After a warmed-up dinner, I took my growing pile of paper into the front room and curled up in his big chair. He had gone to the horse barn with our son Thomas to admire the new foal, dropped while he was away.

Comfortable in my favorite spot, I read through this account, still uncertain if I should have written of that experience with the wrangler. Duncan and I have never said much about it, not in all the years of our marriage. I decided to wait up until he came in to get his opinion.

They came in just after eleven. Thomas gave me a goodnight wave and went upstairs. Duncan took off his coat and came into the parlor. It must have started raining, because his hair was wet. He passed a hand over his grey hair and wiped it on his jeans.

"Thought you'd be in bed by now, Smiley. What's the matter? Got a bit of wind on your stomach?"

Now doesn't that sound like twenty-three years of marriage? I ask you. "I...I wanted you to read something."

I vacated his chair and handed him what I had labored all day to write. He sat down, held out his arms and invited me back to his chair. With his arms around me, he tilted the lamp closer and started reading. His arms tightened, and I nestled close to his chest. "Shh, shh, shh," he murmured, when I shuddered.

That alone kept me from tears. Here I am, past forty-five, and the memory of that degradation is as fresh as yesterday. How strange. I have had so many lovely and joyful moments in my life that it still seems wrong to dwell on such a mean event, quickly over, in the greater scheme of things. But I do. Do other women?

Duncan set down the pages and shifted in his chair. "I wondered if you would write about that day."

"I had to, didn't I? I mean, it was part of the whole journey."

He held my hand and kissed it. I snuggled closer to him. "When was the last time I told you I loved you?" He shifted me a bit and slid my hand against his inner thigh.

"Maybe when you rode away last week," I said, and moved my hand higher.

"I love you, Smiley. You still want to hitch your team to my wagon?" He said that now and then, usually when things hadn't gone as planned.

"You know I do, Duncan. I love you right back."

He kissed me. It's been a while since I've been kissed like that. I'm happy Thomas didn't take it into his head to come downstairs for a late snack. I do believe his old parents would have embarrassed him.

Chapter Sixteen

I remember little about the next few days. My eye throbbed and my other eye drooped in sympathy, making vision difficult. Each day seemed to bring some new ache or pain. When I couldn't stop my tears, Hawk insisted that I ride on the pony drag. When I was situated, he covered me entirely with a trade blanket, creating a safety nest where I could burrow down and shut out the world. How did he know to do that?

My throat hurt too much to swallow, which was just as well, because there was so little food. Hawk shot two prairie dogs with the wrangler's rifle and showed them to me when the march slowed for a much-needed rest. It was not my imagination that The People were moving slower and slower, even the horses.

"Mother will cook them for you," he said.

I opened my better eye as wide as I could with my fingers and nodded. That got me a half smile, which made me immediately suspicious. That particular smile usually meant he had something else on his mind.

He did. "She will cook them for you, but there are many children who will smell the cooking."

He was right. Besides, I told myself that even small lumps of *chien de prairie* would be challenging. "Save me the broth, if you please." I hadn't forgotten all my manners.

He brought me water then, and broth in a tin cup later when we stopped long enough to warrant cooking fires. (Small ones. We had no idea where scouts and troops lurked.) He held me up and close to his chest so I could drink. When he lowered me down, he gave me a gentle squeeze.

"You're a good girl, Elizabeth Ann." He left me a canteen with US stamped on it, and swung onto his horse again.

Blue Mountain Woman rode by me most of the time. Although her English language skills were rudimentary, they weren't really needed. I could tell without words how deeply it pained her to see me lying there, drawn up into a ball. I resolved to get on my horse the next morning no matter how I felt.

We stopped that night near Reed's Fort, a wind-scoured trading post presided over by an old coot who, from all appearances, had subsisted in Judith Basin since the earth's crust was still hot. The People seemed to know him well. Everyone went trading and came away with a dab of food and ammunition, though not much. He said he was expecting supplies soon from the closest river drop at Cow Island, some twenty miles north on the Missouri River.

I've asked myself a time or two why the Nimiipuu didn't leave me there with Reed and his mixed-blood family. All I can surmise is that they feared Reed would jump to conclusions if he saw me with my black eye and battered face. Or they might even have decided that as well as they thought they knew this white man, maybe they didn't know any white man's heart, and didn't want to chance more injury to me.

Peeking out from under the protection of my blanket, I watched Reed move among the different families, visiting here and there, admiring new babies, looking for all the world like a favorite uncle. I didn't feel up to visitors. I could be cynical and write that Mr. Reed was in no position to argue with his customers. He was significantly outnumbered. I'll give him the benefit of the doubt, though. He knew these people and they knew him. Whole sermons have been given on that subject. Too bad the wrangler never listened to one.

Through the exercise of real grit, I mounted my horse in the morning. Fair One looked gigantic, but I threw a leg over and hauled myself on board less than gracefully. I discovered it was much easier riding in Indian clothing. I also discovered that my world was a better place when Blue Mountain Woman looked less anxious.

To my further relief, the sun shone, although it was a cold sun because wind blew steadily from the north. Only stragglers in the bird kingdom were still heading south, almost as if they missed the message. I reckoned we were near the end of September, in the white man's world.

That afternoon, I was privileged to witness a display of aboriginal zeal that might have terrified Elizabeth Ann Everett back in Omaha, but which satisfied some less-cultivated part of Liz.

Our scouts chanced upon a hunting camp of River Crows. No words passed between anyone, but Ollokot painted his face in record time and dashed out with a silent knot of warriors right behind. Hawk went along, of course. He daubed on some of his red and white paint, took a quick count of his arrows and charged out behind Ollokot, after handing me the wrangler's rifle with a meaningful look and the command to use it if something went amiss.

Several of us followed at a discreet distance. A few days ago, I would have been too frightened to do anything but wait behind with my hands over my ears, but that hell with the wrangler had left me without much of the burden of fear that had cluttered my summer journey. After all, what else could happen? I wanted to watch.

Some of the older youths and I waited on a rise not too far distant from the Crow camp. The Crow had obviously enjoyed good hunting. The men were cutting up two buffalo when the Nimiipuu swooped down on them, silent no longer.

I doubt those River Crows could have been the scouts who gave us so much heartache at Canyon Creek, but revenge is sweet. Several of the hunters managed to escape on horseback and split for Reed's Fort. The rest were cut down as they worked over the slain buffalo. It was a singularly gory sight, with its mounds of red meat, and the hunter toppled into them with red blossoms on their chests and heads.

When it was over, Ollokot motioned to us to join them in the Crow camp, where his warriors set fire to the Crow tipis. They didn't scalp any of these Crow, although the young boys who had ridden down with me played at counting coup until Poker Joe ordered them to stop. The warriors loaded us down with meat and we rode back to the rest of The People, singing. I sang, too. I didn't know their songs, but "We'll Rally Round the Flag, Boys" worked for me. I think it was the first song I ever learned, right before the Civil War ended.

I should be embarrassed to admit that the encounter with the Crow cheered me up, but it did. I have never been an advocate of violence, but there was something so satisfying about the raid. Didn't General Robert Lee say it was a good thing war was so horrible, else we would grow too fond of it? Maybe he was a traitor to his country – you know, that country trying to work such mischief among these people I rode with – but there's definitely something to what he said. I felt a curious lift to my heart, almost a sensual emotion, as I watched the Nimiipuu wade through the Crows so systematically. I can't explain it really, except to say that I felt better for the first time in days.

Poker Joe insisted we travel on that day and we did, but it was a half-hearted kind of movement because all we wanted to do was eat. This irritated Poker Joe. His efforts to hurry up young and old alike met with stares and downright hostility.

After one of his attempted to hurry along stragglers, he slapped his hand on his thigh and burst out, "God-damned bunch of savages!" I couldn't help my whoop of laughter, which earned me a glare from him.

We ate a lot that night. I was impressed how carefully the leaders divided the meat among the families. As soon as Chief Joseph called a halt, everyone rushed about preparing the meat. Children ranged across the prairie hunting for buffalo chips, as the rest of us scrounged around for what wood we had brought with us. A portion of the meat was cut into strips and readied for drying.

It may have been the best dinner I ever ate, and I've eaten at

Delmonico's. Nobody felt like hanging around for well-done. I had to school my feelings to keep from cramming it in and reaching for more, all in the same motion. I ate slowly and with as much dignity as I could, considering that all I had to work with was one of Hawk's knives. I doubt there was a fork within miles.

The flavor of the meat was piquant, perhaps owing to the buffalo-chip fire. The nicest part of the impromptu banquet was knowing there was more if I wanted seconds. I did.

Considering what awaited us in a few weeks, something more important than a rousing dinner happened that night, although it didn't mean much to me at the time. After dinner, the chiefs of the clans and the leaders withdrew for a council, rather than brandy and cigars in the drawing room. I was certainly not invited, nor were any of the women. What I learned, I learned later from Hawk.

"The chiefs have chosen Looking Glass," Hawk said when he returned to our own campfire after the session.

"And?" The subtleties of Indian commentary were still beyond me, as you might note.

I received that look-down-the-nose stare I was already familiar with. "Poker Joe will no longer lead us on the trail."

I peered closer at Hawk. He squatted on his heels by the fire, running a finger in little circles in the dirt. His unease seemed to seep out of his pores and into our space.

"That's not good?" I asked, still wanting more information.

"It's terrible." Hawk turned around and started running his fingers through his hair, an absent-minded, homey sort of gesture I was used to from other late nights. You know, like putting out the cat and locking the front door. Freed from its confinement, his hair fell in curly waves to his shoulders. "All Looking Glass wants to do is slow down." He spoke with a dourness that did sound Scottish.

"We're almost to the Canadian border, aren't we?" I asked. "And isn't General Howard several days behind?"

"Come on, Liz, when was the last time you looked at a map?" he exclaimed.

He had me there. Geography has never been my strong suit. Still, Montana Territory struck me as the perfect place to disappear, and so I told him.

Hawk looked at me like he wanted to bite off my head, but sighed instead. "Do you honestly think that Old Day After Tomorrow hasn't telegraphed all the forts between here and the Dakotas for reinforcements?"

"Did you mention that in the council?"

"No. I cannot say yes or no in councils yet, but I can tell you that Poker Joe got excited and asked Looking Glass how he planned to deal with Bluecoats who would ride at him from many directions."

"What did Looking Glass say to that?"

Hawk shook out his buffalo robe and lay beside me. By tacit agreement after the wrangler, we had abandoned the notion of one side of our tiny shelter for him and the other for me and Blue Mountain Woman. He turned to face me. "He ignored Poker Joe like he was not even there. It seemed rude to me, but no one challenged him. Not even Joseph." He stared up through part of burned canvas to the sky. "We are all tired."

That sad fact had come to govern our travel, with the choosing of Looking Glass to replace Poker Joe as leader. I was weary, and I had only been traveling since July. The People had been on the run since early spring. They would have to trust to luck, a notoriously fickle companion, to get them across the border.

Blue Mountain lay down on the other side of me and we composed ourselves for sleep. After drowsy words with Blue Mountain Woman, I turned toward Hawk. His hair smelled so fragrantly of wood smoke. I've always liked that aroma, and to this day, I can't smell wood of a dying campfire without thinking of the journey and The People.

I looked at the sky through the wreckage of the canvas. The stars seemed closer here tham anywhere. I remembered holding out my hands to stars like that in Omaha when I was a child. I knew they were the same stars, but lying there between two people who meant a surprisingly great deal to me, I saw them as The People's stars. I gazed and wondered how Phil was doing. Eugenie told me once that she wanted my bedroom because it overlooked the back lawn, where we played croquet and lounged about. I thought she had probably moved her things in there by now. My parents must have given me up for dead.

For one frightening moment, I wondered if they had been killed in that clearing after Methuselah raced me out of it. I must have gasped with the thought, because Hawk put his hand on my arm. He gave it a little shake and whispered, "Liz? What?"

I edged closer and whispered my sudden fear. "They were unharmed," he said softly, his lips close to my ear. "Others stayed to watch, then joined us."

"Thank God," I said, then thought to beat myself up a little more. "Why in heaven's sake did that thought never occur to me until now?"

"I would suggest that you have been busy for many days." It was as dry a statement as I ever heard from one of The People and made me chuckle, which I think Hawk intended.

He said something strange then, something that a few weeks ago would have earned him a sharp rejoinder, at the least. "When all this ends, and it will, do something for me."

I didn't tell him that I would do anything for him. He had saved me on more than one occasion. He had only to ask. "I will," I whispered.

"No matter what happens to The People, or me or my mother, ask yourself, when you are back in Omaha, if you wish none of this had happened."

It was an odd request. I considered it, and couldn't help a smile in the dark. Maybe I was being flippant and shallow. "I *am* certainly happy my school friends can't see me now," I said. "I doubt they would even recognize me."

"Would *you* recognize you?"

Would I? He slept then, his hand still on my arm. I relished the way his body relaxed in sleep, as if he trusted me. His deep and peaceful breathing became more soothing than I could ever have told him. I tried to scold myself into remembering that this was all a terrible fix to be in. With any luck, this awful experience would fade, and I would go back to being Elizabeth Ann Everett of 303 McDermott Street, Omaha, Nebraska. If not Vassar this fall (no loss), parties and card games and flirting and new dresses loomed in my future, all those comforts familiar to me.

Were they essential to me now? I lay there asking myself why they suddenly seemed trivial. Had Elizabeth Ann Everett been left behind, a casualty of war between a peaceful tribe making hard choices and the U.S. Army? Who was she?

Chapter Seventeen

We crossed the Missouri at Cow Island, where the river was not so wide, and shallow this time of year. The U.S. Army had a supply dump at Cow Island. A soldier in the Fifth Infantry told me later that ordinarily, the goods would have been transported by steamship up to Fort Benton, but the river that year was too low. The supplies at Cow Island were to be freighted this time to garrisons upriver, and also to some settlements in Canada. A contingent of eight or nine soldiers guarded the supply.

Even now, I can't help but wonder if that little group of Bluecoats was a decoy to delay us. Remember, please, that no one in the army knew precisely where The People were going to emerge from the vastness that was, and still is, Montana. Cow Island seemed a logical spot.

Whatever the merits of speculation from a woman's writing desk in Oregon twenty-seven years later, I do know that The People hit the jackpot at Cow Island. The last steamship of the season had unloaded a pile of goods. I recall a mound of kegs and barrels along the riverbank.

Chief Joseph and several others, Hawk among them, rode to the supply dump to bargain for some food. The sergeant in charge was reluctant to part with any of his goods, which I thought foolhardy of him. He did unbend enough to hand out some hard tack and a little bacon, and grudgingly, some sacks of flour. It was obvious to everyone that such a stingy amount of food wouldn't go far among five hundred or so people. Perhaps he figured Joseph could duplicate the miracle of the loaves and fishes.

We camped near the supply dump on the opposite side of the Missouri. Under the cover of darkness, which came earlier and earlier every day, many of the braves raided the dump and burned what they couldn't liberate. You could smell bacon for miles. The sky lit up with the great fire until the night turned bright.

The soldiers dug themselves in near the supplies and kept up a steady fire all night, until the Nimiipuu sharpshooters showed them a few things about marksmanship. They retreated then to a discreet spot farther from the river and why not? The supplies were all ablaze. I doubt that sergeant was given too many more independent commands, once the army got around later to fixing blame for all the weakness and error displayed from Lapwai to the Canadian border.

We did appreciate the quantity of flour and hard tack from the raid on Cow Island, but it wasn't as huge as government reports would have you suppose. I didn't get more than a modest piece of fried bread and the slices of bacon were nice. There were beans aplenty, but beans are hard to cook when you are on the move. Come to think of it, we could have used them a little later as ammunition at the Bear Paws when cartridges ran out.

The night at Cow Island remains in my mind for several reasons. I spent half of it sitting on my buffalo robe, hugging my knees and watching the flames across the river. Hawk had a side of bacon to show for his participation in the raid, but that was all. He sat with me and we stared at the flames and sparks that roared higher.

I found it almost as entertaining as the fireworks on the Fourth last year, which were better than usual because 1876 represented the nation's centennial. It was the first time my parents let me attend any function with a young man, a student at St. Mark's Episcopal Academy. The St. Martians, our name for them, often paired with Miss Sumner's Female Academy for harmless events, and this was one.

I don't even remember his name, but my escort spent the entire time between "oohs" and "aahs" trying to hold my hand. It wouldn't have minded it so much, except that he had clammy hands. All I will add here on the matter of the bonfire, courtesy of The People and the U.S. Army, is that Hawk did not have clammy hands.

He didn't say much of anything, which was nothing new to me. He finally leaned closer and nudged my shoulder, which for him was an amazing liberty. "We ought to leave you here when we pull out tomorrow."

"I suppose you could," I replied, after a silence of my own that gave the word "dubious" all sorts of new meaning.

He asked (cautiously this time), "That's what you want, isn't it? Isn't it?"

Now that push had finally come to shove, I didn't know how to answer him. This *would* be a safe place to be left behind. I could stay on my side of the river until my friends the Nimiipuu were long gone, then wait for the soldiers to find me. There wouldn't be any danger to me from Bannock or Crow scouts.

He let go of my hand, politely setting it back in my lap, which touched me somehow, even as it saddened me. I couldn't have told you why then, or maybe I didn't want to admit why. He cleared his throat. "Of course, Blue Mountain Woman will miss you," he said, then add quickly, "So will I." I knew he wasn't serious because he grinned. "I have gotten used to your silly white questions and you have greatly improved my English."

I could take both a cue and a light tone. "And you and this journey have cured me of complaining."

"Well?" he prompted.

Well what? Was this a preliminary, granted a clumsy one, to get a compliment, an agreement, or a kiss? Probably not the latter. I had never seen Nimiipuu kissing.

"I don't know." I didn't know anything, from how I felt, to the state of the union, to what happens when you combine ketchup with mayonnaise. I realize now I was experiencing a great shift in my view of everything I had thought of value and useful for a young woman in the last quarter of the nineteenth century. I was changing in unheard of ways, but I didn't recognize it.

"Don't you think your folks are worried about you?"

I knew they were. I also knew then and there that this was a moment unlike any other. Whether Hawk knew it or not, and I never asked him, I was taking my first steps toward womanhood, even more than that, personhood. I was growing up in a way I could never have predicted a mere few months ago, when Phil and I plotted our escape from Omaha to Yellowstone National Park.

"I can telegraph my parents from Canada." I said it quietly and I meant it. This was no time to abandon The People, even though I knew I was no real asset to them.

Hawk regarded me with that long, unflinching gaze that made me nervous at the beginning of this adventure, but which had turned into welcome introspection, compelling a person to think, and not just regurgitate words because it was that person's time to speak.

"You are strange," he said.

"Strange in a bad way or a good way?" I asked impulsively.

"A good way, I think," he replied quickly, too. "Listen to me, Liz. I can tell you that Joseph wants you in safer hands than ours."

Well, that was final. What about you, I wanted to ask, but felt too shy. Hawk released my hand and left. Saddened, I stayed there alone. With my chin on my knees, I watched the Nimiipuu sharpshooters keep their army counterparts across the river busy earning their thirteen dollars a month. The firing slowed on both sides and The People began filing back to their campsites. Some carried bolts of cloth, though what they planned to do with them I couldn't fathom.

One man held a bag of sugar and scooped it into his mouth by dirty handfuls. He saw me watching him and held out the bag. (The People are like that.) It didn't look appetizing, damp and grey in his outstretched hand, but I wasn't about to offend his kindness. I took a pinch. Why not?

I took longer than expected to return to our campsite, mainly because there were babies to tickle, and ladies of Blue Mountain Woman's age to assure that I felt pretty good now. One of them insisted I apply a little of her bear grease concoction to my yellow eye. I think they knew this was my last evening among them, and that I would travel no farther. Drat Chief Joseph anyway for starting that rumor.

Blue Mountain Woman was spreading out the robes under the stars when I returned. Few but the most discriminating – my own mother would have fallen into that group – had bothered to erect shelters, so most of us had a good view of stars.

I kicked off my moccasins, lay down and scrunched as far down in my robe as I could. Hawk lay next to me, his hands behind his head, staring at the stars. He said nothing to me, and finally his eyes closed.

I couldn't sleep. After an hour I sat up, just me and a quiet camp. Blue Mountain Woman's face had relaxed in slumber. She was such a pretty woman. Too bad she had no daughters who looked like her. Hawk slept, too. Thirsty, I pulled back my robe and reached for the canteen.

As I drank, I noticed a couple lying nearby. They had flung back their blanket, too, and they were making love. I had never seen anything like that before and I watched. They were so wrapped up in each other that I am certain they were unaware of a voyeur. Their attention was centered on each other. I should have felt embarrassed perhaps, or some shame, but as I watched the two of them twined together, moving in perfect rhythm, all I felt was great emptiness. I wanted someone, as well.

My Omaha upbringing finally got the better of me and I slowly lay down and turned away toward Hawk. To my horror and embarrassment, his eyes were wide open and he was smiling at me.

"I thought you were asleep," I whispered, which has to be one of the stupidest things I have ever said. There is no advice in etiquette books to gloss over such a situation.

"No. They are kind friends. I wish them joy."

His whispered words took away the embarrassment, because I wished them joy in each other, too. Instead of shame, my heart was touched to see love in this time of horrible stress and questionable outcome.

"I do, too," I said, and I meant it.

I also wanted Hawk to take me in his arms. That I would want love so close on the heels of my horrific experience with the wrangler told me something even then about resiliency. I have thought about this through the years, and I continue to wish that couple well, as I sit here in Oregon writing at my kitchen table. I don't know if either of them survived Bear Paws, but I hope they did. Hope is all we have, when everything else is gone.

Chapter Eighteen

My last chance for safety before Bear Paws came the next day. Even now, my brother Phil wonders why I didn't take it, which tells me that I have done a poor job in the intervening years explaining to him my life and how it changed – in my opinion for the better – after my weeks with the Nez Perce. As reluctant as I am to share some of the harsher details of that time which remains vivid in my memory, I will share this manuscript with my little brother. If he reads it with a good heart, as Hawk would have said, he will come to know me better.

We had another dust-up with the Bluecoats, who I assume came from Fort Benton to check up on the supplies at the landing. They should have chosen a better day, but orders are orders, I suppose.

It was comparatively minor and I might not have known of the incident at all, except that I rode in the rear of The People and saw Ollokot lead out with warriors back down our route.

Blue Mountain Woman and I watched them. As composed as always, she sat on her horse and kept her eyes on the braves until they disappeared behind another of the many coulees in that Missouri River drainage.

"Do you worry?" I asked her, puzzled by her serenity.

She gathered up her reins and turned her horse back to the line of travelers, so I followed. "Would worry help?" she asked.

"I don't know," I replied, "but he is your only son."

"I had another, but he is gone." She pointed with her lips toward this vanished son. "It is not his time yet."

A month ago, I doubt I would have understood; now I knew she was right. Hawk would either come back or he wouldn't, and nothing we could do or say would alter that fact. I pushed back from that sort of calm acceptance, but had the good sense to say nothing more. In my defense, remember please that I was only eighteen. I also wasn't Indian enough and never would be.

They did return, all of them. Apparently, the man with shoulder straps chose discretion over valor. I must applaud his good sense. The lieutenant did tell a newspaper reporter later that he was responsible for slowing down our retreat, but this is not true. Our march slowed because Looking Glass was our leader.

Unlike Hawk, I have to give Looking Glass the benefit of the doubt. His rise to leadership coincided with the fight at the Bear Paws, but he was not leading people who in their full strength had fled from Lapwai months ago, and whose talent and energy had been hemorrhaging every step of the way. The People could not miraculously raise from the dead those warriors who had given their all at what is now called White Bird Canyon, or Camas, or Big Hole, or Canyon Creek. He could not replenish food supplies. He could not reset the clock to summer, when winter was close at hand. When he died at Bear Paw, I doubt anyone was happier about it than Looking Glass, himself. Forlorn hopes and thankless tasks are well-named.

Now to my last chance. When Looking Glass and his warriors returned at mid-morning, Hawk and Poker Joe didn't change mounts for rested horses, but came directly to me and Blue Mountain Woman as we rode steadily on. Chief Joseph was with them, so we pulled out of the line of travel.

Joseph spoke and Hawk interpreted, as usual. Like so many of The People, Joseph had rudimentary English skills, but I know he has always felt more comfortable with an interpreter, at least, one he can trust. Through the years, some of the newspaper reporters seem to have taken a fanciful approach to his words. (Note to self: More on this later, when he became a bit of a celebrity.)

"He tells you that trail riders have found a white man and woman. We will leave you there."

I shook my head as the memory of the last attempt came back like an unexpected slap on the back. I put my hand to my throat, where the wrangler's fingermarks at least were no longer visible. I felt that pain all over again. "No."

More conferring. "Joseph says you will be safe this time. He won't take no."

I had no choice, as I had had no choice for weeks. I pulled Fair One toward the men but stopped, more unwilling, when Blue Mountain Woman began to wail. "I can't leave her," I tried, but I knew my argument was feeble and destined to die aborning.

"Sorry, he says. He had decided."

Hawk faced me and not Chief Joseph, so I saw all the sympathy in his eyes. Still, I had to obey. I joined the men, but looked back at Blue Mountain Woman, which only made her mourn louder. I felt worse than before.

Accompanied by an escort – no one trusted white men after the wrangler – we rode for over an hour until we came to a sod house, well-hidden in the side of a cutbank. I am certain I would have ridden right past it and never noticed a thing.

Chief Joseph dismounted in front of the soddy. Poker Joe joined him and gestured to me. Against every fiber of my being, I dismounted and followed, Hawk right behind me.

The man and wife stood in the doorway. I heard a baby squalling in the gloom behind them. I can't recall what they looked like in any detail, except that the woman's eyes were red-rimmed and her mouth set in a tight line. I know she was terrified. She also had a child to think about.

The man cradled a rifle in his hands. When he saw the line of mounted braves behind us, he slowly let it drop to the dirt floor of the soddy. He looked neither defiant nor resigned, but he carried the air of one who had, to use that delicate Western phrase, seen the elephant.

Poker Joe listened to Joseph, then moved forward. The woman took a step back.

"We will not harm you," he said.

The man worked his mouth and spit just out the door. I gather he didn't believe Poker Joe. I had the crazy notion of telling him that he really should hang around with a better class of Indian, if he thought Poker Joe intended harm, but had the good sense to keep my mouth shut.

"We are leaving this woman with you," Poker Joe continued. He gestured me forward and so did Hawk. The man and woman looked me over.

I thought I looked quite nice. The skin around my eye was still faintly greenish yellow, but I had lost every ounce of baby fat I had ever been cursed with. My skin was a pleasant shade of tan, with no blemishes. I wore that wonderful deerskin dress with fringe on the bottom. I had braided my hair that morning, so it looked especially orderly. I've always wished my mouth weren't quite so wide, but who can remedy that? (I mention it here because my husband chides me when I get a little critical in front of the mirror. I promise to take this bit of vanity out of the finished manuscript.)

For a moment, I was at a loss to interpret the look of disgust in that woman's eyes as she measured me up and down. Then I realized what she thought of me. I took another step forward and looked down, suddenly self-conscious of the beaded moccasins I was so proud of, and my beautiful dress. The dress even had a row of elk teeth, and those are highly prized.

"You don't understand," I said.

The woman turned her head, so she looked at me out of the corner of her eye. "You whore."

I felt my stomach turn over as if someone had jabbed me there. There I was again, flat on my back, helpless, and trying to protect myself from the wrangler, who hated me, too. "No. No. You don't understand," I said over and over.

Poker Joe came to my defense. "The woman was forced to go with us through no fault of her own. No one has harmed her."

I guess the man felt he had a leg to stand on, or maybe he didn't want to appear less forthright than his wife. "Yeah, well, explain that shiner she's sporting."

Poker Joe had no idea what a shiner was, but I had a little brother. "That was from a white man who tried to do me harm," I told him.

"And what if I don't believe you?" he countered.

What could I say? Joseph spoke to Poker Joe again, more emphatic this time.

"We must leave her here with you. The Bluecoats will be here soon enough," Poker Joe explained. "You can turn her over to them. We will leave you her horse for your troubles."

There followed one of those long silences which are only comfortable if you are sharing them with someone you care about. I was afraid to look at the woman again.

You might wonder why Hawk didn't say anything. His English was at least as good as Poker Joe's, but he remained silent. Remember, please, that Hawk hadn't yet been invited to speak in the tribal council. His role now was to listen and learn. I did notice that his breathing had become louder. He was not a happy man.

The woman was obviously in charge in that marriage. She cleared her throat. "I suppose it is our Christian duty. Come here, you."

She reached out to draw me into the soddy. Her hand closed around my wrist like a talon and I shuddered. I couldn't help myself. Her hands were dirty and she smelled bad. I had become accustomed to being around The People, who smelled of woodsmoke and leather.

I know I shouldn't have shuddered. She jerked herself up straight and said something under her breath I couldn't quite hear, maybe because I didn't want to.

I started to back up and bumped into Hawk. I know it was an involuntary move – at least I think it was – but he put both hands on my shoulders. When the white woman saw that, her mouth worked a little and she spat on me.

What followed can only be categorized as a tense moment. There. I just underlined it. Tense moment. Hawk dropped his hands like my shoulders burned and drew out his knife. I didn't see that, but I heard it. I reached behind me to wave him off.

The settler started moving his foot toward his rifle on the floor. Poker Joe kicked it away. We stood there staring at each other, then the man grinned in a sickly way. "Aw hell, we'll take her in," he whined, careful not to take his eyes off Hawk. "She'll be all right."

I glanced at Joseph, who was observing that settler in the aloof manner particularly his. The strain showed in his eyes. I loathed to see him humiliated and forced to deal with such scum on my behalf. I writhed inside to think of all the trouble I had caused him since Yellowstone.

I had to end this. I walked toward the couple again, until I stood between the two groups. I looked over my shoulder at Hawk, even though I knew he was the Indian with the least power among the three of them.

I couldn't read any clues in his expression. Poker Joe was pulling his best poker face. Joseph looked back the way we had come, as if he wanted to be anywhere but where he was. (That was probably true of the whole, long flight from Lapwai, but why quibble now?)

I couldn't do it, not to save my soul I couldn't. I turned around. "I can't. Don't make me," I said quietly.

"Then do not," Hawk said.

Joseph spoke to me. "The way ahead is hard."

Gratified that he had actually said something to me gave my battered heart a lift. "I don't mind," I told him. "I can't stay where I am not wanted."

Hawk put away his knife. I thought he looked relieved, but I wasn't certain. We mounted and rejoined the line of outriders. The woman shouted after me with something that I prefer not to immortalize on paper.

A couple of the riders squeezed off some shots into the soddy and I heard glass tinkle. The couple darted inside like rabbits. They slammed the door and drove the bolt home.

We rode in silence, then Hawk looked back, where the soddy was hidden again. As much of a mollycoddle as the settler seemed to be, he must have been brave enough at one time to strike out on his own for Montana Territory.

"How can people live in the ground like that?" Hawk asked no one in particular.

We rode through buffalo grass turning that memorable yellow which signals winter. It doesn't grow too tall, so if I were you, I'd discount those elegiac passages in settlers' memoirs where they mention riding through grass that grazed their horse's belly. Maybe they had short horses, but not that short.

The buffalo were gone from that nutritious range. Maybe they were already going going gone, sold to the highest bidder, slaughtered for bone and hide, which was used to make belting in factories back East. These men I rode with were already relics; they just didn't know it yet.

I decided to seize the moment, the same as they did, but for different reasons. For the first time in my life, I felt that I not only lived on the earth, but that I belonged to it. I was part of Blue Mountain Woman's great circle, inseparable to my surroundings. The feeling was heady and altogether satisfying. I am certain none of The People wanted to lose that mastery of their land, and I wasn't going to be the person who told them that loss was inevitable. Now was a moment to cherish.

I wanted to talk to Hawk about what I felt, but his eyes were closed, and he had tipped his face toward the sun. I watched him, liking what I saw and wishing for a tiny moment that we had been that couple last night. What an impish thought! I waited for it to go away, but it didn't. I thought of the times in the shelter when he was preparing for sleep and he told me to look away. I always did. I decided then that if he said "Look away" again, I wouldn't.

I suppose the feeling was too radical to discuss. When Hawk opened his eyes and looked my way – he is one of those people with a sense to know when someone is watching – I settled for a blush and half smile.

To my pleasure, he tugged on Fair One's bridle until I stopped. "I'll race you, lassie," he said.

I came in last, of course, although Hawk had the charity to slow down as we neared The People and allow me a less-dignified loss. Blue Mountain Woman burst into tears all over again when she saw me, and it took nearly all evening to assure her that I would not leave her again.

When we moved on in the morning, our journey ended at the Bear Paw Mountains.

Chapter Nineteen

We have a neighbor, Bill Barton from Georgia, who lives on the ranch adjoining ours. After dinner at our house one night, I chatted with Mr. Barton about the Civil War, in which he participated on the losing side. "You know, Mrs. Stuart, every time I think about the surrender at Appomattox, I can't help ('cain't hep,' as he says), wish the ending would be different. Like mebbe this time we'll win."

He said it apologetically, certain we would laugh at him. Neither of us did. We knew what he meant.

When I think about the Bear Paws, I also cain't hep but wish maybe this time the ending will be different. Foolish, I know, but I wish it anyway. I know the ending too well, and I do not want to write about it.

My husband feels the same way. I've been showing him some of this manuscript as I go along. After reading what I wrote yesterday, he said he didn't want to read anymore.

For several days, the Bear Paws figured prominently in our line of march. As we neared them, I began to see how the mountains got their name. Rising out of a relatively flat plain, a series of gorges and cutbanks radiated out from the center of the formation like gigantic digits. The land was gullied and eroded, with a stream running through it. Snake Creek, Hawk said. You'll also see it spelled Bear's Paw or Bearpaw, so take your pick.

Something else competed for my attention: hunger. We had so little to eat and I found it hard to direct my thoughts away from my stomach. I couldn't ignore the fact that I was starving, no matter how hard I tried.

My traveling companions didn't seem to be troubled as much as I was, raised as they were by the reality that you eat when you can, and starve when you can't. The children were still learning this lesson, though, and I knew how they felt because I saw it in their eyes.

We pushed on, the wind blowing colder by the time we stopped in early afternoon, sooner than usual. The women set about putting up shelters, those who had any shelter left. Hawk saw to his horses, then squatted on his heels with other warriors. When Looking Glass joined them, Hawk gestured several times toward the ridges that rose above us. Looking Glass made some sharp signs right back and shook his head. Hawk left the circle abruptly.

"What's wrong?" I asked, as I took our remaining blankets off the pony drag and set them inside our shelter.

"He's not even going to put up any sentinels," he said. He put his bow and arrows and the wrangler's rifle on the blankets. "When I told him I would sit up there by myself, he laughed and called me a white man."

"The last soldiers we saw were three days back and riding in the other direction," I reminded him.

"I know that. I also like to think that I have learned more about soldiers since we started this little trip."

His unease seemed to become mine. "You think we should keep going?" I tried to sound casual, because he was frightening me.

"I do. We're only some thirty miles from Canada. I can stand another day or two without food."

I couldn't, but I didn't tell Hawk that. Looking Glass had no objection from me, if anyone had inquired of me. Yes, stop and hunt. Still, there was something about this place.

Hawk turned away, his head down. When he looked up, I knew he had made up his mind. "I don't care what Looking Glass thinks," he said quietly. "We are going on in the morning, even if we have to travel by ourselves."

I sighed, which earned me a sharp look. I wished I had something of value to trade for a bite to eat. Up until then, I was skeptical of that Bible story where Esau sells his birthright to his twin brother Jacob for a bowl of soup. I understood now. Esau was probably as hungry then as I was now.

If I couldn't eat, I could at least find some conversation. Since Hawk looked uncommunicative, I went in search of Poker Joe for some sympathy. That turned out to be a smart idea. Poker Joe sat cross legged by a cooking fire with Chief Joseph, whose wife had left him in charge of stirring a cooking pot. He stirred every now and then, but mostly as punctuation to his conversation. They looked up when I joined them.

A smile playing around his expressive face, Joseph looked toward our shelter. "He has a bad heart?"

I nodded. "Hawk wants to leave for Canada right now."

"It would be wise," Poker Joe agreed, which didn't exactly advance my own case. "Well, wise if we were led by wise men."

Even though Looking Glass was nowhere in sight, I lowered my voice. "Why does Looking Glass do this?"

Poker Joe shrugged. Chief Joseph ran the stick around the cooking pot. He dipped out a modest serving with a tin cup and handed it to me. I couldn't believe my eyes to see chunks of actual meat in the broth. I ate, hardly stopping for breath, despite the fact that I had noticed in recent days that the Nimiipuu dog population was on the wane.

Hawk was gone when I returned. I saw him walking toward the ridges that rimmed our stopping place. He had wrapped Blue Mountain Woman's trade blanket around himself. He walked steadily to the top, working his way up easily enough. He stood there for the longest time, looking toward the south and east, seemingly unmindful of the wind blowing colder by the minutes.

We three ate our handful of partly cooked beans in silence that night, and prepared ourselves for sleep as soon as the stars were out. I wondered if I would ever get to sleep. My stomach felt like a washcloth wrung out and wrung out and still twisted again to squeeze out the final drop of moisture. As my middle continued to tighten, the only benefit I could see about this adventure was having the smallest waist in Omaha, if I ever found my way home.

I know Hawk liked to tease me about my naïve approach to geography, but even I knew that Montana Territory wasn't really that far from Nebraska. What he didn't understand, and what I didn't know how to tell him, was that the distance was more than miles. It ran from the Stone Age to the Bronze Age, to the Iron Age and on and on to what the writer Mark Twain dubbed "The Gilded Age," with railroads and timetables and watches and calendars – my world.

Did I miss it? I considered the matter. I didn't miss corsets, or which fork was the correct fork, or worrying that my dance card wouldn't fill up fast enough, or that it wasn't ladylike to sprawl on the sofa and read magazines.

I knew my career with The People wouldn't last forever. We would get to Canada, and I would find a policeman who would telegraph my father to come and get me. (Heavens, but I was naïve, as if Canada had well-laid-out towns and constables!) Then it would be back to the usual round of corsets, correct forks, dances, and turning into someone I wasn't, all to secure the right husband with the proper career, living in the best neighborhood.

I would have to leave the freedom of my deerskin dress behind, and Fair One, too. That would be hard. Harder still would be saying goodbye to Blue Mountain Woman, who had burrowed into my heart and wouldn't be dislodged easily. I lay there in the cold and the dark and realized that I loved her as much as my own mother.

That wasn't all. How in the world could I leave Hawk? I rehearsed in my mind the whole wretched, splendid journey from Yellowstone Park to the Bear Paws. At every turn, he had been my protector and my friend. We had laughed together, cried together, fought together, suffered together. I glanced in his direction. He lay close to me now, which had been a mutual decision arrived at with no discussion. I wanted to stay with him, even though it was surely the worst wish of my entire life. We had nothing in common. Stone Age doesn't meet the Gilded Age and dissolve into happily ever after. Did it?

I could tell myself this was so, even as some part of my brain wanted this capable, charming man. I also knew – how, I wouldn't tell you – that if I touched his shoulder and he raised his buffalo robe for me, there would be no going back, no looking away ever again.

I lay there in utter frustration, knowing my situation was impossible. Once I returned to civilization, everything would end. Chief Joseph and Looking Glass might not know it, but their day was done. I think Poker Joe knew it, and Hawk, too. A great winnowing was sweeping the land and the Indians of all nations were as chaff in the wind.

Dreary thoughts! My head ached from cold and hunger, but my senses seemed to sharpen. I started to smell things that weren't there, like bacon and eggs and pepper, then corned beef and cabbage. The imagined odors made me want to weep. I was such a poor excuse for a Nimiipuu; I was a counterfeit Indian. Shame on me for trying to blend in.

I heard horses nosing around on the frost-covered ground, searching, as I did, for something that wasn't there. The herd that had looked so endless to me in Yellowstone Park had shrunk noticeably. Every day, more and more of the beautiful spotted animals lagged behind like some of the old men and old women. Sometimes a horse collapsed from sheer exhaustion and lay there as we passed by, beseeching us with a glance almost human.

Some of the fallen horses whinnied to each other, as if speculating on the nature and depravity of man. The People let others wander away, some limping, all worn down past bearing. I asked Hawk once if it wouldn't be better to shoot them. He said no man could bring himself to do that. "Some will live, and they will grow strong on prairie grass," he told me.

"But you'll never find them again," I protested.

"Probably not, but at least they won't be dead, and that is something."

Many in the camp were still awake. I lay there listening to a mother singing to her baby. Over there, someone laughed. I heard the loud slap of cards, and wondered if some man had lost his moccasins. Looking Glass had broadcast it about that there would be a buffalo hunt tomorrow. Many of the young men were readying their rifles for the occasion, the same rifles that had protected the people from Bluecoats who wouldn't, couldn't, leave them alone.

I wrapped my blanket closer around me. The sky had been overcast earlier, but the clouds cleared away. Our joke of a shelter let the stars in, which suited me well that night. They appeared to hang so close that I reached up. The points of light tipped and leaned toward me as I stared in fascination.

I was an idiot. I couldn't touch stars. No one could. I tried though, and something happened.

Chapter Twenty

I must have fallen asleep. That was it. I was asleep. That was why I had the dream that didn't feel like a dream. It was real and there I was in the middle of it. I was staring up at the sky when out of one particularly black corner a shooting star blazed.

It fell for thousands and thousands of feet, leaving behind a trail of wispy plumes that wound around each other like corkscrews. It bathed the whole camp in its light.

When I knew it must surely crash, the star shot skyward again, its glow gentler and softer now, a sort of half-light. It pulsed and brightened, then faded to nothing, leaving the whole sky black and devoid of planets and stars. I blinked my eyes, realizing that all the brightness had rendered my night vision useless. I waited for my eyes to adjust and they did, with the stars and planets in their usual alignment, gazing on The People.

I sat up. The fire was only ember now, so I put a few more chips on the coals, happy to occupy my hands because my brain whirled. I looked at Blue Mountain Woman, asleep. I had to speak of what I had seen, so I knelt by Hawk's buffalo robe and shook him gently.

He sat up so quickly, completely awake, that we nearly bumped heads. He glanced around then back at me, a question in his eyes.

"I didn't mean to startle you, Hawk." I felt shy then, as if in the early days of our journey together.

"What's wrong?" He yawned and propped himself up on his elbow.

"I'm not sure."

I hesitated and he waited. That's another thing I like about the Nimiipuu: they'll wait with you without feeling the need to fill space with chatter.

When in Rome… I took a deep breath. "I…I…think I had a vision."

I cringed inside, waiting for him to laugh at me, but he didn't

"Tell me about it, Liz," he whispered, his voice kind.

It took me several starts and stops, and fumbling for words, but I told him about the falling star that swooped around, and the brilliant light. "So…so.. I think my name should be Bright Star," I finished in a rush of words. I looked sideways at Hawk, too embarrassed to do anything else.

He lay back and propped his hands under his head. I thought he had returned to sleep, so I started to slide over onto my buffalo robe. He took my wrist and pulled me closer.

"Bright Star." He said it in Nimiipuu and in English. "It is a good name."

"Then you do think I had a vision?" Oh, me of little faith.

"Certainly I do. You are entitled to your own *wyakim* to protect you, Bright Star."

He said nothing else, but I could see by the moonlight that he was smiling. I felt warm for the first time in days, and my stomach didn't ache.

I started to shift away once more, but he kept his hand lightly on my wrist and opened his buffalo robe.

"Lie down here with me, Bright Star. We will both watch the stars."

I glanced over to make certain that Blue Mountain Woman still slept, then lay down next to Hawk and rested my head on his arm. I knew I was precisely where I wanted to be, but I still felt cold and nervous all over.

What a man. He didn't object when I put my cold feet on his legs. For days I had begun to think I would never be warm again. I snuggled closer. He obliged by turning sideways until our bodies fit together.

I never had the courage to ask, but I have wondered if he was as ready for love as I was right then. The only thing stopping me was supreme exhaustion of such depth that it took months for me to revive. No matter. I had been learning well from the Nimiipuu and understood their unwritten wisdom of enjoying the small moment. It was enough to be close and warm.

I was almost asleep when Hawks put his lips to my ear. "Do something for me."

I mumbled a reply. I suppose he considered it adequate.

"If anything happens to me, take my necklace."

I still regret I was too tired to fully register what he was asking and why, but I mumbled something else. He shook my shoulder. "I do not want the Bluecoats to take it off me. Promise me."

I promised, then fell asleep. Strangely enough, or maybe not so strange, I dream of Thomas Jefferson and his medallion that Lewis and Clark carried west. I didn't dream of the profile of our third president, but of what was on the back: Two crossed peace pipes, two clasped hands and the words, "Peace and Friendship."

I woke before dawn, roused by my stomach, a trusty alarm clock. In this case, it was someone else's alarm clock. Hawk sat up, folded his arms across his middle and rocked gently. When he saw I was watching him, he nodded. "Good morning, Bright Star."

"How can you say it is morning? It's pitch dark."

"Look again around the edges."

I looked, and sure enough, the faintest fringe of dawn was curling up from the east. The cold winds of last night presented themselves, too. I shivered and tried to move closer to my source of warmth.

"Where are you going? It's so early."

"I feel the need to be moving, to be away from this place." He put on his Jefferson medallion and reached for his moccasins.

I shivered at his words, and got up quickly, too. I tried to poke a little life into a dead fire while Hawk woke up his mother. When she rose in one swift movement, I wondered if she had even been asleep. If I got up the nerve, I might ask her if she heard our talk last night.

We ate the few remaining beans from last night's handful, then started for the horses. Others moved about, too. Joseph and one of his daughters passed us on the way to the herd and waved. Hawk, Blue Mountain Woman and I walked slowly to the horses and watched the sky lighten. The first blush of dawn brushed the eastern sky, the clear, cold air making the colors sharp and strong.

I took a deep breath and slowly let it out, watching the vapor that curled from my lips. Eugenie and I used to do that at home, pretending we were smoking pipes. I realized with a start that I hadn't thought about Eugenie in a while.

Blue Mountain Woman saddled her horse and started for the campsite to gather our possessions. By unspoken thought, we were leaving. She stopped and turned back. In all the years that have come and gone, I am so pleased that she did, because I knew her heart. That knowledge has sustained me like a blessing through many trying and joyful years.

She took my hand, took her son's hand, and joined them together with hers. She had a strong grip. When I feel lonely because she is not with me now, I remember the grip.

"I heard your words last night," she said, then smiled. "Be good to each other always."

She touched my cheek with hers, gave Hawk that deep look, and walked toward camp.

I had to grin at that, which made Hawk smile, too. "You know you have a fine smile, Bright Star," he said, I think mainly to cover his embarrassment, because Nimiipuu men are modest in ways that might surprise you. "Let's get the nags together."

He was soon mounted. He started to cut out his other horses while I walked toward Fair One. I heard sudden thunder and looked at the clear sky. Odd, that. The early-morning planets still worked their way across the sky in the new light. The thunder continued in one long roll.

The horses were beginning to snort and move restlessly. I spotted Fair One and called to her, but she began to step around in nervous circles. I looked for Hawk, who stared beyond my shoulder. He opened his mouth to say something when the thunder burst upon us.

I don't suppose any of you reading this – provided it sees the light of day beyond my own family – have ever seen a cavalry charge. Although my father's wartime service was decidedly sedentary, he relished the stories of others' bravado. As a child, I was nourished on tales of Gettysburg and Chancellorsville. I used to think it would be high adventure to gallop along, guidons flapping, sabers held high, and rush at the enemy.

But they were rushing at *us* this time.

Had I been mounted, I still don't think I could have moved, even if I thought I had any place to go. What looked like hundreds of troopers charged at us. In the early light, I could just make out red and white guidons with the number seven – Custer's regiment. I stood there with my mouth open and watched them gallop toward us.

Chief Joseph stood to my left, as transfixed as I was. We looked at each other, and I knew this was the end of the journey.

He didn't stand still for long. He whistled to his horse, slapped a halter on him, tossed his daughter up on the animal's back and pointed north. His daughter stared at him and he pointed north again, then slapped the horse. The Appaloosa leaped forward and his daughter bent low over the horse.

Blue Mountain Woman rode toward us, calling me. Hawk shouted from the middle of the herd for her to make a run for it, but she hesitated. I came out of my trance and called for Fair One again. No luck. I couldn't see Hawk. I tried not to panic, truly I did, but I stopped running and started screaming.

As I screamed, the line of soldiers divided evenly down the center, half of them surging for the awakened camp, and the rest pouring toward the horse herd across the open prairie. I stuffed my fist in my mouth to stop screaming and closed my eyes. I was only eighteen, and confronted now with certain death. Even in the middle of this crazy summer, certain death was something that happened to other people. Now it was my turn.

A horse stopped right in front of me. I put my hand over my ears and crouched down. I hoped death wouldn't hurt too much.

"Get up, Bright Star."

Hawk leaned down, his hand out. I looked past him to the line of solders, some of them scouts. I couldn't have counted the freckles on anyone's face yet, but it was close. They fired their carbines, filling the arm with smoke and popping noises.

I grabbed his hand. He jerked me up in front of him and pulled me over his lap. I struggled into a sitting position and threw my leg over, while he turned his horse around and started north.

He reined in before he had gone too far, because there wasn't any point in going anywhere. The troopers had split into smaller groups, some driving off horses and others bearing down on The People running here and there like rabbits.

Not fifty yards in front of us was a most formidable knot of Indians. I still couldn't tell one tribe from another, but they did not look happy and relaxed.

"Our brother the Cheyenne," Hawk said in a conversational tone right in my ear. "So much for friends and trading partners. See if I ever trade them another horse."

The scouts bore down on us, screaming and yelping. I put my hands over my ears again. I wanted to close my eyes, but I was too fascinated by those scouts, stripped down to their war paint and making ready to kill us. I felt as if I were standing outside myself, watching the whole thing.

Hawk dug his heels into his horse's flanks and started toward the Indians. My first impulse was to implore him to go the other way, but he didn't really have a choice of directions. He wailed his death chant – high-pitched and spooky and right in my ear – as we rode forward. The goosebumps marched up and down my spine in continuous ranks.

I caught the spirit of the thing then. We obviously weren't going to get out of this one, so I saw no sense in hanging back or moping. I knew "Battle Cry of Freedom," was a rousing Civil War song, so I started to sing. "Yes, we'll rally 'round the flag boys, rally once again…" I felt better and better, the closer I rode to death, "…shouting the battle cry of freedom," at the top of my lungs. There were some things I wished I could have done before I died – mainly make love to the warrior on whose lap I sat – but there you are. Onward.

We were near enough to pick out individual faces, but I knew this wasn't the time for me to tell Hawk that I still thought they just looked like Indians to me.

I finished the chorus, and was trying to remember The Apostle's Creed when someone rode in front of us, hunched low over a fast-moving horse. Blue Mountain Woman. She dashed past us, then pulled her horse to a halt so fast that it nearly sat down. She leaped from her horse and stood there, her arms open wide, waiting for the Cheyenne scouts.

On quiet walks around our ranch in the spring, I have watched mother birds drag a wing to across my path to entice me away from a nest of fledglings. My husband assured me that other momma critters do that, too. I always walk carefully on prairie grass, careful not to disturb the young ones, as I remember Blue Mountain Woman with perfect clarity. And I thank her.

The Cheyenne scouts couldn't resist. They paused in front of that woman with her arms outstretched and gave us an open path to the bluffs above the camp. Canada was out of the question, but not the bluffs, where already I saw puffs of smoke from Nimiipuu rifles, picking off the troopers below.

I heard nothing then but Hawk's deep breathing as he slowed his horse, knowing full well what his mother was doing and knowing also that he could not save her. We screamed our defiance anyway as the scouts, too busy for us right then, jabbed and hacked at Blue Mountain Woman. As tears streamed down my face and my nose ran, I watched as one of the scouts snatched off her basket hat, jerked back her hair and started peeling off her scalp. I don't think she was dead yet, but she didn't make a sound.

I heard a terrible sound right behind me, Hawk dissolved in tears. He bowed his forehead on my shoulder and his tears ran down my back.

I wiped my nose on my arm, grabbed the reins from Hawk, and started our run for the bluffs. It seemed to me that if Blue Mountain Woman had sacrificed her life to give us a chance, the least we could do was oblige her.

Chapter Twenty-one

I wasn't sure where I was heading. All I wanted to do was put distance between us and the Cheyenne scouts, who were regarding us with renewed interest again. I was so scared I probably could have beat Hawk's horse in a footrace to Canada.

Our trip came to a sudden halt when the horse went down, struck by a Cheyenne bullet. The poor thing grunted and rolled over after we tumbled off his back. Hawk hesitated a moment. I knew he wanted to shoot the horse and get it over with, but the wrangler's rifle was nowhere to be found and I had his bow and arrows.

We ran for our lives to the nearest cutbank. The sharpshooters already there held off the scouts while someone reached down and with no ceremony, yanked me up by the neck of my dress. I was in no position to protest; I couldn't breathe.

Poker Joe leaned over and gave Hawk a hand. We piled together into a heap behind a growing mound of rocks and dirt. Another Nimiipuu farther back dug furiously with his bare hands. That seemed like a sensible thing to do, so I joined him. Hawk watched me, then turned back to the rocks and fit an arrow to his bow.

I lost my fingernails in the first few minutes of digging, but I don't remember any pain. I was too busy. I wanted a nice, deep hole to crawl into. If I could have pulled the earth on top of me, I would have done that, too. Fear galvanized me and I burrowed like a madwoman.

Soldiers were digging in a short distance away from us. Puffs of smoke billowed out at intervals on the bluffs and ridges around us. The Bluecoats fired more often than we did, but with less effect. Since that awful siege, I have read some soldier accounts of the whole summer's journey. To a man, they all mention the superior marksmanship of their opponents.

Soldiers with gold on their shoulders went down first. Hopefully, on those still alive, this created a melancholy reflection on the folly of seeking rank. One soldier, shot in the throat, fell halfway out of the breastworks. He stayed that way, because, as Hawk put it, the Bluecoats had small hearts and feared to raise up enough to pull his body in.

Every now and then the body moved as another bullet slammed into it. Hawk put an arrow in the man. I knew it wasn't a mistake and told him if he did that one more time I wouldn't speak to him again.

When we had dug in as best we could, I was assigned to reload the rifles. It wasn't a bad job. The rifles were warm and felt good in my cold hands. Our piles of ammunition grew smaller and smaller. I felt I ought to mention the fact, but didn't have the heart to say anything. The sharpshooters could see as well as I.

Our hearts turned bad in the early afternoon when more personal disaster struck. Poker Joe took a good look at the mound of shells remaining and shouted to another group of Nimiipuu sharpshooters in a nearby rifle pit. They shouted back. On his hands and knees, Poker Joe crawled over to the next rifle pit.

Hawk stood up to cover him and I nearly fainted from fright. "Sit, you idiot!" I yelled and he did, but not until he squeezed off a really deliberate shot from a borrowed rifle.

Poker Joe got a handful of shells and stuffed them down the front of his shirt. He started back to us, crawling low, a smile on his face. He looked pleased about something, but all I wanted him to do was hurry up.

He had just about reached us when one of those unfortunate incidents of war happened. A Nimiipuu in the rifle pit on our far side caught his stealthy movement, must have thought he was the enemy sneaking up and shot him, bam, right in the head. Poker Joe happened to be wearing blue jeans that afternoon. Maybe the sharpshooter mistook them for soldier pants. I don't know. I do know that the rifleman was devastated and wailed long into the night. No one blamed him; The People understood war and chance. But Poker Joe? What a loss for us all.

I doubt he knew what hit him. He slithered into the pit next to me, drenching me in his blood. I stood up, goodness knows why, and tried to get away from him and out of the pit. Hawk grabbed me and threw me down. "No, no, Liz," he said. "Get the shells out of his shirt."

I had to touch that dead man? Me? I barely could force myself to squish spiders and I was supposed to get shells out of a man's shirt when the man's head was mostly gone? I knew *I* couldn't, but I knew Bright Star was going to start insisting.

I took a deep breath and turned him over. There was little left of his face except his chin and part of his jaw, but I ripped off his shirt and the shells tumbled out. A deck of cards tumbled out, too. The wind picked them up and they fluttered around the rifle pit before blowing away, a dead man's hand. I know aces and eights were Wild Bill Hickok's dead man's hand, but not to me. It's fifty-two cards exploding across a battlefield.

During a lull in the fighting – it didn't sound like a lull to me – someone pulled Poker Joe from the pit. I tried not to look at the body, but it always seemed to be in the corner of my vision, no matter where I glanced.

The rain that started in the morning turned into snow by mid-afternoon. We didn't dare move around to get warm, or build a fire. I shivered until I retched. To distract myself from the constant firing from the enemy, I thought about Phil and those silly adventure novels we pored over in Omaha. I was living one of those adventures that very afternoon, but there was no thrill. Shock settled over us in the rifle pit and we all stared at each other like mannequins in Wannamaker's. Whenever he wasn't firing Poker Joe's rifle. Hawk leaned until his forehead rested on the earth mound we had dug, his eyes closed.

The wind picked up as the sun began to make its descent. I cannot tell you with what relief we watched the sun go down. We sat there another hour, saying nothing. Below us in the Nimiipuu camp we heard the howling and screams of women mourning their dead. The sound tugged at my heart and I wanted to join in, but I didn't know the words.

Every time I closed my eyes, I saw the look on Blue Mountain Woman's face as the Cheyenne wrench off her scalp. Then her expression gradually blended into Poker Joe, disintegrating before my eyes. These images still bother my dreams, upon occasion. Duncan shakes me gently awake. We usually lie there in each other's arms, remembering.

When the moon was still biding its time, Hawk reached for my hand. With no words spoken between us, we slipped out of the rifle pit and stumbled and slid down the slope to the remnants of Joseph's camp.

The camp was a veritable ant hill. Everyone who was old enough or not too young burrowed with tools or hands into the side of the cutbanks. Babies sobbed, but softly, little ones with no energy, either, a fatal loss in the young. The wounded groaned, and women lamented as they dug into the hillsides. Small fires illuminated but little, and gave off even less warmth.

This might make you chuckle, or at least appreciate irony, that delicious dry humor of Indians and people who have earned their cynicism. Later on, after the surrender, those insufferable, shoulder-strapped grads of West Point, America's premier engineering school, had much to say about the impressive breastworks and rifle pits that The People threw up on such short notice. I heard someone, maybe General Howard himself, called them engineering marvels. Hawk would have enjoyed that. They were the result of mothers digging to save their babies, using tin cans, their fingers, and tin cups.

Not letting go of my hand, Hawk and I wandered among the survivors. Some of the women called to him. When he finished speaking to them, Blue Mountain Woman's friends mourned her, too.

We found his kinsman Joseph sitting quietly with his blanket pulled up around his face. He rocked back and forth and in that high falsetto sang a nameless tune the prickled the back of my neck. I had seen Joseph toss his young daughter onto a horse and point her toward Canada. Who did he mourn?

Hawk bent over Joseph. "Ollokot?" he asked. Joseph nodded, then looked up at him, his eyes red and swollen.

I couldn't stand one more minute of this; clearly I wasn't composed of the sterner stuff used to fabricate The People. I wrenched loose from Hawk and stumbled toward the edge of the cutbank. I didn't know where I thought I was going, but I had to get away from all this suffering. I was on my way out of the puny shelter of the cutbank and probably would have been shot for my pains, but I tripped over somebody and fell.

Right behind me, even though I hadn't heard him, Hawk grabbed me and pulled me back. He didn't say anything. What could he say? I don't think he was angry. He sat me down, pulled me onto his lap and held me there until I calmed down. I couldn't bear to look at him. He was suffering, too, and I was nothing but trouble. I felt young and stupid and foolish, out of my depth, treading water, sinking.

When my breathing returned to normal, I leaned back against him, sort of testing the water, if you will. I shivered as more snow whirled around us. He tightened his arms around me, and I mourned Blue Mountain Woman silently in my heart. I think he knew it. "For many years, it was the two of us, until you came along and we became three," he said finally, which took my breath away. "She told me to take care of you. I think she knew."

Knew what? That she was going to sacrifice herself for us? That I more than likely had fallen in love with her son? That life was going to be neither easy nor just? I wanted to ask him, but I was too shy and we had no time for frills.

Maybe I was too exhausted for what he said to register right away. It sank in now. "'We became three,'" I repeated.

"We did," he said quietly. I heard him above the moan of the wind and the wounded, and the laments of new widows.

I thought he might kiss me, because his face was so close to mine. I tried to flog my tired brain into memory, but try as I might, I didn't think I had seen any of The People kissing. He pressed his forehead to mine, then rubbed his cheek to mine until I was comforted and content. Maybe we rubbed cheeks too long, because I was definitely feeling livelier by the minute.

As tired eyes looked into tired eyes, he held me off. I looked around, wondering if anyone had seen us. I do know for a fact that The People are reserved about overt displays of affection, the exception obviously being that amorous couple of a few weeks back who, to their credit, had no idea I watched them. This time I noticed smiles on several women's faces and felt gratitude that we two had given them something to smile about.

To work. Hawk turned to one of the women and engaged her in quiet conversation. He came back to me holding half a tin cup. "Here you are, Bright Star, start digging."

I took the cup, shaking my head, well aware that half a tin cup was no earth-moving equipment with which to attack a mountain of dirt. Maybe I was finally catching on, because I moved toward the cutbank without any questions. Hawk borrowed some red paint from someone and applied it to his face, his whole face, and not just the Blue Mountain Woman side.

I stopped digging. "You're not going back up to that rifle pit, are you?" I felt my lips getting stiff.

"Yes," he said, sounding faintly surprised. "You didn't think I would stay here, did you?" He was putting red paint around his mouth and his words came out muffled.

I threw my arms around him, not caring who smiled. I touched his chest for good luck, then returned to my task. I didn't want to see him leave. Dig, Elizabeth, dig, I told myself. Work hard, Bright Star. Save The People. Hurry to the rifle pit, Hawk. It is dark and the night will save you.

Then the worst thing happened, worse than everything that had happened since Methuselah reared back and sent me on an adventure I did not want until it became the crowning event of my life.

To my real gratitude, the firing stopped from the soldier pits and breastworks. I sat back, relieved too soon, as I heard most distinctly, "Fire!"

followed by an ear-splitting whump. The sky exploded with light and rained down shards of hot metal on the camps of The People. The women at the breastworks screamed and grabbed for their children, pushing them deeper into the side of the cutbank.

There was another whump, which lit the night sky with exploding stars, beautiful to see, deadly as they fell. Silence, everyone tensed around me, waiting for, dreading a third and louder roar as another cannon belched fire.

This one was different. The barrel must have been pointed more toward the sky at a steeper angle. Again, the shell exploded, this time much closer to one of the rifle pits. Silence. I heard the crank of metal as artillerists elevated the tube. When it fired again, the shell exploded directly over a rifle pit. I covered my ears as men screamed when hot metal rained down.

Twice the other two cannons roared, then silence. I've asked myself since then, and I have asked others why the U.S. Army didn't dispatch us all that night. A few years ago, I even asked General Miles, the man who was the author of our misery. "My dear Mrs. Stuart, we wanted surrender, not annihilation," he told me.

Oh, thank you, sir. How kind of you to see that we were…that The People were not all killed that night, but sent to a humid hell in Indian Territory to ponder the sin of being Indian and repent somehow. Why didn't I think of that myself?

I can tell you why I had to ask him, and it forms the worst part of this narrative, because I knew when those shells exploded with the bright stars of death, that my name could not possibly be Bright Star. That was no vision I had; it was a hoax. I was fooling myself. Bright Star was a fraud. Maybe she was even an angel of death. Vision? My *wyakim* was no *wyakim* at all.

Chapter Twenty-two

If you are reading this for accuracy as to what happened on what date, don't coming crying to me. I had no idea of time or day. All I knew was that we were cold, and all the birds had flown south; winter was coming. I had bigger worries, and they concerned *me*, glorious *me*. After a life of privilege, I knew I was a fraud. That's hard to swallow when you are eighteen, white and invincible.

Luckily, Hawk was the only person who knew my other name was Bright Star, and he was in a rifle pit. Imagine my relief. If these dear ones in the camps under the bluffs had an inkling that it was Bright Star who had rained fire and death on them, they would have killed me. Or so I imagined, as I dug in silence. To say that my thinking was muddled is correct. I doubt any of us were in a normal frame of mind, not with all this confusion and misery. That was my reasoning, however; I am not proud of it.

I've wondered about that sudden display of cannon and howitzer and can arrive at no opinion. Is it worse to be regularly fired upon, or worse to *expect* to be fired upon at any moment? Personally, I think it is the expectation that terrorizes. Every little sound might be *the* sound, every creak *the* creak that means a deadly blast to follow. Even though this century is young, I suppose someday a physician of the mind will consider the matter. There will probably be other wars in this twentieth century of ours, still almost brand spanking new, to test all sorts of theories.

I spent what remained of that night digging into the cutbank with my puny tin cup. It snowed off and on, but the snow melted into miserable Montana gumbo. Most of us were silent, exhausted nearly to the point of derangement, in some cases. Now and then, one of the women would shriek and groan as she thought of a loved one killed in the day's sharp fighting. Everyone would wail in sympathy, then settle down again to the business of digging.

The dirt from our excavation was packed into the barricade in front of us. Some of the dead horses found a place of honor in the breastworks, after sizeable hunks of them had been removed and added to otherwise empty pots. Deeper and deeper we dug into the cut banks and coulees, working mainly in family groups. Since Hawk and Blue Mountain Woman were of Chief Joseph's clan, I stayed with these now-familiar faces. Hard to believe there had been a time when I couldn't tell one Indian from another.

Off and on, the cannon roared, aiming accurately for the rifle pits rather than the individual family camps below them. The troopers and soldiers were well aware by now that the marksmen must be silenced before anything could be done about the well-defended non-combatants.

We stood in muddy water, our feet so cold that we couldn't feel them. I took turns propping one knee and then the other against the side of the cutbank to get a foot out of the water. This was nearly as tiring as standing in the freezing slush.

One summer we took our children to Seaside, Oregon, not far from the mouth of the mighty Columbia. My older children spent much of the time playing in the sand, building castles with moats and palisades. They enlisted me to dig with them, knowing that I was generally up for any sort of fun with them when I wasn't in the family way, and bending became a chore.

I didn't last more than five minutes. The simple act of digging nauseated me as it brought back terrible memories. If my children read this some day, they will understand why I begged off digging in perfectly wonderful sand on a fine beach.

The day began cloudy and misty, with high winds. None of us had slept, so by the time it was light enough for firing to commence, the women and children had mostly completed their digging and were out of sight of the soldiers who tried once to creep closer to fire upon them. That effort proved reckless, as Nimiipuu sharpshooters, Hawk among them, rained down accurate fire.

The unspoken fear: we knew how little ammunition remained. Once it was gone, we were done for. Everyone knew it; no one said it out loud. God help me, but my bigger fear was that someone might find out that I had thought to call myself Bright Star. Even I had had enough of the shelling of those bright metal stars overhead.

We were so hungry. Someone broke open a box of bacon purloined at Cow Island and passed around the raw, salty slices. The children ate most of it, because most of us lied and said we were not hungry, not really. Then the little things found a flour sack and scooped out handfuls and ate it, too, licking it off their arms and clothing until I wanted to cry.

No one had the heart to comment upon a silent gathering of war leaders in Chief Joseph's coulee encampment. No one raised a voice in that circle. We knew we could not last much longer.

Somehow, I slept through most of that afternoon, curled up in a corner of our tunnel, my legs drawn up close to my stomach in an attempt to get warm. I missed out on the day's adventure by sleeping through it. Chief Joseph was chosen to parlay with the commanding officer, someone called Bear Coat. You would know him as Nelson Appleton Miles, who commanded the Fifth Infantry, and who had ridden from the Tongue River Cantonment with his command. As it turned out, Bear Paw Mountains, plus plenty of self-aggrandizement, burnished his career and eventually led to his promotion to Commanding General of the Army in 1895. Bear Coat retired last year in 1903.

The stars certainly did align in his favor after Bear Paw Mountains, but I cannot recommend his behavior there. After the parlay, he decided to detain Joseph overnight, trussed up like a bug in a rug, apparently, an unwilling guest of the U.S. Army.

This act naturally caused great consternation in our camp, and more weeping of women and then children, too, who cried because their mothers cried. I huddled in my little Eden in the tunnel and kept quiet, doing my best to be overlooked.

Some of the sharpshooters came down from the rifle pits as soon as it was dark. I watched for Hawk, but he was not among them. I tried to ladle calm acceptance on top of anxiety, but it didn't sit well there. I reckoned he had figured out that Bright Star was a hoax, too, an imagined vision of a hungry white girl. He was an intelligent man. Flowering shells from a Hotchkiss gun would remind such a man of Bright Star.

When the sharpshooters gathered near the remaining war leaders and learned that Chief Joseph had been detained, there was much arguing and gesturing. No one seemed to know what to do. Looking Glass spoke at length, probably offering a few suggestions, but the young men turned away, ignoring him, which pleased me. Had he urged the march with more fervency, I knew The People would be in Canada now, instead of stuck in a bad place getting worse.

The big guns boomed again, but I think many of us had finally reached that point at which – you know what I mean – that point when everything bad has happened and there surely can't be anything worse. There was, of course, but no one knew it at the time. We were helpless of remedy, and above all, defeated, but not yet ready for that final step of surrender.

To be so near and yet so far! From a clear day atop the Bear Paws, I could probably have seen Canada. There were no clear days, no way out.

Is anything worse than waiting? There was no food. My command of Nimiipuu language was nonexistent. I was white and frightened. All I could do was hide in the tunnel and dream of returning to Omaha, which left me more depressed than ever. Somewhere not really too far from Montana was my father with his tobacco-scented shirts and his comfortable laugh, and my mother with her lovely frocks and high-priced sneer.

Also out there, lying in the snow with her body mutilated beyond recognition and her hair gone was Blue Mountain Woman. She had thrown her life away for me and I knew it. I ached all over with love for her and worry for Hawk. Where was he?

As you can tell – and I might make changes before I tuck this away – I say I was worried about Hawk, but still wasn't ready to admit that I loved him. That I loved him will surprise no one, but I was young and none too sure about anything. Some people of my husband's acquaintance call me a wise woman. I was not wise then.

Shortly before morning on that day – maybe the one before – four or five braves slipped out of camp and started north. Looking Glass had convinced them earlier that Sitting Bull was waiting across the border to come to our rescue (Honestly, that Looking Glass…). I hardly need add here that help never came. We didn't know it then, but Sitting Bull had been warned against giving any aid to the Nimiipuu. Instead, he had drawn his own band one hundred miles farther north in Canada. The People had not a friend anywhere; they just didn't know it yet.

Chief Joseph was returned to our lines that morning, exchanged for an eager-beaver lieutenant who had fallen into our hands the day before. Joseph spent the next hour or two in quiet talk with the remaining war leaders. And we waited.

I made myself some dinner that night. I rinsed out my half of a tin cup, put a handful of flour in it, stirred in some muddy water and drank the concoction. It could have used some salt. I spent the rest of the evening shivering and blowing on my hands for warmth.

The children were quiet this night, too exhausted and hungry to complain. They crowded close together, their eyes full of confusion. Poor things. Their ponies were gone, their warrior-fathers dead or missing. They had nothing left but the rags they sat in.

I perked up when the sharpshooters came down from the firing pits. I strained my eyes to see if Hawk was one of them. I had nearly given up looking when he came into the tunnel, muddy and his hair matted in one clump. He leaned on Poker Joe's rifle. As I came closer, I saw that his leg was bloody. Wordless, I took his gun and eased him down.

He closed his eyes and almost but not quite smiled. "I knew you would be here," he said, sounding almost as content as if he had come in from tending the stock and wanted his dinner. I suppose I could have joked and said something stupid like, "I just got back from shopping and found the most wonderful pair of shoes," but no. I leaned against his shoulder and savored his muddy, bloody, stinking presence, because he was Hawk and I loved him.

I wanted to blurt out that my name couldn't possibly be Bright Star because of the exploding shells, and it was all a mistake, but I knew I had no business loading my childish, selfish problems on his shoulders. A bigger matter loomed, obviously.

I looked around for something to bandage his leg. I finally resorted to pawing through someone's possessions and found a bolt of cloth that must have come from the government stockpile at Cow Island. It was a gorgeous, impractical hunk of lavender brocade probably destined for obscurity on some post trader's shelf. Goodness knows what use anyone would ever find for it.

I unrolled a yard or so until I found clean fabric. Using a knife nearby, I hacked off a portion and hurried back to Hawk, who was alert and watchful. There was no overlooking his sigh when he saw me, which gratified my heart.

He gave me a wary face when I explained my intentions, but offered no argument. I felt his forehead, which did not reassure me, because he was the warmest thing in that tunnel. I found some cleaner water than I used in my delicious dinner, waited for the mud to settle to the bottom, then wiped off as much of the dirt and blood as I could.

The wound seemed to be the result of shrapnel from one of the big guns. It made a jagged path above his knee, with the bone blessedly intact. The disturbing flap of skin hanging down seriously unsettled my aforementioned dinner. All I could do was plow ahead, even though the whole mess looked like it needed a long row of stitching. I gritted my teeth and held the flap of skin down tight where I thought it belonged and wrapped the lavender brocade around as snugly as I dared.

Hawk sucked in his breath a few times, and made one or two involuntary moves with his hands to stop me, but didn't say anything. I wanted to close my eyes, too, but someone had to perform a surgical procedure and I saw no volunteers.

When I finished, I fixed a flour and paste stew for Hawk. He opened his eyes when I put the cup in his hands, and drank the glue almost like it tasted good. He must have noticed how anxious I looked because bless his heart, he had the energy to tease me.

"Bright Star" – oh, don't please – "who taught you to cook?"

"I learned from the finest chef in Omaha. If I mentioned his name, you would be deeply impressed."

He smiled at that and touched my face. No, he did more. He held his hand against my cheek. "You're going to make some lucky Nimiipuu a fine wife. Your father will probably get half a chicken for you."

He was hilarious and I laughed. "No, no, at least two chickens," I teased back. "My father is a shrewd trader."

More laughter. I am certain the other occupants of the tunnel though we were completely barmy. He held my hand then and his eyes softened with memory. "My father paid Meopwits ten horses for Blue Mountain Women, four three-point trade blankets and that copper pot."

He had me then. Who knew a half-dead Nimiipuu with nothing to his name could make me an even better offer? "You're worth twice all that," he said simply. "Maybe someday I will be able to make your father a wealthy man like Meopwits. As it is, take this."

He handed me the brass trade ring he wore on his little finger. I held out my hand and he found that it fit on my forefinger. I couldn't bring myself to tell him I was a fraud. It would keep.

He didn't kiss me. I didn't expect him to. We touched faces, his feverish and dirty, and mine merely dirty. After a long and wonderful moment, I helped him to his feet and he returned to the firing pit.

Chapter Twenty-three

Two twelve-pound Napoleons and a Hotchkiss revolving cannon treated us to reveille after the sun rose, collapsing our tunnel. I tried to scream, but my mouth filled with dirt when I opened it. I gagged instead. All I wanted to do was get out of that place. And go precisely where? Hmm? the more rational side of my brain inquired.

I couldn't leave. Mothers and children all around me dug frantically, not for the tunnel's mouth, but to find the ones buried when the cannon roared. We dug like demons in the mud, but as we scraped and shoveled at the mound of earth, the screams and scrabbling from within grew fainter and then stopped. A little girl and her grandmother were dead when Joseph and one of his kinsmen lifted their limp bodies from the debris.

We continued our frantic digging and pulled out three other women, blessedly alive. The guns lobbed more shells our way, and we knew we were done. We spent most of the day crouched in the tunnels, hungry and wretched beyond belief. I grew up some more that day, when I became fully aware that my plight was miniscule because I had no children to worry about. As I watched a young mother trying to nurse her baby out of empty breasts and fighting back tears, it was as if some cosmic hand slapped the side of my head. I grew up.

I vowed that if I got out of this alive, I would make sure the soldiers knew that the Nimiipuu had not made war on me. I would tell them, and gladly, that The People had kept me alive by not abandoning me in a wilderness where I could not survive alone. I would tell all this to their soldier Bear Coat.

I waited and waited for Hawk to come down that night, but he did not. I jumped up every time anyone came into our tunnel. I wanted to look at his wound again and rebandage it. I wanted to tell him thank you for everything, and that even though I was probably not worth more than half a chicken, that was enough for me.

I sat there on the damp tunnel floor, hugging my knees to my chest, trying to stay out of everyone's way. I didn't belong there, but neither did they. Canada and Omaha were so far away that they might as well have been suburbs of Vienna.

It was a long night. Since this was the sheltering cutbank of Chief Joseph's clan, I watched with the others as two strange men wearing the flowing hair of the Nimiipuu, came into the shelter. I sought Mary, the older woman who, with Blue Mountain Woman, had helped me after the debacle with the wrangler. To my whispered question, she said they were Captain Jack and Old George, trusted interpreters she knew.

"I think they have come from the camp of Old Day After Tomorrow," she said. She sighed. "I suppose he is here now, too, and his troops."

So General Howard had joined his soldiers to Bear Coat's. "Why are these two Nimiipuu here?" I asked.

Old Mary took my cold hand in hers. "I think they are here to talk of surrender."

Ah, the S word. Someone finally said it. We sat together. Mary closed her eyes. I knew she was praying to her Presbyterian God. Please listen to her, I thought. Please. We have suffered enough.

So much for prayer. There was more rifle fire in the morning, then another blast or two from the big guns, then – could it be? – silence. We waited as Chief Joseph dressed carefully in his best clothing, and twined otter tails in the two braids framing his face. His wife smoothed out the rest of his hair so lovingly, so kindly.

Someone had prepared his favorite Appaloosa and brought it to the tunnel entrance. We gathered around the entrance and watched as White Bird handed him his rifle. Joseph bent down and they conversed quietly. I have no idea what was said, but I do know that in the middle of the night to come, White Bird and fifty or so adherents struck out for Canada.

As tired and disillusioned as I felt, I knew as I watched him ride into a halfway place between our camps and the camp of the soldiers, that I was a witness to history. Bear Coat and the one-armed soldier Old Mary identified as Old Day After Tomorrow joined him. I watched Joseph try to give his rifle to General Howard, who shook his head and pointed to Colonel Miles, triumphant man of the hour. Joseph handed his weapon to Bear Coat and surrendered.

None of us heard his "I will fight no more forever" speech, but we saw him gesture to the sun, so I think he said all that, probably allowing for a flourish or two from the journalists present. Writers like to embellish, don't they?

Which reminds me: Here is a good place for me to insert something I alluded to earlier, when I asked Bear Coat later, point blank, why didn't they just blow us to smithereens. As I recall, he said something noble sounding, but the truth of it was that from the beginning of their flight to now, the Nimiipuu had also been pursued by journalists who knew a good story when they saw one. By the time the flight culminated not forty miles south of Canada and possible freedom, the American reading public had swung completely to the side of Chief Joseph and The People, fleeing oppression and only wishing to return to their peaceful life in the beautiful Wallawa Mountains of eastern Oregon and western Idaho.

Bear Coat, a man of vast ambition, didn't dare blast the Nez Perce into oblivion. Yes. I will call them Nez Perce now because everyone else does. Maybe I will. Maybe I won't. Oh, you sly dog, Bear Coat.

And that was that. Many readers had bought lots of newspapers to digest along with breakfasts of bacon and eggs, toast and cereal, and public opinion is a might thing. It is also somewhat fleeting, but that is for later in this story.

Throughout the afternoon, the sharpshooters came out of their firing pits, holding their precious weapons high and away from their bodies. They worked their way to the valley floor to join their families, those who had families left to join.

Bluecoats filed into our encampments, their rifles ready. It makes me shudder even now, when I think what could have happened if a child had moved suddenly, or someone cried out. I am certain we would have been mowed down by those troopers of the Seventh Cavalry, those Custer avengers. I saw it in their eyes.

Hawk was one of the last men out of the rifle pits. Even helped by a friend, he could barely walk. In fact, he stumbled and fell halfway down the slope. I wanted to run to him, but I was too terrified to move out of the surrender line. Friends helped him to his feet and he leaned on Poker Joe's rifle, which I am certain was empty. His tired eyes lit up when he saw me.

He started toward me, then changed his mind, which broke my heart into a thousand shards, even though I understood why. He knew, and I did, too, that the less involvement any of The People had with me, the better for all of us. I don't know when I have felt so low. I would have cried, but why bother? I doubt I had a tear left.

With the women and children, I watched as the men dropped their rifles in a growing pile, then moved forward toward the soldier camp. We moved along, too. Wait for it, wait for it, Lizzie Everett. Now.

"Goddamighty, Sergeant, look at this! A white woman!"

The line stopped. I knew this would happen, but I was not prepared for the terror I felt. I stood there, gazing back at the soldiers, all warm in buffalo-robe overcoats and wool caps with earflaps. They all looked the same to me, like the Nez Perce had looked to me six weeks before.

None of the soldiers approached me, but the word passed along. Soon the line parted to let two men through, Colonel Miles and General Howard. The jig was up.

Miles pushed ahead of the general, because that was Miles. He came too close to me and I backed away, unaccustomed to such rudeness. The People never crowded around. He stuck out his hand. "Miss Everett? Miss Elizabeth Ann Everett? We've been looking for you!"

I couldn't help myself. I started to back away. I would have run, but there was no place to run. All I knew was that I wanted nothing to do with someone who could smile like that and hold out his hand after stomping us forty miles shy of the Canadian border.

"Get away from me," I muttered.

Maybe he didn't hear me. I had gotten used to speaking softly, like the people around me. He kept coming toward me with that toothy smile. "It will be all right, Miss Everett," he said, now using a tone of voice he probably reserved for children. "You're safe."

He took my hand to shake it. I hauled back with my other hand and slapped him across the face. Since he wore one of those wool caps, I only connected with his nose. I would have scratched his face, but he had me by both hands now, still talking in that silky tone.

"My, my, we've been through quite an experience, haven't we?" He glanced over my shoulder. "Lieutenant, take Miss Everett to the surgeon's tent."

As I struggled, he transferred my hands to another bundled-up officer who pulled me along to a tent. I wanted to say goodbye to my friends, to Hawk, but he wouldn't let me. He sat me down inside on a folding stool and put my hands in my lap. I discovered I was too tired to jump up, so I stayed where I was, defeated like Chief Joseph. I had no weapon to hand over, nothing but me, and I already sensed that I was going to be an embarrassment to the U.S. Army.

The hospital tent was full of wounded men. They lay in tight rows in the tent, vivid testimony to the accuracy of the Nez Perce sharpshooters. The surgeon didn't notice me for several minutes, his attention claimed by a soldier who twisted and turned on a cot. When he did turn around, he stared at me until I blushed and looked away. The lieutenant whispered to him, and he nodded, understanding.

He was far kinder than Bear Coat. He sat down by me on another stool and made no move to touch me, to my relief. "The telegraph wires have been buzzing with real speculation, Miss…Miss…"

"Elizabeth Ann Everett of Omaha, Nebraska," I supplied. "You mean, people have been looking for me?"

"Oh, my, yes," he said. "Once your parents got out of Yellowstone Park, the whole world heard. Your father is a man of some importance."

"He is," I agreed. "I'm glad they are well."

"I believe they are home in Omaha." He looked up when an orderly called to him and held up two fingers. "I have to hurry because I'm needed. There were other tourists in the park who had scares, too. Why did the Indians carry you off?"

I knew he had two minutes, so I told him quickly about Methuselah and his sudden urge to ride with the Indians. The surgeon – his eyes looked as tired as mine – smiled at that. "You've had quite the adventure," he said when I finished. "Do you need any medical attention?"

I shook my head. "I'm hungry," I said simply. "Pretty dirty, too."

"We can fix both. Orderly?"

With a small salute to me, he returned to his patients while an orderly ran to the mess tent. In short order I was addressing a plate of hot beans and salt pork. I ate faster than I should have, but I had never eaten anything better, not before and not since. I even ran my finger around the rim of the plate and held it out for more. When it came back full, I set to again. By the time I came to the bottom of that helping, I resisted licking my fingers. I only hoped that my friends were eating, too. (They were, which relieved my heart when I found out.)

Wouldn't you know it, but Nelson Miles was not a man to leave a person alone. He came into the tent hospital when I set down that empty plate. He held out his hand again, and this time I shook it, noting with satisfaction that there was a red mark beside his nose.

"Elizabeth Ann Everett," he began, repeating my name as he had outside, as if afraid he might forget it. "I am Colonel Miles." He stopped, as if I ought to make something of this. I couldn't think of anything to say about his name, so he continued. "Your parents are mighty anxious about you."

"I suppose they are," I replied, which I didn't think he quite expected.

"I thought it wisest that they not follow my command," he said.

"Good idea," I said, wondering where my courage came from. Maybe it was all those beans and a full stomach. "It wouldn't have done for them to see you shelling innocent women and children."

I know he didn't expect that. I'm not so sure I did, either. "Ah well..." He paused, perhaps waiting for me to apologize for my conduct outside the tent. I had nothing to say, and I saw the affront in his eyes. He got up to leave, then sat down again and waved away the surgeon, who wisely did not budge. I had an ally there.

He leaned forward and I leaned back. "Miss Everett, I hate to remind you of any...any abuse... you suffered during your captivity..." He looked down at his boots. "If you have any name or names to mention, we will see that the guilty parties are punished."

I stared at him and spoke louder than I intended, because he winced and glanced around.

"Not one of The People laid a hand on me."

"Come come, Miss Everett," he said, his face as red as his nose now, all pretense of kindness gone. "You needn't fear these savages now! We know something happened, because General Howard came across ...um...a bloody petticoat at one of the Nez Perce campsites. It had been partially burned – I suppose to discard evidence."

I knew Hawk had carried that petticoat and my riding skirt toward a campfire. I also knew that the morning was misty and we were in a hurry, as usual. Damn! I wanted to tell Colonel Miles that was mainly the wrangler's blood, but the words wouldn't come. I could tell by the colonel's expression that he was certain I had been raped twenty-four hours a day with time off for meals. It seemed to me that Nelson Miles had also read too many of those lurid novels about frontier heroines and the Fate Worse Than Death. I knew as I watched him that no amount of truth could change the mind of a man already convinced. Time for other tactics.

I shrugged. "I cut myself shaving."

Right then, sitting there more alone than ever before in my life, I knew the name of my *wyakim*. I had known it all along, but after a summer with the Nez Perce, I *knew*.

I was Elizabeth Ann Everett. She was me and I was she and it was more than enough to help me find my new way.

Chapter Twenty-four

"Cut yourself..." The colonel had been leaning forward like a priest in a confessional. When I said that, his head snapped back and his eyes narrowed. I narrowed my eyes and stared right back at him, enjoying a tiny victory when he looked away first. I had a feeling that my life was going to be tiny victories from now on, maybe so small that only I knew.

He slapped his gauntlets on his knee and rose, maybe thinking to intimidate me by standing up. I stood up, too, knowing I was a lot shorter than he was, but much taller inside.

"Miss Everett, my adjutant will take you to your tent. We haven't a change of clothing for you, but at least there is soap and water." He bit off each word like good peanut brittle.

I thanked him with amazing serenity, which made him glare, but what could he do? He left the tent.

He allowed me to stew there for the rest of the afternoon, maybe thinking I would break, or at least show some remorse for my sass, but no. Dr. Tilton and Dr. Gardner needed help and I did what I could, which amounted mainly to washing dirty faces and holding someone's head over an emesis basin.

After dark, I was escorted to my tent by a lieutenant who must have been told by his boss that I was a recalcitrant female who didn't know what was good for her. His disdain for me was probably obvious to ships at sea. He did pull back the tent flap, which was nice of him. I thanked him.

"Where are the Nez Perce?" I asked.

"Over there," he said with a vague gesture.

"Have they been fed?"

"Yes."

"Their wounds tended to?" I wondered what the surgeon thought of that purple brocade around Hawk's knee.

The lieutenant wasn't a happy man. His expression more than suggested that I wasn't like the white girls he probably knew. He did have some dignity, though. "The assistant surgeon is seeing to them now, Miss Everett."

"May I go to them?

He leaped back as if I had spit on him. "You…you want to join those savages, after all" – he coughed delicately – "…all they have done to you?"

Sigh. Here was another man who would never believe that I wanted to see those Indian because of all they had done *for* me. I wanted to see with my own eyes that they had been fed. I wanted to thank Old Mary for her kindness when I felt so alone in the tunnel. Mostly I had to see Hawk and tell him what I had learned.

"Yes, I really want to see them." I started forward but he put his hand on my arm to detain me. "You're welcome to accompany me, lieutenant, if you think I need an escort."

"Colonel Miles said you are not to leave this tent." He gestured to two privates watching this whole exchange. "They are here to make sure no one comes in, and no one goes out. For your protection, of course."

Of course. "I'm a prisoner in this tent?" I asked so sweetly.

"For your own protection," he repeated.

"Good night then. Pleasant dreams," I told him. Too bad you can't slam a tent flap shut.

I sat down on the cot and stared into the blue flame of the lamp until spots danced in front of my eyes. The flickers of light leaped and sparkled until I blew out the lamp and sat staring into the darkness. It had been an awful day, one that had only gotten worse with the surrender.

I lay down and closed my eyes, feeling some measure of peace simply because the guns were silent. If there hadn't been a guard outside my tent, I do believe I would have lit out for Canada.

Old Mary had said that White Bird was going to do precisely that. I hoped that Hawk traveled with him. I knew his horse was dead, but Fair One was out there in the darkness somewhere. He would never make it on foot, but Fair One would carry him away from this place, and, sadly, away from me. "It's 303 McDermott Street," I said softly. "Omaha, Nebraska. Please don't forget me."

I opened my eyes next morning to the sound of loud talking outside the tent. When I poked my head out, I saw one of my two guards staring at something in his hand while the other poked it. I looked closer, then threw back the tent flap and snatched the object from the private before he had time to tighten his grip.

It was Hawk's Jefferson peace medal. He must have somehow left it here for me. He told me once that only a person with a warrior's heart could wear it, and he gave it to me.

"Where did you find this?" I asked the trooper.

"It was right here in front of the tent." He scratched the back of his neck. "I can't imagine how it got here. I mean, me and my bunkie, we been watching your tent all night."

Oh really? I put the medallion around my neck and tucked it down the front of my deerskin dress. It chilled my skin. "I believe it is a gift to me," I told the guards. "I won't tell the colonel about it. After all, we can't have him thinking that you fell asleep while on watch, can we?" I rummaged around in Civil War stories I had heard. "I know that in wartime it is an offence punishable by death, and you seem to be at war with the Nez Perce."

After horrified glances at each other, they nodded and resumed their stance outside the tent, protecting me from who knew what.

With this gift, I knew Hawk was gone. He must have left during the night with White Bird. I hoped he rode Fair One, because she had a gentle canter and he had a bad leg. Another storm prepared to break over the Bear Paw Mountains and I shivered to think of Hawk and the others struggling through snow. Please let him be riding Fair One.

As it turned out, he wasn't, but I still felt encouraged. He was on another horse and Fair One was still mine.

After a solitary breakfast in my tent, I heard someone clear his throat outside my tent, then spit. One of the new guards swore and the other one laughed. I waited, wondering, then heard, "Miss Everett? Miss Everett? Care to see an old Yellowstone codger?"

I knew that voice. I pulled aside the tent flap and there he was, scratching away. I still didn't know where to look, except that with the other hand, Muskrat Watkins led Fair One to the tent. She looked as glad to see me as I was to see her. "Are you hungry?" I asked her, wiping at my tears.

"I gave her some oats." Muskrat stopped scratching and whispered. "An Indian brought her by the corral. It was darker'n pitch but whoowee, I knows a pretty piece of horseflesh when I see one."

"I was hoping that Indian who left him would ride Fair One to Canada," I said in a low voice.

He whispered back, that old reprobate. "Oh, Miss Everett, I managed to look the other way when he picked out a pretty good cavalry remount and rode off." He laughed, spraying me and Fair One with tobacco shreds. "I think it was the adjutant's horse."

I laughed, too, but softly. "Well, in that case…Mr. Watkins, what are you doing here?"

"I threw in with General's Howard's banda merry men after we got outta Yellowstone. I had enough of tourists. Most uf'um got no common sense." He pulled a sad face, then brightened noticeably. "'Cept for yer pap. He made some kinda deal with that one-armed general, and what do you know, I'm temporarily working for the U.S. Army."

So they really were trying to find me. My father and his deals. Maybe they weren't as far-fetched as Mother made them seem.

"Promised him I'd find you and bring you home," Muskrat Watkins said. "Here we are." He peered at me closely, but not in an intrusive way. "You had quite a trip, didn't you?" There was no condescension or embarrassment in his voice.

"I did, Mr. Watkins." My eyes filled with tears. "Please keep Fair One safe."

"I'll take'r back now, Miss Everett," he told me. "Never you mind. I promised him I'd get you to Omaha. Promised your father I'd get you home and I will. Fair One, too."

"I know you will, Mr. Watkins," I said. "Did...the Indian say anything?"

Muskrat scratched himself thoughtfully, and not on his face. Dear me. "He said sumpin' that made no sense."

"Try me."

"He said maybe he'd pay two chickens for you, if you kept Fair One alive."

He laughed again and so did I, but I sidestepped the tobacco spray this time, then looked around as that insufferable adjutant headed toward my tent. "I'll take care a this one," Muskrat whispered. "Don't you pay no mind to what them shoulder-strap know-it-alls are saying about you, missy. Sure is a cinch they don't know their Indians. Now, if they hadda been Kiowa or Comanche that caught you, you wouldn't be standing here."

Muskrat Watkins made a dignified retreat with Fair One. Lewis and Clark's Jefferson peace medal was safely hidden against my skin, and no one was the wiser. I think the adjutant knew something had been put over on him, but I could tell he had no idea what. He did inform me stiffly that Colonel Miles had made some sort of promise to that disgusting man leading away the Indian pony and he hoped I wasn't too upset. "And by damn, if some thieving redskin didn't pilfer my remount last night," he exclaimed. I nearly laughed, but resisted. Still, it was the one bright spot in a bleak day.

The day was spent in preparing to leave and travel to the Tongue River Cantonment – later named Fort Keogh – where the Tongue River flows into the Yellowstone. Howard's ragged detachment, so many miles from their own Department of the Columbia, would remain a little longer in place until the more severely wounded were ready to travel down the Missouri by steamboat.

I was not allowed near the Nez Perce, argue as I much as I chose, but I did witness the final heartbreak of the journey. Amid an undignified squabbling, Miles's Cheyenne Scouts and Howard's Bannocks divided up the spotted horses among themselves. Each scout must have gotten at least twenty ponies. I know that some were part of Hawk's herd.

As soon as the beautiful creatures, worn down with travel, were in others' hands, the scouts rode away with them. A great lamentation rose from the Nimiipuu as warriors, women and children cried for their lost horses. They were now afoot, and afoot they were nothing.

I had hoped to travel with the Nez Perce, but they were to travel downriver to Fort Buford, where the Yellowstone meets the Missouri, and then on to Bismarck. General Howard did assure me that he and Colonel Miles had arranged for them to return to Lapwai in western Idaho. That relieved my heart, and I had to be content with that welcome news.

I was not allowed to ride Fair One when we left the Bear Paws in the morning, but was relegated to one of the army ambulances. Colonel Miles couldn't fathom why I wanted a reminder of my cruel treatment at the hands of my captors, and nearly ordered the animal shot. I raised such a commotion that he feared I would do myself an injury if I didn't have my way. His patience with me was wearing thin, but I know General Howard had given him a letter from my father, saying that Muskrat Watkins was to see me safely to Omaha. Somehow that old reprobate Watkins convinced Miles that Fair One was part of the deal. For that, I will be forever grateful to him.

We were ten days traveling from the Bear Paws to the Tongue River. Most of the Nez Perce came, too, but I was not permitted to get near any of them. I rode with my head down mostly, amazed at how endlessly it was possible for my heart to break any more. It rained and snowed and we were all in perfect misery, At least there was food.

Finally, Colonel Miles forced me to ride in one of the ambulances. I helped the two doctors as much as I could, and Muskrat rode Fair One. The surgeons were kind to me, but I avoided the other officers and their knowing glances. I had spent six weeks with the Indians, and I was worse than dirt to them. The inference was cruel and unfair, but Elizabeth Ann Everett, the new and improved Elizabeth Ann Everett, wasn't about to pick that fight. I knew I would have to get used to my shredded reputation; might as well begin now.

At Tongue River Cantonment, some of the sergeants' wives were kind. I ended up with white women's clothes again, an item here and an item there. Nothing fit, because I had lost so much weight during my "captivity" – they never called it anything else – that everything hung in a straight line from shoulders to toes. I had a suntan that would have looked more appropriate on a railroad section hand, and the hollows in my cheeks almost caved in my face.

The officers' wives were less charitable. One lady assured me that if I would come to Jesus, my sins and the stain of my incessant ravishings by heathen captors would wash away in the blood of the Lamb. I couldn't really follow the logic, but knew better than to argue the matter. They were convinced.

Colonel Miles said goodbye to me and Muskrat on the morning we left, traveling down the Tongue to the Yellowstone on a mackinaw boat, accompanied by a highly skeptical Fair One, of course. Miles declared he had no hard feelings. He took me aside to whisper than he and his fellow officers had agreed never to mention that I was part of the flight of the Nez Perce. In other words, if I played my cards right, my weeks of degradation and shame could be swept right under the rug and forgotten. Apparently he was thorough. I doubt any of you have heard of the Everett party of tourists, have you? I didn't think so.

I knew he expected me to be grateful for this piece of nonsense, so I thanked him prettily, then shook the dust off my moccasins before I boarded the mackinaw boat. (The Nez Perce would follow a week later.) Aside from my morals and my wardrobe, the only other thing the good women of Fort Keogh had been unable to remedy was my shoe size.

Chapter Twenty-five

And so I came home to Omaha, accompanied by Muskrat Watkins, a beautiful Appaloosa, and the growing conviction that Elizabeth Ann Everett had powerful *wyakim*, indeed.

Everything looked the same: the sheltering cottonwoods, the brass door knocked shaped like a hand, the deep front porch. The geraniums blooming madly when we left in July were dead now, but the dried-up stalks still nodded in the window boxes, silent testimony to Mother's state of mind. She ordinarily would have had them uprooted and gone after the first frost.

I don't know what I expected, but I saw things differently. My first though when the house came in view was, "Gracious, do the five of us really need all that room?" After a season with my Mother the Earth, three stories plus servants' quarters in the attic seemed pretentious.

My parents were relatively the same, which surprised me at first until I considered the matter. They had no more idea how to deal with my return from the grave than I did. They didn't know the new Elizabeth Ann, and I was still getting used to her.

Father folded me in his arms and patted my back. He held me out at arm's length and said, "Let's go see what there is to eat in the kitchen." Poor Father. He always thought he could solve the world's problems with a leg of lamb.

Mother took me in her arms, too, a special event for both of us. She hung on longer and tighter than I thought she would, then released me.

Her hands went to her hair. She patted it back in place, looked at me and sighed. "Elizabeth, you're so brown. Almost like an Indian."

She gasped and her hands flew to her mouth. I could tell she hadn't thought about that common expression. As tears welled in her eyes, I think I loved her more at that moment than I ever would have thought possible. I have wished many times since then that I had said something.

Eugenie hurled herself at me, pelting me with questions even as she hugged me over and over. "Lizzie, what was it like how did they treat you were you hungry did you ride astride?" tumbled out. Her face had a pinched look, so unlike Eugenie, and I knew she had worried. Dear Eugenie. I wish you had lived long enough to know my children. Our daughter Millie is so like you.

Phil stepped forward most formally to shake my hand and kiss my cheek. I could tell he was bothered about something above and beyond my homecoming, so I asked him what was wrong.

"Lizzie, I tried to ride with General Howard. I really did." He started to cry. "He wouldn't let me!" He sobbed, his voice high and strained. "I nearly got into a fight with him. Can you imagine?"

I could; I knew my little brother. I pulled him close. "It's over now, Phil. General Howard himself told me how hard you tried. Believe me, it was better you didn't follow."

"Really?" He didn't believe me.

"Yes, really," I assured him. I leaned closer, for his ears alone. "You wouldn't have believed how bad it was."

He managed a brief smile. "Not like *Nancy Ames, Heroine Schoolmarm*?"

"Not even like *Daring Dick, Boy Rancher*," I teased gently, smiling back.

That was my homecoming. It was at the same time better and worse than I could have thought possible. The frozen geraniums in the window boxes testified that Mother worried about me more than her reserved nature could say.

It was worse in a more important way: I didn't want to be there.

I have never forgotten my first morning at home, waking up to the scratching of bare branches against the window. I heard no children crying, no big guns booming, no wounded groaning, no women wailing. I heard no loud English voices, no soft Nimiipuu tongue. I lay there listening and thinking, Doesn't anyone in Omaha know what's going on?

I had one nightmare nearly every night: Blue Mountain Woman bludgeoned and scalped before my eyes, then turning into Poker Joe disintegrating, and Bear Coat Miles chasing me across the plains, grinning and grinning. Too often I woke up with my heart being abnormally fast and my bed wet with perspiration.

I still haven't entirely outgrown that nightmare. Sometimes after a busy day, or a day with too much frustrating correspondence from Washington D.C., I still have that nightmare. Duncan pats me back to sleep. I do the same for him.

Phil and Eugenie sustained me during that first difficult year at home. I told them the entire story of my weeks with the Nez Perce, leaving nothing out. They cried with me and tried to be my champions in the neighborhood. All they got for their earnest endeavor was a resounding snub from the good homeowners on McDermott Street and its environs.

I did not go out into society at all in 1878. No invitations were extended to me, and we gave out none ourselves. Mother chafed a bit at this, but she bowed gracefully enough to social pressure and learned to tat. She seemed to become more thoughtful, as well, especially after one night when my nightmares overwhelmed me, and she held me close in bed. After that, she made no complaint.

Eugenie took up needlepoint. I still have my favorite sampler of hers, framed and situated over my writing desk. *I am Elizabeth Ann Everett*, it reads. Mother and Father didn't understand that one, but I never told them about my *wyakim*.

During our year of community ostracism, Phil's grades improved. An indifferent student, he applied himself, eventually graduating from Omaha Academy with nearly all A's. He parlayed that into Harvard Law and a brilliant career. Now and then he'll take a pro bono case for me dealing with Indian rights, but that is a story for a better writer.

I spent much of my time in my room. I wore a track in the carpet by the window. I paced back and forth, usually late at night, only to stop and stand facing northwest toward Canada, where I thought Hawk might be, and where my dear friends had been returned to their ancestral homeland in the Pacific Northwest.

I erred in this fiction of the Nez Perce returning to their homeland, which brings me to public opinion, that fickle mistress. I had mentioned the favorable power of the press earlier. Father didn't really like for the ladies in his life to read the newspaper, but I wore him down on that issue. I wanted to know more.

At first, the news of the Nez Perce remained in the readers' minds. I read with some relief and no real surprise that after their trip from the Tongue to the Yellowstone, then the Yellowstone to the Missouri, Chief Joseph was greeted with great acclaim downriver in Bismarck. There was a band, and a banquet, and all the papers reported the happy event.

Then everything fell to pieces. I believe that General Howard and Colonel Miles were sincere in their promise to return the Nez Perce to their homeland, come spring. Instead, and over those officers' objections, The People were sent to Fort Leavenworth in Kansas, a total of 87 men, 184 women and 147 children. Some others, mostly the Christianized Nez Perce, were sent back to Lapwai Reservation in Idaho. I could only hope that Old Mary was among that number.

At Fort Leavenworth, the others spent a winter and summer at a race track near the Missouri River. Many were stricken with malaria, and quite frankly, who in the world has anything nice to say about humidity, especially people acclimated to the cool and dry uplands of eastern Oregon and western Idaho?

As if that weren't bad enough… In August, they were assigned to the Quapaw Reservation in northeast Indian Territory. Malaria, that generous host, was also there to greet them with open arms. One hundred of the people died in mere months. I still hate to think about the babies and little ones, and their parents helpless to do anything to change their fate.

I only learned the grim statistics later, by pestering the Army for records. The newspaper reporters so eager to follow the news of Noble Red Men dropped the story with their arrival in Indian Territory. Apparently valiant resistance and a yearning for freedom only sell so many papers. Editors and reporters understood that people really didn't want to read about malaria and squalor over coffee and doughnuts, not when there is some other human interest for reporters to chase after.

Part of the problem was the citizens of Oregon and Idaho, who had informed their elected representatives that the Nez Perce were not welcome in their former homeland. (You know, that place where they had lived for hundreds of years before a single covered wagon rolled West toward them.) As soon as the Nez Perce bailed out in 1877, pursued by the U.S. Army, settlers had snatched up all the Indian land. Think how embarrassing it would have been if The People had returned to claim what was theirs by inviolable treaty. Better keep them on a reservation in Indian Territory, where they might oblige by dying.

I never asked him, but I know that Chief Joseph never would have surrendered if he had known what was really in store for The People. He would have walked to Canada or died fighting.

I didn't know much of this, as I scoured the paper in Omaha for scraps of news about my friends. Occasionally, if the paper needed some small piece of copy, there might be a small article about the tribe, now dying of malaria and homesickness at a rate that would have alarmed anyone except Congressmen or the Bureau of Indian Affairs.

My personal first year of exile ended when it became obvious to Omaha's better crowd that I did not – let me put this delicately – display any overt signs of Indian alliances. Oh, the irony; the only danger to my virtue had been that odious wrangler. Gradually, Mother had a few trusted friends over for tea, where I was exhibited, allowed to say a few words, and given permission to pour. My tan faded to a more appropriate and privileged pallor and my cheeks filled in. I smile about it now, but even my bosom regained its former majesty.

There was nothing Mother could do about the starkness of my expression, coupled with an odd tenacity that the new Elizabeth Ann displayed. Mother had high hopes that the bleakness would pass, as all things did. The tenacity? It's still with me.

How could the bleakness pass? I yearned to know what had happened to Hawk. Did he get to Canada? Was he in Indian Territory? At Lapwai? Was he even alive? The thought of that dear man lying dead somewhere shook me to the marrow of my bones. Don't be fooled by what you read in those vacuous stories that *McCall's* and *Ladies Home Journal* print. Love hurts, especially when you have no way of knowing what has happened to the man you adore. You feel torn in two, and hope seems like a distant memory.

As I paced and anguished in the quiet of my room, I asked myself when I began to love him. I couldn't put a finger on it until it occurred to me one night that first of all, I *liked* Hawk. (Oh, don't scoff.) He was smart, clever, witty in that way of The People, and honestly, really nice to look at. I'll admit to admiring his legs, something your average proper white lady could never say about any gentlemen caller in an Omaha parlor. Let's be honest here: A man in a loincloth is easy to look at, if you catch my drift.

But love him, with the idea that this is the man you want to marry and have your children with? Maybe I could trace it to that awful scene at the horse herd, when I raked him verbally over the coals and tried to strike him. He could have done anything then, but he chose to comfort me. Yes, that was probably the beginning, even though I didn't know it at the time. Yes. He was kind when he didn't have to be, because maybe, just maybe, he loved me, too.

There you have it. By 1879, I was declared redeemed and valid for all general purposes. I spent less time pacing in my room, but more time in our stable a genteel distance from the house, watching Fair One, my Nez Perce horse. She returned to health and vigor much sooner than I did. After some unnecessary coaxing on my part – he loved horses, too – Father had her bred to a dignified roan. Her colt was a delight – all legs, ears and those wonderful spots. I named him Poker Joe and took great pleasure in watching him frisk about with his mother, who appeared content in her relatively small paddock. I suppose she had had her fill of journeys. Another year added another spotted delight, a filly this time.

As my Indian mare was not deemed a proper animal for a lady, I had to content myself with riding sidesaddle again on a gelding whose ancestry was impeccable enough for the renovated daughter of the Union Pacific treasurer. I did make certain that our groom – Muskrat Watkins, of course – exercised Fair One and her little traveling circus.

Incidentally, Muskrat – he owned to Henry Watkins now – never gave up chewing tobacco, but he did consult a physician about his lice and pubic crabs. He was cured, and lived happily ever after with our housekeeper, who took him to church regularly and saw that he bathed. When Father bought a finer pasture on the edge of Omaha, the happy couple moved there with the horses. This meant Mother finally got the German housekeeper and French chef she wanted. Everyone was happy.

I presented a serene figure to the community, as the new Elizabeth Ann fumed and plotted below the surface, yearning for news, any news. I never let on how really bored and unhappy I was. Everyone who meant anything to me, besides my immediate family, was either dead or gone. I figured I was to mark time until I either made an advantageous marriage or dwindled into spinsterhood. I only confessed to my mirror that I felt older than I cared to admit.

Upon one subject I remained firm. Mother came into my room one morning not long after my return and caught me in my chemise. Her eyes widened to see Hawk's Jefferson peace medal before I had time to stuff it inside my chemise.

"What are you doing with that…thing?" she asked in shocked tones, as if she had chanced upon me worshiping the Sun God Amun-Ra.

I explained to her that it was a gift that had originally been given to a long-defunct Nez Perce by Meriwether Lewis himself. Never a student of history, Mother was unimpressed. All she saw was a heathen relic (Thomas

Jefferson? Heathen? Well, perhaps a little.) She ordered me to take it off. I refused. She drew back, her mouth open.

"Mother, the only way I will ever take off this necklace is if the owner shows up and claims it."

At the thought of that, she paled, swallowed a couple of times, and left the room. Although she never bothered me about the medallion again, she gave me a beautiful silver chain a month later for my birthday. I loved her for it, this woman of contradictions who was my mother.

The year passed rapidly enough. I went out into society more, and even received a proposal of marriage from a junior executive with the railroad. I considered his offer carefully. He was an attractive man with good manners and few bad habits, but try as I might, I saw no fun in him. He wasn't the sort of man who could perplex me one moment, and make me laugh at the same time. I told him no, but with regret. He seemed disappointed, but he married someone else later in the year.

The only other matter of interest in 1880 was a reception held for now-Brigadier General Miles that we attended at Fort Omaha. I had misgivings about attending the reception. I should have stayed home.

The reception was held at the quarters of General George Crook, then commanding the Platte District. General Miles looked handsome and trim in his uniform, with all his medals on display. He stood in line as if posing for his portrait. I knew at whose expense he had raced across Montana and won those stars. As Hawk would have said, my heart was bad.

He didn't even recognize me. Some officer, probably his adjutant, murmured my name as was customary as I went down the line, but perhaps he did not hear. The post's band was playing a little too enthusiastically. I smiled at him, then moved on down the line and right into the cloak room. I didn't look back, but vowed to stay away from all military functions, a vow I have kept.

By 1880, Mother had tracked down another worthy suitor for me, this one a middle-aged widower with two children who ranched in Red Cloud, Nebraska. His banking interests and some connection to the railroad took him to Omaha now and then, which brought him to Mother's attention. After a few sedate parlor visits and one dinner in a good restaurant, I had enough experience by now to know he was working up to an offer.

I considered the matter. I was almost twenty-two, and too old for college. All of my friends from Miss Sumner's Female Academy were long since married, and some were mothers already. I had devised no scheme for maintaining myself independently, as skinning dead horses was not a ladylike trade. I knew my parents wanted me off their hands, because here was Eugenie, about to make her social debut. I had become an impediment, and I knew it.

Why I didn't marry that ranching empresario with the pleasant children and become the cattle queen of Nebraska will occupy the remainder of this document.

Chapter Twenty-six

A surprising thing happened in October, a thing which gave me a heartful of hope. I love that phrase. It has become a beloved expression in our family.

Another autumn had come to Omaha. I thought in terms of seasons then, more often than I realized. It had been three autumns since I was sent by the army to the Tongue River Cantonment and away from The People. This autumn, the autumn of 1880, I was still marking off each day on my calendar, as if it mattered. I don't do that now.

That Thursday began as most Thursdays, with Mother going as regular as clockwork to an old friend's house to play bridge. Father was in his office downtown by eight in the morning as always. Eugenie and Phil were at their respective academies. I promised the housekeeper I would polish the silver. Winter's more active social schedule, even in Omaha, demanded the niceties, which meant – ugh – polishing the silver. Bridget was hanging out the week's wash in the backyard while I made faces in the polished serving trays in the butler's pantry.

Bridget pounded up the back steps, calling for me. I heard something close to panic in her voice and hurried to the door.

"Miss, miss," she began, then pointed at a man standing by the carriage house, a valise at his feet. "He wants Lizzie. Oh, miss, he's…he's…"

I saw what he was. For the tiniest, most wonderful moment, I thought it was Hawk, but no. "Go inside," I said, my eyes on the distant figure. "I'll see what he wants."

"Aren't you afraid?" she asked, her eyes wide. Bridget had come from County Cork only last spring.

"Heavens no," I assured her. I shooed her inside and closed the door. I hurried down the back steps as the Indian came closer cautiously, clearly more apprehensive than I.

"Yes? May I help you?"

He gave me that swift scrutiny I was familiar with from The People. He must have seen what he liked, because he lowered his shoulders and relaxed. "My Aunt Mary said to look for dark red hair. You are Lizzie?"

"I am," I said, my voice soft to match his. With a sweet sort of ache – I can't explain it better – I remembered the way everyone called me Lizzie, only it sounded like Lissie. "Mary? A Presbyterian lady who made the journey to Bear Paw?"

When he nodded, I tried to swallow my ready tears and nearly succeeded. I had last seen Mary, Blue Mountain Woman's friend, at Bear Paw, before I was forbidden to mingle with the captives. I dabbed at my eyes with my apron, wondering what news he brought.

He had no wish to linger. "I have to hurry," he said. "My train leaves in half an hour." He held out his hand. "I am Thomas Adams, from the Lapwai Reservation in Idaho Territory."

I shook his hand, knowing it would be a soft handshake, almost a feminine one, because that was how The People shook hands. "I am Elizabeth Ann Everett." I couldn't go through the preferred mode of Indian conversation, which meant lengthy pleasant chatter before arriving at the heart of the matter. I needed information and I needed it now. "Please tell me you have news of Hawk."

"I have for you what Aunt Mary knows," he hedged.

"Please tell me." I looked over my shoulder. "I would invite you inside, but.."

"No need," he said. "It is only this: some of The People who made it to Canada have been making their way to Lapwai."

"Hawk? Oh, please..."

"No, except this is what my aunt wanted you to know. One of the braves who snuck back mentioned Hawk, who gave this to Old Mary."

He handed me a creased and grimy piece of paper. I opened it and read, *Lizzie. 303 McDermott Street. Omaha.* "You found me," I said simply, thinking of the times I had so lightheartedly mentioned my address.

"The brave also told my auntie this from Hawk," Thomas Adams said. "He told her, 'Make sure Lizzie knows I am alive.'"

"Thank God," I whispered.

"The elders at Lapwai discussed the matter. They decided that if anyone was ever going near this city, they would find you and give you the words of Hawk. That was a year ago and several more months."

I couldn't help my dismay. Anything could have happened in the intervening year and a half. My *wyakim* of Elizabeth Ann Everett gave me a mental shake then, asking me to think of a time when any of the Nez Perce would be making a trip east. It could have been another ten years. It could have been never. Who said they would ever be free to travel?

I had to do better. This nice man had given me something to hold onto. "Mr. Adams, thank you," was sufficient, especially as I fought back tears.

Thomas Adams picked up his valise. "Message is delivered. I am on my way to Indian Territory and Omaha was in the way."

I tried to be polite, but Indian Territory? "You're going to Indian Territory on *purpose*?" I asked. "Oh, dear, that sounds rude."

"I want to go," he informed me firmly. "The People had permission to ask for a teacher from Lapwai."

"You're a teacher?"

That brought a smile. "I will be by the time I get to Indian Territory! Actually, there is a young woman there, kin to Chief Joseph like Hawk." He left the rest unsaid, but I understood. I held out my hand this time and we shook hands again. "Thank you for the message. It's nice to know."

"My auntie has a heartful of hope. She said you should, too. Goodbye."

He left me as quietly as he must have come, startling the maid. I had to smile, because quaintly enough, Omaha *was* in the way. I was no closer to Hawk, except that I now had a heartful of hope from Old Mary in Lapwai.

* * *

Winter followed, and I learned no more. No, that isn't true. I learned a great deal about myself. I have always been an active person, working hard and involved in busy-ness. Thomas Adams's visit brought me to a complete halt and the stark realization that there was nothing I could do to change my situation. In Nez Perce eyes or the eyes of my family and society, I had no way or means or reason to go to the reservation at Lapwai. I was a white woman and an outsider. No doors were going to magically open.

All I had, ultimately, was a heartful of hope. I would have to wait in patience and humility for my circumstances to change. The matter was out of my hands. All I could do was wait and hope, and do it bravely, such as I had witnessed among The People as they traveled toward that forty-miles-too-far Canadian border with their own heartful of hope. It could be years, it could be months, it could be never.

My tears were bitter and angry at first, matching the mood of that interminable winter, with blizzard after blizzard. I began to long for bedtime, when I could put aside the mask I wore of a proper lady, safely back in the fold of her privilege and society. In bed, I could press a pillow to my face and sob out my frustration and sorrow. I looked forward to that like a drunkard yearns for the next bottle.

Things changed as time passed so slowly that winter. A little at a time, I let myself hope. I started remembering Blue Mountain Woman's many kindnesses to me, from helping me find that moss I needed, to combing my hair and braiding those little shells in it. She had given her life for me and her son and I honored that memory with the resolve to never shame her with poor conduct.

I remembered the mothers shielding their children with their bodies, every time the cannon roared. No one shook a fist at the Bluecoats who rained down hot metal and terror; they simply kept digging until that which they prized the most was safe, their little ones. They accepted the terror and the hunger and the vast disquiet of going toward…what? They were kind to each other because this struggle belonged to all The People.

I doubted I could be that good, then I remembered times when I *was* that good on the march. I guess what I am saying is that I finally allowed myself the privilege of being human. I knew I was not perfect, and I knew Hawk knew it, too.

Christians call it "waiting upon the Lord." I never asked Hawk what he called it. I doubt the Nez Perce even have an expression for that sort of holy patience that burns away the dross, simply because it is already part of the air The People breathe.

I just sort of let go. I can't express it any better than that, really. I stopped crying every night. I went about the business of being a good daughter and a good sister, because I knew I had no control over anything else. I could be good. I could be kind. I would wait.

The winter helped, as much as it aggravated, because it gave me a respite from the increasing attention of that Red Cloud Nebraska cattle baron. Mother brought his name up in conversation often enough to remind me that time was marching on. (In an idle moment, I counted all the calendars in our house: ten. None of them marched.) She told me I could do a lot worse than marry the man, which has never struck me as a ringing endorsement. I know she was right; I hoped she meant well.

Oh, that winter. I know the winter of 1886-87 broke records, which is probably why no one remarks on that winter of 1880-81. Still, we live in a fickle state, regarding moisture. The year before had been somewhat parched, so the everyone welcomed more snow, including me. And as our Episcopal priest said, to the ire of the congregation's more censorious busybodies: "For what Nebraska is about to receive, may Nebraska be truly thankful. Amen."

I welcomed our overlong winter. Red Cloud is some ten miles from the Kansas border. With livestock challenges and his distance from Omaha, my determined suitor had to content himself with letters. We wrote – him more frequently than I – and I relished the pause in his headlong courtship. Because Mother was certain that the rancher had already captured my heart, she did not foist other suitors on me.

I did have social obligations that winter, as it turned out. The bright spot for my mother was my appointment to head the refreshments committee for the annual Knights of Saint Mark grand ball and fundraiser. In my mother's mind, this signal honor indicated that Omaha society had declared all to be forgiven and forgotten, and that I was now like everyone else. I established my committee, and dutifully held meetings to discuss the merits of macarons over eclairs, and where to get champagne, if trains from the East weren't dependable. You know, thorny issues.

The Knights of St. Mark, you ask? My father was one of the founders of this philanthropic organization, which sponsored an orphanage for children of deceased railroad workers. It seems to me that if the Union Pacific made railroading a safer occupation, there would have been no need for the orphanage; perhaps I am quibbling.

In an idle moment, I looked up St. Mark, and couldn't see any obvious connection between the New Testament St. Mark to railroading. (I am being facetious.) The matter became more clear when, while I was supposed to be dusting Father's study, I thumbed through an old annual report of the Union Pacific Railroad. There he was, Mark Hopkins, first treasurer of the Union Pacific and the man who chose my father to succeed him. Oh. *That* St. Mark. My father seldom missed an opportunity to move upward.

I must point out here that all winter on the sly, I had been sending letter after letter to the Quapaw Indian agent in Indian Territory, asking for word about a Nez Perce known as Kaya, or Hawk. I never received a response. It was as if the agent looked at the return address, rolled his eyes, remarked to himself, "Hell's bells, her again?" and tossed it. My letters to the Bureau of Indian Affairs also vanished into the government mist.

No one cared. By winter's end, my efforts to patiently let go of whatever events I had no control over anyway were wearing thin on my battered heart. And now I had a committee meeting today after luncheon. Life was unfair.

Matters worsened. The morning of my committee meeting, the widower from Red Cloud sent me a telegram, informing me that he would be in town in two days. He hinted of a great surprise in store for me.

I had a bigger one for him, and for my committee, and my family, and it happened that very day.

Chapter Twenty-seven

To say that my mind was in turmoil that day would be to greatly understate the matter.

What an afternoon. For any of you who duck and run when asked to serve on a committee, even you would have enjoyed this meeting. I have certainly never forgotten it.

We were sitting in the parlor, pads and pencils at the ready to make final assignments, when the doorbell jangled. Dawson, our butler, answered it. My committee was all accounted for, so I assumed Mother and Father were expecting guests. Consequently, Dawson startled me by banging open the parlor doors and scurrying to my side.

You have to know Dawson to appreciate this. Dawson never banged doors or scurried anywhere. He stalked about in such stately fashion that the less informed mistook him for the head of the house.

Eyes wide, he stood by my chair practically plucking at my sleeve. His mouth open and closed several times. One of the committee members, a tiresome girl named Agnes Wilson, started to titter.

"For heaven's sake, Dawson, whatever is the matter?" I asked. "Can't it wait?"

He finally found his breath or his wits. I think it was the former, because all he said was "Miss, miss, miss," over and over. Agnes's titter turned into a choking sound behind her handkerchief.

I fixed him with a stare that was a perfect imitation of one of Mother's,

199

and he started to shake. Pulling himself together before he rode off in two or three directions at once, he said in a great stage whisper, "Miss Everett, there is an aborigine in the foyer!"

I jumped up, dumping off a handful of notes that fluttered to the floor. Agnew stopped tittering. I grabbed hold of Dawson and shook him until his spectacles slid off his nose. "What did you say?"

"An Indian, Miss Everett, a real Indian. At the front door!"

I waited for nothing more, because I had a heartful of hope. I picked up my skirts and dashed toward the door. No one in recent memory had galloped in such fashion down the corridor. Heads popped out of doorways. It was Friday, but Father had taken the day off. He came out of the billiards room in his shirtsleeves. Mother's dressmaker stepped out of the sewing room after I tore by. I can see her yet, with a mouthful of pins falling down the front of her smock.

Hawk stood by the open door, shaking off his umbrella. His hair was cut short in the usual manner of gentlemen in and around the United States and he wore a well-cut suit, complete with vest. I didn't see a watch fob, but I remembered that he was pretty good at telling time without a watch. When I stared at him, mouth open, his eyes crinkled small in a familiar grin that took me right back to better days on that trail from Yellowstone to Bear Paw.

When he held out his arms, I took a deep breath and walked right into them. He held me close – I doubt you could have slid a piece of onionskin paper between us – and pressed my head against his chest, wordless. I have never felt happier.

By now, the foyer was crowded with Everetts and committee members, everyone as silent as we were, until Agnew Wilson gasped and fainted. Poor thing, everyone ignored her. Phil was the first to recover. He dropped his copy of Ovid's *Metamorphosis* that he was translating and came forward, his hand outstretched.

Hawk released me and shook hands with my little brother. "You must be Phil," he said. "I've heard so much about you."

It sounded so prosaic and polite, and so completely insane. No one except Hawk seemed to grasp the humor of it then, although Phil likes to remind me about that introduction even now.

"Yes, I'm Phil. You must be Hawk."

He nodded, then tightened his arm around my waist. "Yes and no. Call me Duncan now."

"Wh…what?" I was still hanging onto him. Father started forward, his cue stick held like a bat. I stepped in front of ~~Hawk~~ Duncan. "Don't you even think about it, Father," I said, with real steel in my voice.

There could have been an unpleasant scene then, but someone noticed Agnes Wilson lying face down on the parquet. By the time she had been attended to, Phil had the situation in hand. Father quietly returned to the billiards room to set down his cue stick and contemplate his future. Duncan seated himself in the parlor, and the committee fled the house to spread all manner of reckless gossip, I can guarantee. Her face a study in stone, Mother accepted the dressmaker's resignation. Our social standing plummeted again.

We didn't remain long in the parlor. Hawk – No, Duncan now – may have looked every bit the gentleman, but I recognized hollows in the cheek and knew he was hungry. We adjourned to the kitchen except for Mother, who ran around locking up the crystal and silver. I made several sandwiches. While he started on the first one, I cut a thick wedge of apple pie and plopped half a cheese on it.

He ate steadily, almost lovingly, as if it had been days since his last meal. Maybe it was. People in the Midwest have never felt much charity for hungry Indians. He finally finished, wiped his mouth and gave me his full attention.

"It's Duncan Stuart now, Bright Star."

I could correct him later. "Why?"

"It is my legal name, and I think it might be easier that way."

Mother came into the kitchen and sat down beside me. For a fleeting moment, I was reminded of Blue Mountain Woman low over her horse, riding out in front of the Cheyenne scouts. Could I have misjudged my mother? Was she protecting me? I could think about that later.

Still wearing her tennis togs, Eugenie burst into the kitchen, blabbering something about the news up and down the street. She gave Duncan Stuart a huge grin, balanced a tennis ball on her racket, then lobbed it gently in his direction. He caught it with a smile and found himself a firm friend for life. Too short, in Eugenie's case.

"Duncan, tell us," I said quietly. "Leave out nothing."

For the next hour we sat around the kitchen table and listened to as harrowing a tale of survival and starvation as I have ever heard. Hawk sat beside me in the first chair I had ever seen him sitting in, his hand on my knee under the cover of the table. I could think of no objection to that.

He didn't make it to the Canadian border until the summer of 1878. He was found near death not far from the Bearpaws by a buffalo hunter hungry for conversation. When it soon because manifest that Duncan spoke English and could read, the hunter spared no effort to restore him to health. "I ate a lot of buffalo hump and dried juneberries," Duncan said.

The hunter couldn't read, but he had a copy of *A Tale of Two Cities* in his dugout on the Marias River. Duncan spent all winter reading to the man. As soon as he finished the book, he was told to begin again. "I can tell you I got mighty tired of Sydney Carton and his 'It is a far, far better thing I do,' speech the tenth time around," he declared. We all went off in great gusts of laughter, even Mother, and Duncan grinned.

"Along about the time grass starts to grow, I slipped out the only window while that old coot was sleeping off a drunk," Duncan said, when we stopped laughing. "I left the book through, sunk in a pail of molasses."

"Did you find Sitting Bull?" I asked, when I could speak without laughing.

"Nothing easier, really. He was about one hundred miles north of the border. White Bird and his clan were there, too. Still are, some of them."

He was silent then, staring out the window, if there had been a window where he looked. That long stare has never left him, even in good times. I was familiar with Indian pauses, so said nothing, but Phil, less informed then, rushed into the breech when the silence went on too long to suit him.

"How was it?" he asked.

"How was what? Oh. Sitting Bull." He shrugged. "We lived and breathed for two years. Didn't eat much."

That was obvious to me. Duncan has never been anything but lean, and it's taken him twenty-five years to develop even a small overhang on his waist. "Personally, I think Sitting Bull will leave Canada this summer. It's just a guess, but his people have been slipping back across the border for several years." (He was right. Sitting Bull surrendered at Fort Buford, Dakota Territory, on July 19, about three months after this kitchen conversation.)

"And The People?" I asked.

"Some of us left Canada, too."

As the sun moved lower and our cook gave us the evil eye because it was past time to start supper, Hawk described the journey back to Lapwai Reservation in Idaho Territory, the rivers crossed, traveling by night and sleeping by day to avoid detection by watching soldiers, and confrontations with other tribes. "We made it finally," he said simply. "Most of us. I have said enough about the journey."

And he had. I never heard any more about it from him.

They had to hide out at Lapwai, too. "We weren't the first to return," he said. "Everyone from Canada who was found at Lapwai was sent to Indian Territory." His chuckle that time held no humor. "The People call it Eeikish Pah, the Hot Place."

"That's no place for your tribe," Father said. He had joined us not long into the story.

"No, it isn't," Hawk agreed, "but I am going there now."

What could any of us say? Mother did contribute then. She had always been a careful observer of fashion. "You'll travel in style in that elegant suit."

He chuckled softly. His laughter sounded so much like Blue Mountain Woman's that I wanted to hug him. I didn't, of course. Father was looking none too approving, even if he had unbent enough to ask questions, and leave the cue stick in the billiards room.

"Believe it or not, they came out of a missionary barrel, Liz. I'm one of the deserving poor now."

That hurt. I remembered his string of horses, long spirited away by the Indian scouts at Bear Paw. I remembered how grand and fierce he looked in red and white warpaint as he rode against the Seventh Cavalry at Canyon Creek. He knew what I was thinking. He took my hand in his. "Don't think about it, Bright Star. It really doesn't bear thinking about."

"It's still a fine suit," Eugenie declared stoutly.

My sister was always good at breaking tense moments. Duncan Stuart grinned at her. "Why, thank you." He turned to me. "You'll appreciate this, Lizzie. I doubt you knew it, but Old Mary is a fine seamstress. She's at Lapwai and she altered this suit for me." He nudged me. "She said to tell you hello and come see her."

I could tell him later about my visit from Thomas Adams. "But you're going to Indian Territory?" I asked, not ever wanting him out of my sight again.

"I miss my own people. If I was found at Lapwai, I'd be sent there anyway, without a chance to stop here." He nodded when Cook herself slid him another slice of pie. "Thanks. Thought I'd save them the bother. The Indian agent at Lapwai – he's married to my cousin – scrounged up some money for my train fare."

"Going to Indian Territory," Father said. I could tell he was eager to see Duncan gone.

"Yes, sir, as soon as I pick up some things that are mine."

He looked at me, a question in his eyes. Elizabeth Ann the Fierce came out of hiding for the final time; no more hiding for her. I wiped my hands on my apron, not taking my eyes from his. I tugged the Jefferson peace medallion out of my shirtwaist and over my head and handed it to Hawk one final time. From now on he would be Duncan to me.

His fingers closed over it and his eyes brightened. "Warm."

My voice was steady. "I have a surprise for you in a pasture not far from here. Fair One has been busy."

He nodded at that. His eyes still never left mine. I knew he would never ask because he had nothing to offer, not even that half chicken we had joked about in better worst times before they became worse worst times.

"Duncan, I'll pack my bags."

Chapter Twenty-eight

I need hardly bore you with the rest of Duncan's visit to 303 McDermott Street. My parents were surprisingly calm about the matter, Father probably thinking he could change my mind, and Mother? Hard to say. They both urged me not to do anything rash.

Phil got my carpetbag and small trunk out of the attic and gave Duncan some of his own clothes. He let him bed down on the couch in his room that night. Duncan protested and said he would be quite comfortable on the floor, but Phil wouldn't hear of it.

I've since told Phil how grateful I am for his wholehearted kindness to Duncan Stuart. Phil just grins in that maddening way of his and assures me he's never had cause to regret it. "Besides, Sis, I owe him one. If Duncan hadn't come along, I'd have had to eventually support you in your spinsterhood, now, wouldn't I?"

I remembered to send a telegram to the Red Cloud rancher, suggesting that no matter what he had in store for me, I was already engaged, and he might not want to drop by the house. I never heard back, but I wished him well in my heart.

After a somewhat stiff and restrained breakfast that next day, Duncan and I rode the trolley car – he enjoyed that – to the end of the line then walked a mile to the pasture where we found Fair One and her spotted son and daughter, plus the now-gentrified Henry Watkins and our former housekeeper, who had begun a pie-making business.

What pleasure it was to watch Duncan as he leaned his arms on the railing and let himself fall under the Appaloosa spell again. He rode Fair One, then dismounted in front of Muskrat and handed him the reins. "Mr. Watkins, would you keep them here for me?"

"They're your horses," I reminded him. Muskrat echoed my reminder.

"Thank you," he said quietly. "With Mr. Watkins permission, they will stay here until I decide if The Hot Place is a good pasture for what I have in mind."

"My pleasure," Muskrat said. "When you're ready, they'll be ready, sonny."

On the quiet trolley ride home, I told Hawk about Bright Star, and the big guns and the stars that fell like harbingers of death for The People. He held my hand, watching my face with nothing but kindness and love when I told him about Elizabeth Ann and her *wyakim*. "I have no Indian name. How could I? But I don't need one."

He considered that. Duncan is not an overly demonstrative man. That's not who he is. He is still water that runs very deep and I have not one regret for loving him. He surprised me, though.

"I have a suggestion," he said as the trolley clanged along. "Since we parted at Bear Paw, one thing about you kept me alive."

Kept him alive. "The fact that you found a woman silly enough to love you with every breath she takes?" I whispered back. The trolley car was filling up and we didn't need an audience.

He knew I was lightening the mood, even as I deepened it. "Oh, that, too," he teased in turn, then turned as serious as I have ever seen him. "It's this: Whenever things were at their worst in these last few years, I knew I could close my eyes and remember your smile. I have been thinking of you as Her Smile." He said it in Nimiipuu, soft and multi-voweled. "That is *my* name for you."

I liked it and told him so. I would have kissed his cheek, but everyone on the trolley car already seemed too interested in what a woman with auburn hair and blue eyes was doing with a well-dressed man who looked like an Indian but not quite. Besides, Duncan has never been comfortable with public displays of affection. He saves his considerable skills for our bedroom.

My parents went about their usual business of the day. Father happily escaped to his office even though it was Saturday, after giving me a stern warning about Doing Anything Rash. Mother echoed what he said, but I sensed that her heart wasn't in it.

Eugenie and I crammed everything essential into my small trunk and valise, even though we had no idea what living in The Hot Place entailed. She dissolved into giggles when I vetoed two corsets and reminded her that I had lived with The People in one old riding habit and a deerskin dress without a corset in sight. Then it was my turn to laugh when she reminded *me* that the magnificent bosom had returned, and did I want to jiggle around in Indian Territory?

We were so frivolous, mainly trying to hold off tears of separation. Phil kindly took Duncan on a walking tour of Omaha and then lunch at his favorite Chinese restaurant. Over Duncan's strenuous objections, at least until he understood the matter, Phil reserved two seats on the Union Pacific to Chicago, and then arranged the transfer getting us closer to Oklahoma Territory.

Duncan came home stunned. "Smiley, what a racket you have on the UP."

I laughed. I knew what he meant. "You mean that we can ride free forever because my father is a UP executive?"

Duncan nodded. "I had no idea I was marrying into American royalty."

And that was my reminder of Indian humor, which is dry to the point of Sahara Desert dry, and self-effacing beyond belief. "All anyone had to do was live with us for six months and claim the exemption. You can't imagine our steady supply of houseguests through the years."

The all-purpose grunt. "Huh. Live with The People for six weeks and you end up in Indian Territory."

Dinner with Father and Mother glaring at Duncan was uncomfortable in the extreme. Father's day at the office, probably spent complaining loud and long to everyone there, made him dig in with admonition and advice neither of us wanted.

After dinner, he took Duncan into his study and closed the door. Or tried to. Father didn't realize he was dealing with both Elizabeth Ann the Fierce and Her Smile, not to mention Kaya the Hawk. He did not take it well when I barged right in, too, and refused to leave. Father ignored me, told Duncan what he thought and said that there would never be a penny of my inheritance given to me, not one, not then and not ever.

"Sir, we will manage," Duncan said, when the accusations and railings against fate ended, leaving Father in a silent stew, his face red.

"I have twenty dollars," I told my wealthy father. I stood up, still clutching Duncan's hand.

"Then what?" Father demanded.

"We will manage," Duncan repeated, tightening his grip on me. It couldn't have been easy to listen to vitriol directed at him in particular and Indians in general, but I knew he had been through much worse, up to and including a long walk, the loss of his mother and a herd of horses, and total defeat. Father had no idea who he was dealing with. Railroad lawyers? Unions? Huh. Child's play.

Father stormed from the room, grabbed his hat, muttered that he was going to his club, and slammed the front door on his way out. I never saw him again.

Mother was quiet all evening. She hugged me before I went to bed. "I wish I could help," she said. "I daren't." I understood.

We left early in the morning before any of the household was up, or so I thought. Phil had arranged the night before for a carter to take my trunk to the depot, so all I had to carry was my valise, which Duncan appropriated, exchanging his lighter grip for my much heavier one.

"Wait."

We were out the door and on the steps when Mother stopped us. She had thrown on her robe. I had never seen her on the front porch in anything less than full dress, so I stared for a moment, then gladly let her pull me close and hold me tight, also a first.

She tightened my muffler. "Dress warm, Elizabeth. If you get a cough, you know what kind of pharmaceuticals I use. Watch out for drunks and keep your feet dry."

It was a curious collection of wisdom from a woman who generally thought out every careful, correct sentence. She glanced over her shoulder and motioned us closer. She pulled out a wad of greenbacks big enough to choke a giraffe, and handed it to Duncan.

"Oh, I..." he began and stopped when she gave him The Stare that I had grown up with.

"What do you know," she told us, her eyes big, wondrous and childlike, "but I remembered where your father keeps the combination to the safe."

"Mama, you'll get in such trouble," I said.

"Hardly," she snorted, and gave her own version of Duncan's 'Huh.' "Abraham Everett was penniless when he married me, and so I shall remind him, if he gives me an argument. My father – rest his soul – owned that brewery in New York, if you will recall."

Thanks to my mother's light fingers, we were laughing when we said goodbye. She saw to it that my lifetime pass on the Union Pacific Railroad was validated and sent to me. She wrote often and visited us several times in Oregon before she died, always the lady but infinitely more to me.

Oregon? How did we get to Oregon, you ask? First we had to suffer in Eeikish Pah, The Hot Place. But I am getting ahead of myself. For any of you who might be concerned, we were married a day later during a layover in Chicago. We splurged on a private compartment then and enjoyed two pleasant nights in each other's arms from the Windy City to St. Louis, to Westport, Kansas, near Fort Leavenworth.

Insert

I am going to add these pages here. I'll ask my husband what he thinks, since it truly involves him. It's just a scrap, so I can discreetly remove it. See there, I marked it insert.

One doesn't marry an Indian on a whim. Maybe someday in the future that won't be one of the many factors to be considered in matrimony. I have to chuckle at myself. Our daughter Millie – short for Millicent Eugenie – heard all kinds of advice and admonition from Duncan and me, every factor known to concerned parents.

Only eighteen, Millie had accepted a proposal of marriage from a young man several grades ahead of her in high school. After two years at Eugene and a teaching certificate, he had been hired by the district to teach mathematics at Baker High School, where she was about to graduate.

We had numerous reasons why they should wait a little. Millie cut through them all. "I love him. He loves me. I've been watching you two all my life. I know what love looks like."

They were married two months later. Who could have said no after that? His parents were startled, but they will recover.

Duncan and I went through so many obstacles to marry. When it finally happened on that layover in Chicago, I had only one fear. I wanted, needed, to know that he would be gentle with me. My only other brush with sexual union had come at the hands of a terrible, brutal man, who had been stopped in the very act by this man who loved me and wanted to be my husband.

Duncan knew what had happened to me. His remorse that he and Poker Joe trusted the wrangler has never entirely gone away. I have done all I can to assure him that I have put the matter as far as possible from my heart and it's true. What happened to me was an act of rage and war. There was nothing about it of love. It is easy to separate the two, because they are miles apart.

We completely splurged on a private Pullman berth. I doubt you have seen two more shy persons than Mr. and Mrs. Stuart, as the trained pulled out of the depot and we accustomed ourselves to that sensual, rocking motion. That was when I told him that all I ever required from him was gentleness.

That was his gift to me, after the usual awkwardness, which strikes both of us now as amusing. How many weeks had I shared a shelter with a man naked except for a loincloth? After the terror that began my headlong flight with the Nez Perce – thanks to Methuselah, that awful bag of bones – I came to appreciate the sight of well-toned men in loincloths. My goodness, ladies, my goodness.

When he was down to his white man's smallclothes, the humor of the matter made him chuckle. "Smiley, I used to tell you to look away."

"You did." I was down to my chemise by then and had started on the buttons, my hands steady. I knew I wanted this man, my husband now, after so many obstacles.

"Did you ever peek?"

"I never needed to," I said and took off my chemise to expose that magnificent bosom. "What about you?"

He stared and then grinned. "Smiley, let me tell you right now while I can form sentences, that *these* improved breasts of yours are not for the faint of heart."

I think that was the last thing either of us said that made any sense for many, many minutes. He was gentle. When that moment of truth came, so was I.

This is all you're getting from me on the subject, except let me add this: When you make rhythmic love with a delectable man on a gently rocking train, well, what a nice introduction to marriage. Remember, I still have that lifetime pass on the Union Pacific Railroad, and I know how to use it.

End of insert (we haven't decided yea or nay on it)

We traveled next by stage – Russell, Majors and Waddell – until we arrived in the rain at what was known as Fort Oakland, near present-day Tonkawa, Oklahoma Territory. The Nez Perce had been moved farther west, but The Hot Place was no cooler.

We were heartily tired of travel, but stupidly, gloriously in love. Maybe it showed on our faces. When we knew we were finally in the settlement of Chief Joseph, all it took was one knock on one shack to be among friends. Hand in hand, we dealt with startled looks, then recognition, as The

People looked closer at me and saw the quiet white woman who seldom complained on the journey, slapped Bear Coat Miles, and smiled a lot because she didn't know their words.

They still call me Quiet Woman. Duncan was Hawk again, Kaya to all who knew him. We were taken to Chief Joseph's shack and welcomed. We spent the night there under a buffalo robe, and two more nights before we made our presence known to the Indian agent at Fort Oakland.

To say that he was unhappy with us was the understatement of the year. He urged me to use good sense and return to Omaha before it was too late. Elizabeth Ann the Fierce assured him that it was already too late, and besides, she had no intention of leaving.

I remained an embarrassment to the entire Bureau of Indian Affairs for nearly six months. Duncan spent time in and out of the guardhouse on idiotic charges while the bureau tried to figure out what to do with us. Remember, this was at the tail end of former President Grant's Peace Policy with the Indians, when, bluntly put, no one knew what was going on.

Maybe they thought to wear us down by separating us. I spent nights in the agent's house with his slightly sympathetic family. As one of the Peace Policy agents, this one had come through the ranks of Presbyterians. When I mentioned to him that most of the Treaty Nez Perce at Lapwai were Presbyterian, too, he did not find it amusing. He and his wife spent too much time scolding me, trying to rouse in me a sense of shame that I would cohabit with an Indian, even a half Indian. (He really took it hard when I asked which half.)

The whole experience was dispiriting and humiliating. I imagine it might have gone on and on, except that it became obvious after four months or so that I was going to increase the tribal population. The agent gave up and assigned us a cabin and some land, plus seed and tools.

People have asked me why the Nez Perce, who were – as General Miles so condescendingly put it – such superior Indians, were unable to make a go of farming, especially since the government gave them land, seed and tools. What people fail to consider is that the body heals faster than the mind. The

Nez Perce are fine farmers and exceptional horse breeders. For The People from the cool, rainy climate of the Pacific Northwest, hot, humid, malarial Indian Territory was not the place and those were not the circumstances. It was not their choice and they wanted nothing to do with it.

Once the Indian agent gave me up as a lost cause, I was permitted to help with the schooling of the Nez Perce children. I suppose he thought my whiteness would be a good example for the Indians. Naturally, he had no idea that my name was Her Smile, and all of Duncan's relatives knew it now.

He also didn't know that I was already acquainted with Thomas Adams, schoolteacher, who had married his pretty wife Sarah, one of Duncan's cousins, as soon as he arrived in Indian Territory. When we were "introduced," his only comment to the Indian agent was, "I think we can work together." We did, only not long enough.

I enjoyed working with the children and learning their language, when I was supposed to be teaching them English and threatening them when they spoke Nimiipuu. My labors were tinged with sadness, as well. In the months before our baby was born, there were fewer children to teach.

Chief Joseph took Duncan and me to the burying ground once, where I counted twenty-five little graves among their elders. Malarial chills and fever carried off young and old alike. It caused me nearly physical pain, Duncan too, to think that those stalwart children who survived the long march and the surrender at Bear Paw only lived long enough to be sentenced to Indian Territory to die. So much for the promises of our captors at Bear Paw.

Tragedy came flapping in to roost when Thomas Adams died of malaria, and we lost our dear teacher. Sarah followed him to the grave with their unborn child. Duncan held me close as I mourned, his own face impassive. He and the others had seen so much death in The Hot Place. These were my first personal ones.

Thomas was succeeded by a stern and upright Connecticut Yankee who truthfully did her best, but was also defeated by chills and fever. In her case, she could leave, and did. Thomas Adams was never given that choice. I regret his loss to this day, and that of his family.

Duncan and I had our first big argument then. (Well, first married argument.) He urged me to return to Omaha and stay there until and even after our baby was born. I refused. It was a lively fight. Frustrated nearly to tears, Duncan ended the confrontation by taking off his Jefferson medallion, slamming it on the kitchen table and leaving. He told me to wear it, since I was the warrior, and stomped out of the house, not an easy thing to do when you're wearing moccasins.

He came back a day later when I was fixing dinner. He washed his face in the bucket by the door. "I guess there is no reasoning with you, Smiley," he said.

"Your medallion is in the apple crate on top of your clean shirts," I told him, and that was that. In retrospect, perhaps I should have done as he demanded.

We heard from the outside world through letters from Mother and my grandmama of the brewery Caseys in New York. We chuckled over Eugenie's letters, badly spelled but brimming with enthusiasm for her new beau, an attorney. Phil, by now a sophomore at Harvard, wrote when he could. I remember one of his letters, received in late spring. He wrote to tell us that Buffalo Bill Cody's Wild West Extravaganza was to perform in Boston soon, with none other than Sitting Bull in a featured role.

I read it, laughed out loud, then handed it to Duncan. He read it, gave his all-purpose "Huh," and tossed it in the cookstove flames. "That's the Lakota for you," was his only comment. The Nez Perce can be such snobs.

Our baby was born July 22, 1882, in the heat of a blistering summer. She was a darling baby with my auburn hair, and Duncan's brown eyes. Her hair was so long that I could curl it around my finger. That's all I remember of her. She never made it to September. I grieved in all the ways I could, his world and mine. What felt the best, surprisingly, was the gash I made in my arm.

Duncan made a nice marker for her – Eugenie Elizabeth Stuart, age two months. We've tried many times since then to have her coffin shipped up here to Oregon, but have you ever tried to get anything out of the Bureau of Indian Affairs?

You can imagine my enormous guilt at insisting she be born in Indian Territory. Duncan bore me no ill will, but our sorrow was considerable. I don't know what would have happened to me then – to us – if my grandmother hadn't had the superior good timing to die. She and I had kept up a lively correspondence from the time I could write, and it paid off abundantly. Other than some inheritance to Mother and my brother and sister, Grandma Casey left the bulk of the brewery money to me, eight thousand dollars. It was a huge sum then, and it still is.

"What are you going to do with it, Smiley?" my husband asked after he finished reading the attorney's letter over my shoulder.

Something in the last letter from Grandmama before our baby's death had me thinking about this eventuality, although I had breathed a word to no one. We knew a great deal about disappointment by then, Duncan and I. "Do?" I kissed him (incidentally, I taught him to kiss and he is good). "Do? I think I will buy me a ranch in Oregon."

Chapter Twenty-nine

That is why we ranch near Cove, in the Grande Ronde Valley of northeast Oregon. Our hawk brand is becoming well-known in that part of Oregon and western Idaho, paid for with tears, fire, and patience. The only blood was mine, for a baby I still miss. The scar on my arm is a reminder, as if I needed one.

As Western ranches go, it is not large, some two thousand acres of fine pasturage. In the last ten years we have added apple and cherry orchards. This region is already shipping many boxes of cherries to markets from Portland to Seattle and north to British Columbia. We run some cattle, but the pasture is mainly for the horses, children of Fair One and a sire who made that fighting retreat to the Bear Paws, too.

To answer your unasked question, no, nothing about the purchase of my ranch was simple. Until recently, it was in my name only. Now it is the property of Duncan and Elizabeth Stuart, because times are changing.

In faith, trust, and with my heartful of hope, I sent Grandma Casey's legacy to my father, asking him to set up an account for me. Unless you lived in an enlightened, mythical part of the United States where women are allowed to do such things on their own, that's how business was done, before the turn of the century.

Father came through magnificently. Before his death a mere six months later, he had that trust purring along nicely, with Phil as co-signer. I found out later that Father funneled my inheritance from him into that account as well.

"Make sure she knows I never meant to leave her penniless," he told Mama before he died. I have wanted for nothing, except the earnest wish that I could have told him how much I loved him, before he died. Mama knows, though.

Duncan and I bided our time through that winter and into the spring of 1883. I taught the reservation school, which came in handy, as I would eventually be teaching my own children. When Phil finished his third year at Harvard, I kissed Duncan goodbye and met my brother in Omaha, using our lifetime UP passes to go West in style.

Duncan knew where he wanted me to look. Letters to and from Lapwai had mentioned some property going up for sale in Oregon's Grande Ronde Valley. A long-time settler had died, and his widow had no desire to remain in such an isolated place, especially with Umatilla and Cayuse Indians to the north and west and Nez Perce Christians to the east. I entered into correspondence with her and her bank in faraway Portland.

"I'd like to see it with you," my husband said that night before I left The Hot Place.

"Let me assuage your pains and assure you that Elizabeth Ann the Fierce will not fail you," I told him. I assuaged him in other ways that night, too, which was the beginning of our eldest son, as near as we could figure. If any man tries to tell you that women are feeble creatures, I dare him to travel a long distance, stay in indifferent hotels, choke down poor food, and negotiate a good deal during bouts of morning sickness.

The ranch was perfect, with beautiful rolling hills, ample pasturage, and fine soil that eventually became the orchards. There was the added bonus of a warm spring, which we still enjoy, clothed in company and bare otherwise. To call the ranch house rustic would be charitable. As it turned out, the hovel didn't matter. Once both Stuarts arrived and our neighbors got a good look at Mr. Stuart, someone burned it down for us. How thoughtful.

But that was twenty years ago. The final replacement house is lovely, and often the scene of pinochle games with our neighbors. Duncan likes to tell the story how he lost his moccasins in a game of cards with Poker Joe and they all laugh, shuffle the cards, and try to cheat him.

I'm getting ahead of the story. My brother signed for the property and I handed over two thousand dollars to the widow. I now owned a ranch only a day's drive from Lapwai Reservation. Phil returned to Harvard and I went back to Indian Territory, throwing up every morning.

It took us another three months of wrangling and red tape to get Duncan Stuart off the reservation in Indian Territory. I think he would be there still, if I hadn't started the first of several trips through the years to Washington, D.C. In all my pregnant glory, I confronted the Bureau of Indian Affairs, was rebuffed, then turned to a senator that the Union Pacific, through my father, had bought and sold many times.

The senator was more helpful, but the clinching deal came through an unlikely source, General Nelson Miles. He heard of my plight through that senator and invited me to dinner. General Miles and his equally ambitious wife, Mary Sherman Miles (aha, now you see another useful connection) listened to me with sympathy and much more.

I learned that night that Mary Miles's Uncle Tecumseh Sherman, then commanding general of the army, had overruled her husband's and General Howard's initial promise to return the Nez Perce to their ancestral homeland. "Uncle Cump regretted that decision," she told me over asparagus. "Let me see what I can do."

I quickly saw what she could do, especially since her other uncle was Senator John Sherman of Ohio. Nelson (yes, we were now on a first-name basis), had to return to his command of the Department of the Columbia, General Howard's old roost, but I was in capable hands. A few conversations, a few tears, and I had secured my husband's release to return to his homeland. Mary Miles and I were friends until her recent death. I owe her so much.

We arrived at what is now called Hawk Ranch shortly before our son David's birth. Duncan delivered him, because by then the white citizens of the region knew we had pulled a fast one, and no doctor would attend me. That ugly cabin burned down a few months later, but we lost nothing of value. When you are Duncan Stuart and lose everything except your life at Bear Paw Mountains, what is an old cabin?

For the next ten years, we had to drive fifty miles to find a merchant who would trade with us. Again, this was no particular hardship. We had good gardens and livestock. I was able to teach our children, and they learned to play together. After David, we had three more children. I tell Duncan that he should hang out his shingle as a baby doctor.

We also had the beginning of a herd of spotted horses, thanks to Fair One, brought to us with her son and daughter by Henry Watkins, a.k.a. Muskrat, who stayed long enough to help build a new cabin and visit friends on Lapwai Reservation, then leave us with full hearts.

As Duncan puts it, Fair One took an instant liking to a stallion as invincible as White Bird, his owner. White Bird, if you will recall, remained in what became the District of Alberta, Canada. Duncan remembered a fine Appaloosa belonging to White Bird, one he had secretly coveted all during the Nez Perce's fighting retreat. A visit to Canada and an offer proved successful. The stallion returned and sired a number of fine horses with Fair One. Thus began our herd.

When we wouldn't leave the Grande Ronde Valley, and showed signs of being productive citizens, matters started to turn around for us. Maybe our acceptance was hurried along when our nearest neighbor needed help during a delicate foaling, and knew Duncan would not fail him. Later, another neighbor begged us to take in his children for several months after his wife died unexpectedly. He was so grateful.

Duncan has been reading this chapter. "You have written about Phil. You must write about Eugenie, too, Smiley," he told me last night. He looked away until he collected his emotions. She was dear to him, too.

Eugenie married quite well in Omaha to Edwin Babcock, an enterprising attorney whom she adored. We were still in The Hot Place, and both of us yearned for her letters of love for us, love for her good husband, and her general exuberance that leaped through the pages and landed in our single room house with the leaky roof.

One of the saddest days of my life was when we received a letter from Edwin informing us of her death. I could recite it to you, because the words burned into my brain like a branding iron. "'The doctors didn't know what it was. We consulted so many. She didn't want you to know. She didn't want you sad, after your own sorrow.'" I read that letter over and over until Duncan took it away. I mean, we expected such terrible news all around us, but Omaha? With doctors? Money for the best of everything? If I could be granted one do-over in life, I think it would be no letter from Edwin Babcock, and only the good news that all was well, and I still had a sister. Do I miss her? Oh, don't ask.

There you have it. I have written my story. Yes, portions of it are enormously sad, but please don't think that is how we view it. Our happy moments are deeper and well-earned, because of the other moments. I have such moments; so do you. We continue to live with a heartful of hope.

This should wrap up the story, until I think of something else, or decide to subtract something (probably that little scrap I inserted about my wedding night.) Here you are: Our children were finally welcomed in school, and we have done business in nearby Cove and LaGrande for years now. Neither of us can honestly say that all prejudice has been swept away poof! by a magic wand, but we remain ever hopeful, as we must.

I only wish Chief Joseph had fared as well as we did. After many letters, visits, my own lobbying with Mary Miles, newspaper editorials and testimonials from friends in high places, in 1885 the non-treaty Nez Perce still alive in The Hot Place were allowed to return to the Pacific Northwest. These Nez Perce, Joseph's band principal among them, were forced to settle in farther-away eastern Washington near Nespelem, on the Colville Reservation. Of the more than four hundred Nez Perce who arrived in Indian Territory initially, only two hundred survived to make the return journey. I can add no comment to such a statistic that makes me anything but angry, even now.

Duncan made many horse-trading visits to his kinsmen near Nespelem. Each time he tried to get Joseph to visit us. Joseph hemmed and hawed, said yes and then no until Duncan began to feel insulted. He also wondered if Joseph scorned him because he was following the white man's road more than Blue Mountain Woman's way, or even that he had married me.

Chief Joseph was always sensitive to others and he knew what he had to admit. He took Duncan aside on one of his visits and spelled it out. "It is this way, my kinsman," he said to Duncan. "If I want to leave this place still so far from my home in the Blue Mountains, I must sign my name to a paper and ask the agent when he will let me leave and when I must return." He spread his hands out, pleading for Duncan to understand. "This is not the way to treat a man. I cannot do it."

Consequently, Joseph never came to our ranch, although he told Duncan many times that he wished he could see our children and our spotted horses. Duncan's herd is truly a sight to behold. The Old Ones like to visit, walk among the herd, and remember other days. Duncan's herd is not the only one, of course. The People are resilient and so are their horses. The signs are promising.

I last saw Joseph in 1899, when he did sign that paper and visited the Wallowa and Imnaha Valleys, accompanied by Major James McLaughlin, US Indian Inspector. (How does one inspect Indians? This has been a family joke for years.)

Duncan and I met the chief at Enterprise, the county seat. He was glad to see us, and asked about our children and horses. Our little party drove out to the grave of Joseph's father. The landowner had put a tidy fence around the grave and it looked well-tended. Joseph spent several moments in silence, gazing down at the little plot, a far remove from the many thousands of acres agreed upon by treaty in 1855 and then cruelly snatched away, which led to trouble and more trouble and finally, Bear Paw.

The chief looked so old and unhappy that I wanted to put out a hand to steady him. I didn't, of course. One doesn't live so many years with a Nimiipuu without learning what is right and proper.

We turned to go. Joseph gave Major McLaughlin the long stare. "Even this little piece of land would be enough," he murmured. The major shook his head. Apparently, another grave there for Joseph was more land than the good citizens of the county thought they could spare.

It continues to rain on the just and the unjust. My heart is ever hopeful that the inequities suffered by indigenous peoples and others in this land of the brave and home of the free will be evened out. I also know enough about the white man to be certain it won't happen in my lifetime.

We have done well. Our cheerful Millie lives in nearby Baker, where her new husband teaches. David, our eldest and one who follows the old ways, runs a logging concern to the east of us and is courting a Lapwai girl. Thomas, our youngest at thirteen, will probably stay here and take over when we are too old to manage. He has the same way with horses as his father. I've seen him several times in the corral, nose to nose with a horse, murmuring to it in the language of The People.

The only one I worry about is James, in his third year of high school. He has a scholar's heart and wants to go to the agricultural college in Corvallis. I knew he will do well, but I worry. Of all our children, he looks the most like The People. I fear the way will not be easy for him.

I was trying to find a better box this morning for my chronicle and came across Duncan going through the desk. "What're you looking for, oh man of mine?" I asked. (He likes that.)

"Some paper." He didn't look up as he searched the drawers. "Got to write a letter to Governor Chamberlain."

I didn't know he had connections like that. "Well well, do tell."

"I got a letter on official stationery, even. He wants me to train one of our horses for him."

I gaped at him. "Are you really going to do it?"

He straightened up, smiling in that maddening way of his that throws so many years off his shoulders and turns him into the red and white-painted warrior who kept me alive on a long retreat. "Of course I am, Smiley. I'll charge him a small fortune for one of our horses, you know, enough to keep James at Corvallis for at least four semesters. Or why not Harvard? Uncle Phil has connections."

When I stopped laughing, I told him I had used up all the paper – except this page you are reading – and promised to get more when I went into Cove today for the mail. Arm in arm, we went out to the porch. "I told Tom we'd take a look at the fences this morning up around Barton's line. See you later, Her Smile."

He hasn't called me that in a long while, Smiley usually sufficing. He kissed me and I went back inside, thinking about dinner and maybe a pie. I watched him from the window over the sink. I still love to watch him, and he knows it.

He stopped halfway between the house and the barn, put his hands on his hips and watched the sky lighten. He raised his hands to the sun and sang a morning song. Her Smile put her hand to her heart when Tom came out of the barn and sang along.

It's not a song for women to sing, but I had my own, one I hadn't thought of in years. "'Yes we'll rally 'round the flag boys, rally once again,'" I sang softly, "'Shouting the battle cry of freedom.'"

I thought of Blue Mountain Woman rallying to save my life, my mother rallying to keep us afloat in The Hot Place, and my sister Eugenie rallying me with her endless love in misspelled letters. I wished them with me as I sang, "'The Union forever, hurrah boys, hurrah.'"

It was enough. They were with me. They never left.

Acknowledgments

My gratitude goes to Loren Yellow Bird, ranger, friend and colleague at Fort Union Trading Post NHS, for his help in making sure I got it right. Thanks also to Marian Webb and Julie Ward Southworth, for loaning me, respectively, accounts of the Nez Perce in Idaho, and the Big Hole Battle (August 8-9, 1877).

Book Awards

- Two RITA Awards from Romance Writers of America for Best Regency of the Year.
- Two Spur Awards from Western Writers of America for short fiction, and one Finalist Certificate, romance novel category.
- Three Whitney Awards, 2011, 2012, and 2014.
- Lifetime Achievement Award from *Romantic Times*.

About the Author

A well-known veteran of the romance writing field, Carla Kelly is the author of forty-three novels and three non-fiction works, as well as numerous short stories and articles for various publications. She is the recipient of two RITA Awards from Romance Writers of America for Best Regency of the Year; two Spur Awards from Western Writers of America; three Whitney Awards, 2011, 2012, and 2014; and a Lifetime Achievement Award from *Romantic Times*.

Carla's interest in historical fiction is a byproduct of her lifelong study of history. She's held a variety of jobs, including medical public relations work, feature writer and columnist for a North Dakota daily newspaper, and ranger in the National Park Service (her favorite job) at Fort Laramie National Historic Site and Fort Union Trading Post National Historic Site. She has worked for the North Dakota Historical Society as a contract researcher.

Interest in the Napoleonic Wars at sea led to numerous novels about the Royal Navy, including the continuing St. Brendan Series. Carla has also written novels set in Wyoming during the Indian wars, and in the early twentieth century that focus on her interest in Rocky Mountain ranching.

Readers might also enjoy her Spanish Brand Series, set against the background of 18th century New Mexico, where ranchers struggle to thrive in a dangerous place as Spanish power declines.

CPSIA information can be obtained
at www.ICGtesting.com
Printed in the USA
LVHW040707221021
701184LV00025B/1874